MURDER
ON
MUSTANG BEACH

BERKLEY PRIME CRIME TITLES
BY ALICIA BESSETTE

Smile Beach Murder
Murder on Mustang Beach

MURDER
ON
MUSTANG BEACH

Alicia Bessette

BERKLEY PRIME CRIME
NEW YORK

BERKLEY PRIME CRIME
Published by Berkley
An imprint of Penguin Random House LLC
penguinrandomhouse.com

Copyright © 2023 by Alicia Bessette
Penguin Random House supports copyright. Copyright fuels creativity, encourages
diverse voices, promotes free speech, and creates a vibrant culture. Thank you for buying
an authorized edition of this book and for complying with copyright laws by not
reproducing, scanning, or distributing any part of it in any form without permission.
You are supporting writers and allowing Penguin Random House to continue
to publish books for every reader.

BERKLEY and the BERKLEY & B colophon are registered trademarks and
BERKLEY PRIME CRIME is a trademark of Penguin Random House LLC.

Library of Congress Cataloging-in-Publication Data

Names: Bessette, Alicia, author.
Title: Murder on mustang beach / Alicia Bessette.
Description: New York: Berkley Prime Crime, [2023] |
Series: Outer Banks Bookshop Mysteries; 2
Identifiers: LCCN 2022052034 (print) | LCCN 2022052035 (ebook) |
ISBN 9780593336915 (hardcover) | ISBN 9780593336922 (ebook)
Classification: LCC PS3602.E783 M87 2023 (print) | LCC PS3602.E783 (ebook) |
DDC 813/.6—dc23
LC record available at https://lccn.loc.gov/2022052034
LC ebook record available at https://lccn.loc.gov/2022052035

Printed in the United States of America
1st Printing

For Desi

MURDER
ON
MUSTANG BEACH

1

Running the Mustang Beach footpath was the sweetest kind of torture.

To my right, through the trees, wild horses frolicked in the surf, kicking up sand and seawater. They tossed their manes against the backdrop of the Atlantic Ocean, which twinkled emerald and sapphire.

To my left, Toby Dodge trotted alongside me. His breathing was hardly disturbed, and he had barely broken a sweat. His black shoulder-length hair was tied at the nape of his neck except for one uncooperative strand, which he kept tucking behind his ear. A head taller than me, he'd adjusted his stride to my slower pace, one of many chivalrous gestures that I'd grown to appreciate over the past eleven months, as we'd gotten to know each other.

What was so torturous about this run? I could look, but I couldn't touch. That rule went for both the wild horses and my running companion.

"Middle name?" he asked, continuing our back-and-forth quiz game, which we'd been playing on and off since we first met. "I'm sure I've asked you this already," he added, "but I can't think of the answer."

"That's because I don't have a middle name," I said. "I'm just Calista Padget. Short and sweet."

"You're short. I don't know about sweet."

"Ha ha. First job? Wait—I know this. Retail, right? Your mom's gift shop."

"I swept the floors and kept the shelves stocked. You?"

"Boring: babysitting. Best first date you've ever been on?"

"Hasn't happened yet. But it will in approximately"—he consulted the time on his phone—"eight hours."

My stomach fluttered, my head felt full of clouds, and a ridiculous smile, one I couldn't control, made my face feel lit from within. You see, Toby was just coming off a yearlong abstinence experiment. As playful as he could be, he also had a serious side, one that let him accomplish things like start his own business and last a whole year without dating anyone in order to heal from a previous relationship.

That year ended tonight. Which meant that we were going to have our first official date. I didn't know what he had in store, but I needed to be prepared for anything. That's what he kept telling me.

At the end of the two-mile path, we slowed to a walk. The wood chips under our feet transitioned to a ramp that sloped upward. Emerging from the maritime forest, we strolled to the observation platform, and the view stretched open before us. The horizon went on forever, ocean indistinguishable from sky. Dolphins surfed the breakers, their fins glinting as they arced out of the water. A strand of pelicans swept over the crashing waves. And on the beach, two jet-black mustangs stood head-to-tail, flicking flies from each other's faces.

Mustang Beach is the sole domain of Cattail Island's several dozen wild horses. A few hundred fenced-in acres of pristine oceanfront, plus the surrounding dunes and woods, are theirs alone to roam. They forage for sea oats and pampas grass, acorns and Tinnakeet grapes. They drink from puddles and seasonal pools. They survive thanks to the knowledge embedded in their DNA, passed down through five hundred years of adaptation.

Their survival is also thanks to the fence.

A generation ago, wise Cattailers realized that if they allowed the mustangs to continue comingling with humans, the herd, unique in all the world, would soon go extinct.

The fence isn't there to keep the mustangs in. It's there to keep the people out.

So, as much as I wanted to climb the wire-and-wood barrier and gallop for all that cool liquid turquoise and dive in; as much as I wanted to approach a mustang, tell her my name in a soothing voice, stroke the white blaze between her eyes, caress her velvet nose—I had to settle for simply admiring the postcard-worthy view. Aside from the platform holding us above the dunes, the scene of sea and sky, of sand and horses, probably looked exactly the same as it did three hundred years ago.

My breathing back to normal, I rested my forearms on the railing. My baseball cap kept my long hair in place and shielded my eyes, but the morning sunlight reflecting off the ocean was dazzling, and I couldn't keep from squinting. "The pregnant mare must be hiding out," I said. Any day now, one of the herd's adult females was going to give birth. We'd been hoping to catch a glimpse of her. Apparently, though, she was keeping a low profile. Sheltering in the scrub pines, maybe.

Toby and I shared a bottle of water, taking turns gulping until it was empty. "Check out that little house." He pointed north-ward, at a cedar-shake bungalow of traditional Outer Banks architecture nestled in the grass-topped dunes. Bottle-green hurricane shutters were propped open. Rocking chairs dotted the wraparound porch. Three second-story windows were dormered, and above them, three cupolas crested the apex of the green-shingled roof.

"That's Sanctuary Bungalow." I explained that the once home had been converted into a tiny museum and office for the herd caretaker of Mustang Beach. "She lives in an apartment on the second floor, as far as I know."

"I love those old Outer Banks bungalows. I'd like to live in one someday."

"Me too." A fantasy flickered in my mind. Me and Toby, cohabiting. We somehow acquire Sanctuary Bungalow and convert it back into a proper home. Our home. We plant petunias and snapdragons along the path leading to the porch. We pass summer nights in the rocking chairs, sipping ice-cold Cattail Island Blonde from bottles, gazing at the Milky Way, which looks like it's shooting straight up from the black ocean . . .

"What are you thinking?" His baritone voice had a mellow musical quality that I loved.

I tuned back in to reality. My gig at a small independent bookshop would never afford me an oceanfront home—or the means to renovate it, even if it was all of nine hundred square feet.

Moreover, while Toby and I had been flirting hard for the past eleven months, and spending time together almost every day—and while there was an ease between us that I'd never experienced with any other previous boyfriend—the truth was, it was bananas to be daydreaming about a committed, blissful future with the guy.

Just like with running, I needed to take things one step at a time. "I was thinking," I said, "about how excited I am for tonight."

"Tonight?" He scrunched his forehead. "What are you talking about?"

I play-punched him in the gut. Laughing, he caught my wrist and pulled me in for a sweaty hug. "Don't worry," he said. "There is nothing on this planet that could keep us from having the most epic first date ever."

2

Even on a Sunday morning in May, Queen Street was crammed. Out-of-state vehicles inched along, and Toby's seventies-era, fully restored Jeep Grand Wagoneer crawled among them. Our run concluded, we were scanning for a parking spot.

Cattail Island, part of North Carolina's Outer Banks, is named not only for its proliferous cattail plants but also for its shape as viewed from the air: a typical whip-thin barrier island, except for the three-mile-wide northern section. That fat part's where the islanders live, and where the vacationers vacation. And where we all shop.

The commercial district consists of a few quaint blocks of brick boutiques and bistros. Geraniums in clay pots hinted that summer was just around the corner. Bicycle racks were fit to burst, and benches needed a good rain to rinse away sticky handprints. Tourists of all ages strolled the sidewalks, some eating ice cream from waffle cones bigger than their faces, despite the early hour. The warmer-than-usual temperature might deter the out-of-towners from outdoor workouts, but it didn't stop them from shopping. There was nothing like stepping into an air-conditioned store that sold colorful treasures, tempting you to linger, to touch, and to support the local small businesses.

A just-big-enough parking spot opened in front of the Mother-Vine Bookshop, near the shadow of the sign that stuck out over the sidewalk. "Close enough," Toby said as he eased the Wagoneer along the curb.

The bookshop's front window sparkled, thanks to a few handfuls of glitter. The display was my creation. A beach scene, with swaths of green and blue satin forming the ocean, strips of sandpaper for sand, and, front and center, the spring's freshest, most anticipated reads. Books that promised seaside or poolside victories, along with sun, leisure, and a dash of romance. Origami fishes peeped from the waves, and cocktail umbrellas shaded origami people lounging on tiny beach blankets, which I'd fashioned from my uncle's old dish towels. Above it all, origami seagulls twisted from clear fishing line.

My most recent addition to the display: mustangs. I'd made them according to the directions in a children's book about basic paper art. Not on display—yet—was the teensy horse I'd created to represent the newborn foal. I wanted to wait until the real thing officially arrived. Superstitious, I guess.

"My mother sells authentic origami paper in her shop back home in Emerald," Toby said. "She would love that you're a budding origamist. Hey, the mustangs came out awesome. Those new?"

"*Awesome* is a strong word, but . . ." A bubble of pride floated up inside my chest. "Thanks."

We exited the Wagoneer and paused on the sidewalk. Inside the MotherVine, two customers occupied the lime-green papasan chairs. A forty-something woman read a hardcover book, while a man about the same age flipped through magazines. They wore goofy T-shirts custom-made to mark the occasion of a family reunion trip.

A silver tabby hopped onto the woman's lap, and though I couldn't hear her through the glass, her face let me know she was squealing with delight. She set aside her book as the tabby began kneading her legs. The man got out his phone and snapped some photos while the woman smiled, positioning her head close to the shop's mascot.

The cat's name was Tinnakeet Man, and he was sort of Instagram famous.

It being Sunday, I'd taken the day off. Even so, I longed to go inside, give Tin Man a scratch, and make sure my boss didn't need any extra help. During the run, though, I'd become something of a sweat ball, and now the sweat had evaporated, dotting my skin with salt.

As discreetly as possible, I sniffed my armpit.

Ugh—no go.

It was just as well, seeing as I routinely kept a change of clothes at Toby's martial arts studio, where I could shower. After that, the plan was to go our separate ways for the rest of the day. Toby would take some time for quiet reflection to mark the end of his yearlong effort toward getting to know himself—and then he and I were going to meet for our epic first date.

Life felt good. Everything felt good.

It was as if Cattail as a whole had caught its breath and returned to its regular optimistic self, after the trauma that had heralded last summer. Long story short, the island had been rocked by a double homicide, culminating, for me, in a too-close-for-comfort encounter with a ferocious shark. In the wake—so to speak—of the drama, islanders had been stumbling around in a sort of collective shock. Until now. Life on Cattail was getting back to breezy normal. Like the rest of the island, I was committed to putting the scary incidents behind me. To moving on.

Holding hands, Toby and I navigated the busy sidewalk. We stepped aside for an elderly couple. "Have a great one, ma'am, sir," Toby said.

Cattail Family Martial Arts looked as inviting as any other

storefront. Toby had installed window boxes and stuffed them with petunias and verbena. As we approached the door—painted red, like all the other doors of the Queen Street businesses—he leaned over and pecked me on the cheek. For a second or two, he held my gaze, and I melted into his hazel eyes, wondering what he thought of mine, a rusty brown. Like a giddy teenager, I put a hand where his lips had been. We gazed at each other as shivers rippled down my spine.

Grinning, he keyed into the dojo, the muscles of his back flexing against his damp shirt. He pushed open the door, activating bells that chimed a sweet song above my head.

Suddenly, though, a foreboding feeling came over me. Like icicles steeling my veins. A similar trepidation flooded Toby, I could tell by the tension that stilled his limbs.

He thrust out his arm, blocking me from entering. I peered around him into the dim lobby and beyond it, into the high-ceilinged workout space.

In the center of the mat, a man I'd never seen before was lying belly-up.

3

"S ir?" Toby called. "Can I help you, sir?"

On his back on the springy flooring, the man was dressed for a workout—sweat-wicking top, swishy shorts, orange Reeboks. His fitness journey had just begun, judging by his soft belly.

Toby and I crept closer, through the lobby and into the main workout area.

The man's receding hair had been styled with gel. He appeared to be of average height and just shy of forty, the same age as me and Toby.

"Who is that?" I asked. "Is he okay? Oh—" My hands clamped my mouth.

The man definitely wasn't okay.

His eyes bulged, staring vacantly at the Japanese and American flags hanging from beams high above. His neck was crisscrossed with bruises. A hasty bandage had been applied to his hand and secured with medical tape. Blood had seeped through the gauze, spotting it with red.

I felt bile rise in the back of my throat. "Toby?"

"Don't look." Turning, he held me by the elbows. His touch conveyed unshakable composure. But on his face, I detected fear. "Call 911," he said, handing me his phone.

I rushed back to the lobby. Despite the tremors that had overtaken my whole body, I dialed and spoke as succinctly as I could. I'd barely gotten out the basics—that my friend and I were standing in an empty dojo with the body of a man who'd apparently been strangled—when the 911 dispatcher hit me with a flurry of questions. Were we alone in the building? Were we certain the man was dead? Then the dispatcher ordered us to immediately exit the dojo. "Don't hang up," he added—but the line went dead. I'd pressed the phone so hard to my cheek that it touched the red button, ending the call.

Toby, still near the body with his hands clasped behind his back, glanced my way. "Are they coming?" he called, his voice echoing from the high-ceilinged workout room.

"Police are on the way," I said. "We need to wait outside."

"You go. I'll stay with him."

I couldn't remain in that dojo one more instant. Queasiness squeezed my belly, and I wanted the commotion and magnolia blossoms of Queen Street like never before.

Outside, the sunlight was gentle. I sat on the bench in front of Cattail Family Martial Arts and put my head between my knees. About forty-five seconds later, Toby emerged, sat next to me, and rubbed a hand up and down my back. "Hey," he said.

At his presence, I felt myself unspooling. I sat up and rested my head on his shoulder and sighed so deeply it felt like it came from my toes. "Hey."

"I can't believe this is happening again," he said. "Another murder? In Cattail?"

Curbside, a black Toyota pickup screeched to a stop. The driver exited, jumping from behind the wheel. She was tall and lanky. Red hair fired past her shoulders. A badge gleamed at her hip, along with a holstered handgun.

Iona Fusco.

"Who else is in the building?" she asked, pausing near our bench.

"Nobody," Toby said. "It's just us."

"You sure about that?"

"The door was locked when we got here," I said. "We called 911 right away, and the dispatcher told us to come outside."

Toby yanked a thumb over his shoulder. "Come to think of it, though, I didn't check the back door."

"Sir?" Fusco prompted.

"There's a door that leads to the parking area out back. It's rarely used—"

Hand on her service weapon, Fusco charged into the building.

A police cruiser swung up in front of her truck. A large man of retirement age, shaped like a russet potato, barreled out. Drew Jurecki, chief of Cattail police. "Dag nabbit, Fusco," he shouted. "Wait for backup." He was out of breath by the time he reached the sidewalk. He withdrew a handkerchief from his pocket and pressed it above his bushy sugar-and-cinnamon eyebrows. "Stay," he said, flapping the hanky at us before hotfooting it inside.

4

Cattail police's dramatic arrival attracted a crowd. After all, on a beautiful Sunday morning, what interest would cops have in a martial arts studio? Passing tourists cupped their hands around their eyes and pressed up to the windows of the dojo. One woman with a zinc-covered nose pointed her cell phone and snapped a photo, then studied it. "Nothing but glare," she whined.

A man walking down the sidewalk made an arc around the gathering gawkers. He wore suspenders and a threadbare but clean button-down shirt. On his way to Sunday service, most likely. I recognized him as a local, and he must have recognized Toby and me as Cattailers too, because he paused in front of our bench and asked, "What's going on?"

"Someone was killed," Toby said softly.

"We don't know any details," I added.

He shook his head as, behind him, the cars on Queen Street slowed.

The zinc-nosed tourist was just about to venture inside when the door flung open and Fusco barged out. "Move it along, folks," she boomed. "Nothing to see here." Then at Toby and me, she crooked a finger. "You two—with me."

Despite the lobby's many seating areas, Toby and I stood. We could see Chief Jurecki in the big room, walking a slow circle around the body. Meanwhile, Fusco locked the front door. One by one, she closed the venetian-style blinds on the sidewalk-facing windows while rapping her knuckles at any lingering sun-burnt faces.

With the lobby of Cattail Family Martial Arts suitably dimmed, she faced me and Toby. Her promotion from officer to detective explained her plain clothes: a sleeveless navy top, and gray trousers with a pronounced crease down the center of each leg. "Let's see your security footage," she said. "It's Toby, right?"

"Yes, ma'am. But—security footage? I don't have any."

"There's no video surveillance of this place?"

"Nothing like that's even crossed my mind." He looked wide-eyed at me. "Does the MotherVine have security cameras?"

"Antoinette doesn't feel there's a need," I said of my boss.

"I'd guess about half the businesses on Queen Street have them," Fusco said. "You might want to think about it."

"It's not like I have merchandise that's easily stealable, Officer."

Fusco gave her hair an annoyed toss. I nudged him with my elbow, muttering that she was a detective now.

"Detective," he said. "Pardon."

With a curt nod, she snapped on a pair of exam gloves, then produced her small tablet and started taking photos of absolutely everything. The posters on the wall. The watercooler. Toby's immaculate desk. When she shuffled some papers, he bristled but kept his mouth shut. With every pic taken, the electronic version of a shutter clicked.

Next, she went into the big room, exchanged some words with Jurecki, and began snapping photos of the body from every conceivable angle. That task complete, she began rummaging through a container of practice nunchucks. Each pair consisted of two foam sticks joined by a nylon cord. They were like training wheels, Toby had told me. Step one in the natural progression when a student is ready to take on weaponry. The point of nunchucks was not to be a badass but to block opponents' moves without using your body.

Fusco moved on to a container of resistance bands. Selecting a black one, she stretched it out, testing its strength. She pressed it to her throat.

My hand went to my own throat. I swallowed.

The chief headed toward us, his frame filling the doorway that connected the big room to the lobby. "Do either of you know the deceased?"

Toby coughed. "Actually . . ."

Now it was my turn to give him a wide-eyed look. "You *know* the guy?"

"Kinda. I mean—I've met him. His name's Seth Goodnow."

"Have a seat," Jurecki said. "Both of you." We obeyed, opting for the nearest bench, as the chief propped himself against the check-in counter. "Now, then, Mr. Dodge. I'd like some details. From the top."

Toby took a big breath. "You see, I've been experimenting with an open-door workout policy. Unstructured time, when I'm not teaching, for people to come in and exercise. It's been a success. Well . . ."

It had *been a success* . . .

"There's a sign-up sheet." Toby gestured toward the desk. "And a waiver people have to fill out to gain access to the equipment. I don't have much. It's all along the walls in there. Some kettle-bells, some stability balls. There's no gym on-island, so I figured I'd tap into the market for vacationers who want to keep up with their regular workouts. A lot of times it's just too darn hot and sticky to go for a run or walk outside. Even if you get up early. And people are freaked out lately by open-water swimming, ever since . . ."

Ever since last summer, when a shark ate someone in the shallow waters of the Pamlico Sound.

My stomach felt like it was being squeezed in a vise.

"This morning's open workout started at seven," Toby said. "The first person to arrive was Seth Goodnow. He's on vacation here. After Seth Goodnow, this other guy showed up. Followed by two women."

The chief of police shifted his considerable weight and paced the lobby. "You were here earlier this morning, supervising?"

"Of course I was here. Open workout hour ended at eight, and I locked up. But I forgot to check the back door. Come to think of it, last night, I swept the back steps. I might have left the door unlocked by accident."

"Looks like you did just that." Fusco appeared in the doorway. I noticed she was wearing high-heeled shoes—cherry-red patent leather. Since becoming a detective, she'd changed her hairstyle, trading the braid she'd worn as a uniformed officer for long layers that flattered her freckled face. "The back door wasn't locked," she said.

Toby smacked his forehead. He wasn't normally forgetful, but we all had our moments.

"Back to this morning," Jurecki said. "What happened at eight, after you locked up? Well, after you locked the *front* door."

"At that point," I put in, "Toby and I went for a run together."

"Romantic," Jurecki said. "Then what?"

"We got back here at twenty past nine," I said.

"At first, nothing seemed out of the ordinary," Toby said. "The lights were off. All the equipment was put away. Just like I'd left things."

"And then you noticed the body?"

Toby and I both nodded.

"A word, Chief?" Fusco said.

They took a few steps into the big room. Standing there whispering, they reminded me of a number ten: Fusco skinny, Jurecki round. The echo obscured their words, but I heard Fusco saying Scarboro was en route. Scarboro was the medical examiner. Then I heard Fusco say, "We should separate them."

Them meaning me and Toby.

"She's proven herself," was Jurecki's reply. He was talking about me.

If anyone had proven herself, though, it was Fusco. Last summer, we'd shared a harrowing experience. Churning waves, howling winds, sloshing nail-studded detritus—maybe, as she stood there frowning opposite Chief Jurecki, the same memory was flashing through her mind. Unless she was thinking that, right now, by not separating me and Toby, Jurecki was breaking some big cop rule, an infraction she didn't approve of, and she was outranked and had to swallow it.

As they continued whispering, I peered past them, studying the big room. Stand-up punching bags lined one wall, and on the opposite wall, free weights had been neatly stored on metal shelving.

My eyes landed on the body in the center of the mat. Seth Goodnow. His palms were upturned, like he was lying there waiting to receive something. I wondered what friends or family the poor guy had left behind. After all, most people didn't vacation solo. Very soon Chief Jurecki would be making a house call somewhere on-island. Imagine being on a beach trip and answering the door to the news that your loved one had been killed.

Sympathy rippled through me.

And that was when a few details popped out. Things about the body I hadn't before noticed.

5

A slip of paper poked from the pocket of Seth Goodnow's shorts. Sand clung to his calves, and a trail of sand led from the back door. There was his watch too, a duller orange than his sneakers, one of those activity trackers that kept tabs on vital signs. Morbidly, I imagined a skull and crossbones blinking when the watch could no longer detect its wearer's heartbeat.

Jurecki rejoined me and Toby. "Mr. Dodge, tell me what you know about Seth Goodnow. What did he say to you?"

"Nothing much." Toby fidgeted.

Fusco, who had moved behind the desk, held up that morning's sign-up sheet. "Seth Goodnow's got the number one spot, see? Filled out his local address as Nine Love Beach Trail. Batting second, someone by the name of Cooper Payne."

"He was the second person to arrive," Toby said. "A real gym-rat type. Kind of a meathead, to be honest."

"Well, Cooper Payne, the meathead, fancies himself a comedian," Fusco reported. "He listed his local address as Salty Edward's Bar & Tavern. Wrote *ha ha ha* in the margin."

"Hilarious," Jurecki said. "Did you talk to this Cooper Payne?"

"He paid me a compliment." Toby held out his arm, displaying the dragonfly tattoo wrapped around his wrist. A tribute to his Japanese heritage. "He said he liked my ink. Not long after that, the first woman came in."

Fusco consulted the sheet once more. "Heather Westerly is in the number three spot. Local address: Casa Coquina." That was the bed-and-breakfast on Queen Street, a block away.

"Heather Westerly," Toby said, nodding. "Right. Thirty-something. Blond. Told me she has her yellow belt."

"The fourth and last person to sign," Fusco said, "is also a joker. No name. No address. Just a couple of initials. D.S." Again, she held up the sheet. The D.S. appeared large on the page, in a left-leaning, elegant hand.

"D.S. was another woman," Toby said. "Short. Tough. Seemed serious."

Fusco flicked the paper. "Why didn't she sign her name?"

"I asked her to," Toby said, shrugging. "I thought she did. She said she wasn't there to work out. She just wanted a word with the *first* woman. I was distracted because that Cooper guy kept asking me to spar with him. He was pretty annoying about it, actually."

Jurecki held up a hand. "So D.S.—whoever she is—and Heather Westerly exchanged words. What did they say?"

"I don't know," Toby said. "They were in the big room, while I was in here, explaining to Cooper that I wasn't going to spar with him."

"Did anyone speak with the deceased, Seth Goodnow?" Chief asked.

"People aren't super talkative during the open workout hour. They come in, they do their thing, they leave. This group was no different—D.S. and Heather Westerly being the exception, I guess. D.S. left right after she spoke with Heather."

"How long was their conversation?"

"Not more than a minute or two, I don't think. Heather herself left around seven forty-five. I remember because I looked at the clock. I thought, is it eight already? But it wasn't. The other two—Seth and Cooper—stayed until a few minutes later, and left around the same time."

"But they didn't leave *together*?"

"Oh no. It didn't seem that way."

"Let me get this straight. The last time you saw Seth Goodnow, he was hale and hearty."

"Yes, sir. The last move he did was a static plank pose right there in the far corner. Pretty good form too."

"When you two came back from your run, did you touch anything? Either of you."

"Nothing," I said.

Jurecki stood opposite Toby, arms crossed, glaring in a way that let me know his interrogation was going to take a turn. "So you're a kung fu guru or something?" Jurecki asked.

"Just a karate instructor, sir."

"Know anything about weaponry?"

"Sure. Nunchaku, for one." At Jurecki's raised eyebrow, Toby explained. "Nunchucks. Also, in college I spent a few summers in Japan with my mother's family, studying kendo." When Jurecki's other eyebrow went up, Toby added, "Traditional Japanese sword fighting." Then Toby dropped his head into his hands. Probably when he realized that admitting he knew how to neatly slay someone was not, at the moment, in his best interest.

I couldn't read the chief's mind, obviously, but I had a pretty good idea what he was thinking. That it would be easy for someone trained in ancient assassination techniques to defeat a smaller, weaker opponent.

Of course, Toby loved the martial arts because of their purity. They weren't about destruction and death, but preparedness. So you can go about your life calmly—*and* have a way to protect that calm when it's threatened. He opened his mouth, about to defend his beloved self-defense, when Jurecki butted in.

"You got a black belt or whatever?"

"Fifth-degree, sir."

Momentarily, Jurecki gazed down at his sensible shoes. The

expression on his face was one of regret. As if he didn't want to ask any more questions but knew he had to. "So tell me, Mr. Dodge. What motivates a guy like you to devote his life to becoming a violent killer?"

"It's not about that at all. It's about—"

"I know, I know. Use the force, be one with everything, and all of that."

Until that point, I had been freaked out enough to stay more or less quiet, to let the process unfold however Jurecki and Fusco saw fit. But Jurecki's focus seemed to have lasered in on Toby, and I couldn't stay mum any longer. "Chief," I said, "you once told me I was barking up the wrong tree. Remember?"

"Actually, I believe I told you there *wasn't* a tree." He pointed at Toby. "This here's a tree. And you can bet your biscuits I'm barking up it."

"He had nothing to do with this," I said, springing to my feet. "I was with him the whole time."

"Be that as it may, you're both going to need to come with me. Down to the station."

6

The cramped room in the police station smelled like musty carpet and burnt coffee. On the opposite side of a chipped table stained with drink rings, Fusco fiddled with a voice recorder. A portable one, similar to the kind I used in my early days as a print journalist. When she got it working, I provided as many details as I could about discovering the body. Then, as if she'd grown suddenly bored, Fusco pushed back her chair. "BRB," she said.

Alone I sat. Was the mirror on the wall actually two-way glass, like in the movies? My own reflection horrified me. I'd forgotten how grubby I'd become during that morning's four-mile run. I was sitting there in my tank top and shorts, a complete and utter disaster. There wasn't much to be done about that. I offered a finger wave to whoever might be observing, then tucked a wayward hair back under my cap.

I'd ridden in Fusco's pickup while Jurecki had stuffed Toby into the back of the cruiser like a common criminal. Mercifully, the crowd had dispersed, and Queen Street seemed oblivious to what had gone on inside Cattail Family Martial Arts. Word hadn't hit the street. Yet. The commercial blocks were so sunny and bustling, it had been almost impossible to believe that a man's life had savagely ended not long ago, just on the other side of a brick wall.

Cattail's biweekly newspaper had been on hiatus since the double homicide eleven months ago, with the editor in chief still more or less holed up inside her home, for various reasons. The larger news crews from Virginia, however, would come sniffing. The TV vans were probably grumbling down 64 East at that very moment.

And, as anyone living on a small island can attest, the news media isn't the only gossip spreader. No, islands have their own special magic when it comes to that. It was only a matter of time before the rumors spread like wildfire.

I shuddered to think about the hit Toby's year-old business would take once the news broke. Even the less seasonal businesses like his raked in cash during the warmer months. He didn't even have the benefit of the doubt that came from being born on Cattail. He was a dingbatter, as the Outer Banks old-timers would say, a permanent condition even if you'd lived here a half century.

Drumming my fingers on the table, I found myself feeling grateful, perhaps ludicrously so, that he and I had gone for a run together. That we'd snagged some quality time before a figurative pant-load of excrement hit the fan.

Fusco strode back into the interrogation room cradling two cartons of juice and two oranges almost as big as grapefruits. "Chief's wife just got back from some R and R in Florida. She toured an orange grove and went a tad overboard in the gift shop." The detective set a juice and an orange in front of me, plopped into her chair, and dug a ruby-red fingernail into the skin of her orange, sending a plume of citrus spray into my eye. "Go ahead," she said. "Dig in."

"Perfect," I said, knuckling my eye. "I was just sitting here thinking my vitamin C intake was low."

Fusco didn't crack even the hint of a smile.

"I thought we were friends," I said.

"You did?"

With a huff, I tore open the carton and sipped the pulpy juice. Fusco *seemed* like the kind of person who'd sidle up to your poker table, or tip back a few beers with you, or throw darts at Salty Edward's. I didn't think I'd ever get there with her, though. She felt the need to exude authority, perhaps as a way to compensate for her relative youth, as she was still in her twenties. Last summer, she and I had been testing this sort of quid pro quo arrangement where we shared information. But thanks to my near drowning, that mutual back-scratching phase of our relationship was over.

Also over—before it even began—was tonight's epic date with Toby. That went without saying. But there were more important things in the world than my own personal disappointments. "You know Toby didn't have anything to do with this, right?" I asked.

"What's the nature of your relationship?"

It was doubtless evident to the entire island that he and I had been spending tons of time together. I saw no reason to keep my feelings under wraps. "I like him. He likes me. So what?"

"You'd like things to advance romantically?"

I leaned forward. "Have you asked him that? What did he say?"

"This isn't seventh-grade recess. You and Mr. Dodge went running along the Mustang Beach footpath between eight and nine this morning?"

"We already told you that."

"Can anyone else verify it? Did anyone see you?"

I palmed my orange, rolling it on the table. There'd been no one else out running. No one else on the footpath. That morning had dawned into the perfect beach day. It had been so pleasant temperature-wise, and the ocean so inviting, that not even the *chance* of sighting a baby horse could have tempted people to a remote footpath in the woods, ending at a beach they weren't allowed to step onto. "You have nothing," I said. "Am I right? You have no leads. Zero."

"Besides your boyfriend, can anyone confirm all you've told me about discovering the body?"

"Toby's not my—never mind. If he was going to kill someone, why would he deliberately put the body in the middle of his own business? Don't you think he'd put it somewhere else?"

"Maybe he got interrupted. Maybe he wanted to get caught."

"Why on earth—"

"People do all kinds of strange things for all kinds of strange reasons. You were a reporter. You know that."

She was right about that. But she was wrong about Toby. I'd spent almost a year courting the guy. Like everyone, he had a dark side. I don't think you could relish the goriest of kung fu movies, the way he did, without having a dark side. But he wasn't a killer. That I knew.

Likewise, Fusco wasn't stupid. I was sure she had ascertained, as I had, that Seth Goodnow had been killed, or almost killed, somewhere else, before being transported to the dojo. The sand on his legs proved that. I mean, it's not like the dojo has a sandbox.

"Look, A.C.," she said. A.C. stood for Agatha Callie, my nickname among Cattail's police force. I'd earned a reputation as a bit of a Jessica Fletcher / Miss Marple type.

"You don't have to call me A.C. anymore," I said. "My sleuthing days are done. I just don't have the stomach for solving crimes." The words felt true—and yet I couldn't stop thinking about Toby. How he'd gotten a small-business loan and single-handedly rehabbed the space from a clothing boutique into a dojo. Then, student by student, he'd built the Cattail Family Martial Arts community. I'd witnessed how his young charges' eyes gleamed whenever he praised them or offered a congratulatory high five. Now, with the dojo linked to a murder, what if all that hard-won trust he'd built up came crumbling down?

"I can't disagree that Toby Dodge seems like a nice guy," Fusco was saying.

"The kind of guy who'd give you the shirt off his back," I said.

"Exactly. And it's the super-nice types who crack."

"Where is he now?"

She turned off the voice recorder. "I'm asking the questions. You're answering them."

"But this is all formality, right? You're just following protocol. You can't possibly think—"

"Toby's being taken care of. Can we get on with things?" She resumed recording. "When you called 911, dispatch told you to wait outside. Did you?"

I pursed my lips.

There'd been that teensy window of time—less than a minute—after I'd left the building, when Toby had been alone with Seth Goodnow. That was not good optics.

Was Jurecki, at that very moment, questioning Toby in some other room close by? Was Toby admitting to having been alone with the body? Or was he fibbing, saying he was outside with me the whole time? It was hard to imagine him telling even a little white lie—to anybody, let alone the police. More importantly, just what *had* happened inside Cattail Family Martial Arts during those forty-five seconds when we'd been separated?

"You know," Fusco said. "If you peel your orange, you can eat it. But you have to peel it first. See what I'm saying here?"

"Toby and I both went outside." There. Not a lie.

"And yet you disconnected the call."

"My *cheek* did, Fusco! It was an accident." I pushed back from the table. "I've seen enough cop shows to know that you can't keep me here unless you're going to arrest me."

She gave me a squinty frown.

"Am I under arrest?" I asked. "Since we're apparently not friends, I'd love to *peel* my delightful citrus fruit alone, somewhere that doesn't smell like coffee brewed with dust that was then spilled onto this carpet sometime in the previous century."

Fusco was still frowning as she leaned back, the front legs of her chair lifting.

I gathered my tastes of Florida and headed for the door. "Thanks for the snacks," I said.

7

Police tape made an X over the front door of Cattail Family Martial Arts, where a uniformed officer stood guard. I swore he gave me the stink eye as I marched past. On my cell I called Toby, but he didn't pick up. Jurecki must still have him. "Hey," I said to Toby's voicemail. "Are you okay? Call me when you get this."

Walking, I googled the mysterious victim, Seth Goodnow. The first item that popped up: an engagement announcement in a Boston newspaper from January of this year. A photograph showed Seth and his then bride-to-be, Naomi Tri, a slender woman who appeared not simply mug-for-the-photographer happy but genuinely joyful. They were shown in an urban park. Seth was spinning Naomi around, her long hair flying.

The future Mr. & Mrs. Seth Goodnow, read the caption. *The wedding is slated for mid-May on the Outer Banks of North Carolina, with honeymoon immediately to follow.*

My heart shot down to the pit of my stomach. Seth Goodnow had been a newlywed, here on his honeymoon. As was customary for a lot of Cattail destination weddings, the guests stayed on for a few days or several weeks, continuing to celebrate alongside the bride and groom.

I slipped my phone into my cross-body bag. I needed a shower—but I *wanted* the MotherVine Bookshop. I couldn't think of any other place in the world that would make me feel like my feet were on solid ground. And my boss, Antoinette Redfield, its owner and operator, could be a pretty good listener.

"No time for poppycock, my dear." Antoinette's voice reminded me of happily tinkling bells. Behind the checkout counter, she was a blur of movement. A line of tanned customers extended past the Local Interest section.

"*Poppycock?*" I repeated. I joined her behind the counter, but without a second workstation, there wasn't much I could do to make the line go faster. "This is serious, Ant," I said. "I need to tell you—"

"Gift wrap this, would you?" She passed me a hardcover book.

Sighing, I tore off some brown paper and did what she'd asked, making crisp corners and poofing out a raffia ribbon. The man waiting for the gift-wrap job was trying not to turn up his nose. I couldn't blame him. Two hours ago, I'd deemed myself too stinky and disheveled to enter this safe haven.

Antoinette gave her chin-length strawberry-silver curls a toss. "Happy reading!" she told him. "Do come back soon." She beamed at the next customer, a teenage boy holding two deep-space science fiction books. "Step right up, young man."

The air-conditioning kicked on, enveloping me like ice-chilled sheets and making my teeth chatter. Antoinette rang up and I bagged. Within minutes, the line shrank to nothing.

"What the heck happened to you?" she asked, really seeing me for the first time. "You look positively mommicked." That was a Cattail old-timer's way of saying I looked like I'd been strapped to a tree for the duration of a Category 5 hurricane. "What are you doing here, anyway? It's your day off."

"I know," I said. "I—"

A thirty-something woman with big brown eyes rushed toward us, an armful of children's books spilling over. I reached out and grabbed one before it hit the floor.

"Thanks," she said, depositing the load onto the counter. "Sorry. I went kind of crazy."

"That happens in bookshops," Antoinette said. "No apology necessary."

As another small line formed, I realized I wasn't going to get another second of her time.

Next best thing: cleaning.

I headed for the compact storage room that doubled as the office. Even at my most stressed, the MotherVine gave me the sense of floating just underneath the surface of a sunny pocket of ocean. The walls' pale green color, combined with the shelves' deep vine green, created a dreamy quality. Wide-plank pine floors creaked like an old book binding, and scents of paper and ink mingled with aromas of coffee and lavender.

Despite the inviting atmosphere, I felt jerky with anxiety.

Armed with a cleaning rag and spray bottle, I sized up my first target: the children's area's plastic-and-coils rocking horse. The sagging thing had probably been the height of safety standards in the seventies, when it came off the assembly line. But kids didn't give a hoot about fifty-year-old springs that groan like a dying animal. At the moment, a three-year-old boy was bucking the rocking horse like a drunk cowhand on a mechanical bull. Nearby, a girl of the same age waited her turn.

"Break time!" I tried to sound cheerful. "Horsey needs a bath."

The boy slid off. I attacked the toy mount, giving it a thorough wipe down. The more elbow grease I expended, the less freaked out I would feel. "Who's next for a pony ride?" I asked when every inch of the horse was gleaming and reeking of Antoinette's homemade tea-tree-oil solution. Breathing hard from exertion, I plastered a smile on my face.

The kids scattered.

Next target: back patio. My favorite grape-scented wonderland. Pergolas cast shade over wrought iron tables and chairs, where customers sat and sipped and flipped through books and magazines. This was the home of the bookshop's namesake: the mother vine, the oldest known of its kind for Cattail Island's golden-pink Tinnakeet grapes. Twisted and gnarled, the thick vine rose from the dirt, fountaining into a living ceiling of serrated leaves. Bunches of grapes dangled, perfuming the air with the seductive scents of jam and ocean spray.

In the farthest corner, a middle-aged guy with his feet propped on an unused chair was perusing the latest James Patterson. "Pardon me," I said, shooing the crumbs from his table. "Pretend like I'm not even here."

"I was just leaving," he grumped.

At the shadiest table, a woman wearing heavy lipstick turned the pages of the Anne Rivers Siddons novel *Outer Banks*. I pointed to the grape stems at her elbow. "Y'all done with those?" I asked. "My boss uses them for composting in her garden at home."

She handed them over before gathering her things and rising to go.

It was then that I heard a voice, shaky with age, mumble, "I shouldn't have come."

I turned. Addison Battle, wizened owner of Addison's Barbershop, stooped before the mother vine. Tufts of hair sprouted from his ears. His hands looked like tree knots. Even on his day off, the old man smelled like leather and Barbicide. He was smoothing his ever-present yellow bow tie; it was rumored he slept and showered in it.

"You feeling okay, Addison?" I asked.

He attempted a smile that didn't quite reach his eyes. I won-

dered if he'd had a rough night's sleep. Either that or his nona-
genarian joints were finally starting to wear down.

Every Sunday, the old barber shambled among the MotherVine
stacks. Sometimes he bought a card to send to his daughter, but
he never seemed to be looking for anything in particular. I think
he just hated not cutting hair—but not enough to go against his
principles and open up Addison's Barbershop on a Sunday. Perusing the MotherVine was his work-around, a way to enjoy some
social interaction.

"Do your eyes ever play tricks on you, Callie?" he asked.

"Everyone feels like that sometimes."

"I suppose." Munching a grape, he shuffled off, the frayed
cuffs of his slacks brushing the floor.

"Hey, wait up." I followed him inside the bookshop. "You
sure you're all right?"

"I'm not sure of anything these days." With that, he headed
for the door.

"That was weird." Resting my cleaning supplies on the counter, I looked around and realized the MotherVine had cleared
out; it was just me and Antoinette. "At least there's a lull in the
action."

"*Lull?*" Antoinette said. "You've driven away all the shoppers!
You tore through here like a smelly tornado and—"

"I know. I'm sorry. It's just that I'm—sort of freaking out."

"What about?"

Tin Man hopped onto the counter and gave my earlobe a few
purry nibbles. It was almost as if he could tune in to my edgy
mood and comfort me accordingly. Stroking him, I slowed my
breathing to a steady rhythm. With his and Antoinette's attention, I could practically feel my blood pressure lowering. I kissed
his head and said, "There's been another murder."

My boss's hands flew to her collarbone. "Why didn't you just come out and say that in the first place?"

I filled her in.

"Good grief," she said through her fingers. "*Again?*"

"I know."

"How's Toby?"

"The police took him in for questioning. Me too. That's normal, right?"

"Is it? Don't you know how the police operate? You covered crime in Charlotte."

"Here and there. I was a jill-of-all-trades kind of reporter."

The door tinkled as a customer entered and drifted toward the DIY shelves. Antoinette and I both said hello as warmly as we could manage. When he was out of earshot, my boss quietly said to me, "Nine Love Beach Trail. Isn't that what you said?"

"The victim's local address? What about it?"

"Sounds like something out of a book."

"Yeah. The kind of book where an innocent woman goes snooping around and ends up dead. That can't be me. I had enough near-death experiences last summer to last me until I'm old and gray. No offense."

She fanned the pages of a paperback. She always had a book nearby, to dip into during slow times. "A proper literary heroine would never be able to resist checking out an address like Nine Love Beach Trail," she said.

"I am not a proper literary heroine. I am a real, regular, run-of-the-mill person."

"Ah yes. My favorite stories are about average people who experience something scary, and then hide out and boringly mind their own business afterward."

"I just want to sail through the rest of this spring while enjoying some peace and quiet. I've earned it. What's wrong with that?" The truth was, while I wanted my sleuthing days to be over, I had a feeling they'd just begun.

Antoinette's light brown eyes crinkled at the corners. "Maybe you're right. I'm sure another dead body is nothing at all to worry about." From a cubby behind the counter, she selected a slim paperback. "Since you chased away all our customers, how about a delivery?"

8

Turns out the slim paperback was deliverable to Mustang Beach's Sanctuary Bungalow, which Toby and I had been admiring just a couple of hours earlier.

But as I still smelled like fish rotting in a barrel, I said goodbye to Antoinette, tucked the book under my arm, and continued walking down Queen Street, all the way into the residential portion. By Uncle Hudson's mailbox, my Little Free Library looked like a dollhouse on a post. Its white trim and yellow siding made it a perfect miniature of Hudson's place. A tiny sign tipped from the roof: CATTALE QUEEN.

I gave the cattail-shaped handle a twist, deciding that all the morning's craziness was bound to calm down once and for all. Sooner or later. Satisfaction pulsed through me as I surveyed the tidy rows of books. I tended to them daily, so only a bit of rearranging was required. That task complete, I turned toward the house. The Old Fart Van was gone, which meant my uncle was out. I'd have to get him caught up later.

After a shower, I made my way into his garage turned woodshop, which was where I accessed my current—albeit temporary—living quarters. A small loft, reachable by ladder, private and sawdust-free thanks to a shower curtain. I dressed in the new outfit I'd purchased from a boutique on Queen Street during a recent spring sale. The skirt had shorts inside—*the look of a skirt with the freedom of shorts,* the boutique owner had said before factoring in an additional twenty percent off, the standard locals discount. My top was cornflower-blue muslin with a front keyhole closure. My new flip-flops had me feeling like I was walking on clouds. (I'd worn my old flip-flops literally into the ground—just a couple of weeks ago, on Queen Street, one flopped right off my foot when the thong finally snapped.)

In the kitchen, I peeled my orange courtesy of Detective Fusco, placing the segments in a plastic baggie for car snacking. And for the second time that morning, I headed south toward Mustang Beach, this time in my trusty old Honda Civic, which I'd bought, used, more than a decade ago. Not only was a Civic one of the most reliable cars out there; it also had the added appeal of being a palindrome, which counted for a lot, at least in my book.

I took Queen Street the whole way. It was the island's main thoroughfare, curling from north to south, kissing the commercial sound side for a few blocks mid-island. My open windows delivered great gusts of warm sea air. Even with the humidity, I was betting my towel-squeezed hair would be dry—frightening but dry—by the time I arrived. I cranked up some bluegrass and savored the fiddle music soaring on the wind. Fusco had been right: the orange was delectable. And I'd been right about the MotherVine helping to sooth my frayed nerves. At least for the moment.

A brown sign announced the turnoff to Mustang Beach. I bumped along the dirt road, passing the treed, isolated parking area where Toby and I had set off on our run earlier that morning. I parked in front of Sanctuary Bungalow. It had been mere hours since I'd entertained a domestic fantasy about this quaint seaside place, and yet so much had changed. A man had been murdered—and here I was, delivering a book. It felt wrong, but it also felt right. I mean, really, what options were there, aside from letting the police do their jobs while I continued to do mine?

Which was bookselling. Not solving crimes. Not chasing murderers. Good old bookselling.

Sitting behind the wheel, I slid the delivery, a volume for middle-grade readers, from my bag. *The Legend of Rosie Beacon* wasn't familiar to me. According to the back cover, it was a fictionalized account of an actual thirteen-year-old girl who'd lived on the Outer Banks during the time of the American Revolution.

Interesting.

I got out of my car and approached the bungalow. Next to the main door, attached to cedar shingles, a sign bore the year of construction: 1938. The doorbell was rimmed with rust. The door was open, and a second sign read, PLEASE COME IN! My chest warmed. For as many times as I'd admired this dwelling from afar, I couldn't recall having ever been inside.

9

I was greeted by a taxidermied goose suspended from the ceiling, wings and feet outstretched, like it was sizing up a landing on the heads of all who entered. The air smelled of must, salt, and the dregs of a vanilla-scented candle guttering on a table. Straight ahead, a mural stretched the length of the wall, depicting exactly what could be glimpsed outside these windows—ocean, surf, and mustangs. An adjacent panel had a big red slash over it, like a no-smoking sign. It showed a person offering an apple to a mustang. Accompanying text read:

Domestic horses eat apples and carrots. WILD horses
haven't evolved in the same way and DIE from eating apples
and carrots. NEVER feed, approach, or entice wild horses.
It's against the law!

"Forty-eight feet high, fourteen feet wide," said a voice.

A woman had emerged from a narrow hallway. Based on the creases around her mouth and between her brows, I put her in her late forties, though she could have been younger. It was hard to tell with sun-beaten folks.

"Geri-Lynn?" I guessed. That was the name Antoinette had scribbled on the back of the bookmark. "I work for the Mother-Vine Bookshop in town," I said, "and I have a delivery. I'm told this is where a Geri-Lynn Humfeld wanted the book delivered."

"You were told right." Her straw-colored hair swished past

her shoulders. She wore a bell-sleeved tunic so sheer her bra showed through. The fringe of her denim shorts tasseled toward broken-in cowboy boots.

"You were saying something about forty-eight feet?"

"That's how big the billboards are on the side of the highway. Forty-eight by fourteen. Each and every spring, the Mustang Beach Sanctuary rents three billboards along the route most mainlanders take to get to the ferry that brings them here. All told, that's more than two thousand square feet of the same message: *Don't feed wild horses.* Yet"—her boot heels clacked against the wood floorboards as she strode closer—"we average one mustang death per year attributed to some knucklehead luring them with produce. It's a good thing I'm a churchgoer. Otherwise, there's no telling what I would do to someone like that." She jerked her thumb at the painted figure slashed through with red. "If I caught him in the act."

"I'm Callie Padget."

She hardly gave her new book a glance. "You're the one from the news last summer. The pier collapse. The shark attack."

"Oh. Yeah." I felt my cheeks flushing. Thanks to the large news outlets' hypercoverage, I'd been recognized by several people— a few bookshop customers and several pedestrians—who peered at me before getting the guts to ask some version of *Is that you? Were you the one?*

These encounters unnerved me. As a former reporter, I was accustomed to describing the scene, not being part of it. The craziest thing was Hudson watching the news one night when my headshot showed up on the screen. The media had gotten hold of my old newspaper staff pic.

"You solved a crime the police couldn't figure out," Geri-Lynn Humfeld said. "Two crimes, actually. Two *murders.*" It looked like she was mulling something over as she spoke, the way her storm-gray eyes roved me up and down. "Your journal-ism background must've come in handy."

"I was just—" *Doing my job*, I wanted to say. The truth was, I'd become a bookseller, and nowhere in that job description was *hunt down murderers*. "I just like helping people," I said. "Every-body does. Have you been getting a lot of visitors this spring?"

"Tons. You've caught me in a rare lull."

"The bookshop's been like that too."

"Are you the one in charge of Tin Man–stagram? I love how you make it so that he's going around the island taking photo-graphs and dishing." Geri-Lynn's laugh was raspy and conveyed a confidence that appealed to me.

She agreed to pose in front of the main mustang mural, hold-ing *The Legend of Rosie Beacon* and flashing a thumbs-up. I shot her full-body, cowboy boots and all. I couldn't imagine how prickly-hot my feet would be in footwear like that during the warmth of May. But Geri-Lynn Humfeld struck me as com-pletely comfortable—in this room, and in her own skin. I guess you'd have to command presence in order to take charge of a few dozen wild horses and everything involved in their preservation, from fundraising to outreach to monitoring the acreage they roamed.

Good morning, fur-ever friends! I wrote on Instagram, adopt-ing the gossip-columnist persona Antoinette had established for Tin Man. *Look who supports her local independent bookshop! It's the phenomenal lady—and lover of four-leggeds—who single-handedly runs the fabulous Mustang Beach Sanctuary. Did you know the MotherVine delivers? Isn't that paw-sitively delightful? Call or DM for details, darlings. Don't delay. Do it meow.*

I hesitated posting it, considering what had gone down at the dojo that morning. After finding a body, it didn't seem appropri-ate to take a light view of anything at all. But, reasoning that social media could offer some normalcy in times of trouble, I hit share.

A family entered the bungalow—a mom, a dad, and three boys. As Geri-Lynn greeted them, the kids immediately acquired a fascination with a faux sea turtle nest. A clear column displayed eggs buried underneath two feet of sand.

"Go on, bud," the dad prompted the littlest boy. "Ask the nice lady your question."

"How did the mustangs get here?"

Geri-Lynn held out her hand and the boy took it. She guided him across a once golden-hued rug that the sunlight had beaten into a cream color. On the opposite wall, a third mural showed a wooden ship tumbled by giant waves. "Long ago, horses were aboard an ill-fated Spanish sailing vessel called *Tigresa*," she said.

"*Tigresa*?" The boy's eyes widened as he took in the stormy scene.

"That's right. It crashed in the shoals, way back in the mid–fifteen hundreds. Many souls, human and animal, didn't make it through. But a few horses did, swimming over the very shifting sands that had crashed the ship to begin with. Those brave mounts came ashore on Cattail Island. They adapted to its humid, hot summers and windy wet winters. They survived."

"Ask your question now," the mom said to a slightly larger boy.

"When will the baby foal be born?"

Good question. I'd been wanting to ask Geri-Lynn about the foal too. I followed Mustang Beach Sanctuary on Instagram. Posts were regular, just about daily. The past few weeks, most of the photographs had been of the pregnant mare, a deep brown beauty with a long black mane, bulging belly, and backward Z scar between her eyes. A few days ago, though, the posts had stopped. Leaving me and five thousand other followers to wonder if there'd been any developments.

"I was here earlier this morning," I said. "Running on the footpath. My friend and I were hoping to see the pregnant mare, but she didn't show herself."

Geri-Lynn paused. "Mama's likely keeping cool in the shade," she said. "Sometimes, a gal wants privacy to give birth, so she seeks out the shelter of the forest. Her band knows to leave her alone."

"Her band?" the oldest boy asked.

"Siblings, aunts and uncles, mates. We can usually count on several births every spring, but this year there's only one pregnant mare. That makes her very special indeed." Geri-Lynn had taken a seat on the window ledge facing the Atlantic. The waves were calmer than they had been this morning, shining like water-covered mirrors.

"The boys learned about the mustangs in school," the mom said, practically popping with excitement. "We came to Cattail just to see these magnificent animals in person. Getting to see the newborn foal would be icing on the cake."

The dad gasped, pointing out the window at a lone piebald stallion galloping south, sand and tail billowing. The mother and boys rushed to the window amid exclamations of "awesome" and "cool."

"To answer y'all's question," Geri-Lynn said, "the foal should be arriving any day now."

The family left with a handful of pamphlets and Geri-Lynn's urging to climb over the dune to get a closer look at the mustangs— "but not too close."

I was about to head out myself when Geri-Lynn, flipping through her new book, said, "It's not true, you know. What you said a minute ago. About everyone wanting to help each other."

I *had* said something like that. And she was right: it wasn't true. If everyone wanted to help each other, then Cattail wouldn't have had another murder to solve.

She turned a page, her forehead creased as if deep in concentration. "You like horses?"

"I don't really *know* horses. But they're beautiful." I told her about growing up on Cattail in an era when the mustangs roamed free, going anywhere they fancied. It wasn't unusual to let your car idle for five or ten minutes as a big bunch of them meandered across the road. One of my favorite kid pastimes was observing them from my tree house as they swished their tails, snuffled for acorns, and munched grass. In those days everyone knew to plant pasture grass, as opposed to the bright green variety. Golf course–style grass was one of the problems the horses started having. The dingbatters wanted lush lawns, not the sandy, scrubby yards that the locals kept. Common fertilizer caused some of the mustangs to grow sick, even die. Then one night, when I was sixteen or so, a drunk vacationer tried to mount a mustang, got kicked in the head, and suffered permanent brain damage. Special meetings were held, and Cattailers eventually voted to give the herd the entirety of Mustang Beach, an area the horses seemed to favor anyway.

The paradox wasn't lost on anybody. The fact that, in order to keep the mustangs wild, they needed to be contained.

Geri-Lynn listened as I spoke, nodding sagely. Doubtless she knew the history, but it was probably intriguing for her to get it firsthand from someone who'd lived it. "These mustangs have no natural predators," she said. "But that doesn't mean they're not vulnerable. 'To honor their wildness, we must accept our own domesticity.'"

"Who said that?" I asked. "Rachel Carson? The famous naturalist?"

"Geri-Lynn Humfeld. I wrote that in my journal a couple nights ago."

I laughed. "I'm glad the mustangs have their own space, but sometimes I do miss seeing them around town."

A flicker of annoyance made her eyes twitch. "These beasts are wild. They're nobody's pets."

"Oh, of course not. I know that." Was she always this touchy about the mustangs? Had word leaked about this morning's murder and put her on edge? Or was something else altogether eating at her? At any rate, I had the sense that she'd been vetting me—for what, I couldn't fathom—and she'd found me more or less passable, despite a few hiccups.

"Well, Callie, thanks for the delivery here." She swung her long legs up on the ledge. "I was talking to my counterparts on the Virginia-Carolina border—you know, the Corolla Wild Horse Fund? Up there, they've got nearly three times the horses. Much bigger operation. They sell this Rosie Beacon book in their gift shop. It flies off the shelves and they're always having to re-stock it. I was thinking—the sanctuary should have a gift shop. Couldn't you picture it?"

I glanced around the cramped space and couldn't picture much more than a shelf selling the usual gift shop fare—postcards, cheap binoculars, sunscreen. And sure, maybe a title or two. "It's doable," I said.

"Do you know the legend of Rosie Beacon?" she asked, perusing the back cover.

"Not yet."

"Me neither. Promises to be an 'inspiring tale of gumption and daring.' Can't ask for more than that out of a book, now, can we?"

10

While I'd been inside Sanctuary Bungalow, Toby had called. *Hey, you*, said his voicemail. He sounded so tired. *I'm home. Gimme a call.*

Driving back to town, I tried him, but he didn't pick up. He was probably in his backyard, throwing an ax at a target, which was his way of venting stress when the dojo wasn't an option.

Which it definitely wasn't. And probably wouldn't be for several more days, while the police did their thing.

"Hey, you, back," I said to his voicemail. "I'm headed home too. Let's talk soon."

Twenty-five minutes later, I stood just inside the doorway of my uncle Hudson's garage turned woodshop. Scupper, his Scottish terrier, had wagged over and was gleefully nibbling my ankles. Like Tin Man, Scupper never failed to put a smile on my face, no matter what sort of mood I was in. Meanwhile, Hudson, whose hearing wasn't the greatest, remained bent over his worktable. A sweet, earthy scent tinged the air—whatever wood he was scrutinizing, his latest work in progress.

Part of me was bursting to tell him all about my day. Another part of me wanted to keep it to myself. As if, by not passing it along, I could erase it from having happened in the first place.

I took in my uncle, feeling flooded with love. Someone had been murdered, yet here I was, safe inside the small home of the cottony-haired, overall-clad man who had raised me. When I'd been nineteen, grief-stricken and wanderlusty, he let me fly the coop, sending me off with five twenty-dollar bills and a bear hug. Eleven months ago, at the age of thirty-eight, I'd returned. He'd welcomed me back, no questions asked.

Well, there'd been a few questions.

The point was, I'd spent my adult life avoiding Cattail. Now, all that resistance had been replaced with a new feeling. Like I never wanted to leave, not even for a day. Murder notwithstanding.

As the aroma of the take-out chowders I was carrying overcame the scent of wood, he startled. "I thought you *didn't* want me to have another heart attack," he said when he noticed me standing there. Elegantly as a bullfighter, he clasped the edges of a nearby tarp and draped it over the wood.

"What are you working on? And why the big secret?"

"Wouldn't be a secret if I told you."

I'd have guessed another Little Free Library, but the shape wasn't boxy enough. The only other things he'd created since I'd arrived back in Cattail were surfboards, and the object under the tarp couldn't have been that, either. "Can you at least tell me what kind of wood it is? Smells kind of like root beer in here."

"Maple will do that," he said, pinning the edges of the tarp with wood scraps.

"Maple's a hardwood, right? So you're building something you want to last."

"I want all my creations to last."

"Come on. Give me a hint."

"It's for Antoinette. For our anniversary. One year."

I rolled my eyes, but my smile was genuine. For as long as I could remember, Hudson Padget had been a bachelor—and had carried a torch for Antoinette Redfield. Even after her husband passed away, it took my uncle several years to pluck up the courage to make a move. Was it weird having my adoptive father date my boss? Kinda. But they were a sweet match.

I could tell my uncle hadn't heard anything about the murder. If he had, he'd have been all over me about it. "Smells like you've paid Salty Edward's a visit," he said, clearing a space on the unused end of the worktable for us to dine. He plunked down a roll of paper towels.

"Hatteras chowder," I said, pulling up a metal stool.

"No one likes eating hot soup in May, you know."

"I do." I submitted to one of my uncle's signature bear hugs. It didn't matter that I'd just seen him that morning, upon first waking. Ever since my near drowning, he hadn't held back his affection. If anything, his hugs had only grown more bearish. "Easy, there," I said, tapping out.

The protrusion that was his belly had shrunk considerably, thanks to walks on the beach. Almost every night, he and Antoinette met for a few miles of shoreline exercise. They frequently brought Tin Man, letting the cat lead the way on his little harness while Scupper took sweeper position.

There was no doubt about it. Antoinette was good for my uncle.

He and I tucked into our chowder and sipped our favorite beer, Cattail Island Blonde, from bottles. Scupper politely head-butted my shin, and I dropped him a hunk of crabmeat.

"So," my uncle said, his hand dwarfing the plastic spoon. "Trouble in paradise?"

"What makes you say that?"

"Wasn't tonight supposed to be your hot date with the monk?" That was what he'd taken to calling Toby, though not to his face. They'd hung out a bunch of times. Toby and I had joined Hudson and Antoinette on a few beach walks, and there were a few nights he had stopped by for septuagenarian poker. "Why are you sitting here with me," Hudson now asked, "eating out of a plastic tub, surrounded by sawdust?"

"You really haven't heard, have you?"

"Heard what? Ronnie and me were out on the water all day."

"Catch anything?"

"Nothing worth keeping. Well, cheers to the lonely hearts club," he said, clinking his bottle against mine.

"*Club?* Your love life's flourishing."

"I was just trying to make you feel better. You know I've been for more walks on the beach in the past year than in my entire life? It strengthens your ankles, walking in the sand." He went on and on. His and Antoinette's favorite destination was becoming Mustang Beach. Even though you couldn't walk on the sand, the path through the trees was picturesque, and the lookout platform showing off the unspoiled coastline was "out of this world." He'd lived all his life on Cattail, but the love blossoming between them was giving him a fresh appreciation for his home island's hidden gems.

"By the way," I said, "have you seen the pregnant mare recently?"

"No sign of her. Not since last week."

I thought about Geri-Lynn Humfeld. Her hesitation when that boy asked her about the foal. Her irritation at the suggestion that the mustangs were pets. On this island, I knew, strange happenings weren't limited to downtown. Was something dark going on at Mustang Beach too? "You really haven't heard the big news," I said. "Have you."

"What's this you're going on about? Another murder?" He chortled at his own joke. When he saw my sober expression, he flinched. "You're jerkin' my chain."

"I wish." I handed over my phone, which I'd cued to the news report I'd dreaded finding yet was sure would be there: an article

out of a Durham daily paper, detailing the events of the grim
discovery, which had been dubbed *the dojo murder*. "We found
the dead guy," I said when he'd finished reading. "Toby and I."

"What's going on with Cattail? No murders here for centuries, and now bodies are piling up all over the place."

"That's a slight exaggeration—"

My uncle put a hand on my shoulder. "You okay?"

"I'm sitting here before you, in one piece. Does that count as
okay?" I sighed, lifting the hair that stuck to my forehead. "Toby
accidentally left the back door to the dojo unlocked. So *someone*
was able to get in and dump a body in there. But *why*?"

"I see you've already got your detecting cap on."

"I know, I know. You want me to set the record straight, but
you don't want me to get myself killed in the process."

"Just be careful. That's all."

Something else was gnawing at my uncle. I could tell by the
way he was tapping his spoon against the soup container. "What
is it?" I asked. "Spit it out."

"The house you grew up in. Where you lived with your mother."

I pictured the old cottage on Hyde Road. The slanted floors.
The sticky doors. For a long time, it was difficult for me to merely
think about the place where I'd lived as a child. Lately, though,
that reluctance had turned into something like nostalgia. In fact,
just a few months ago, before Christmas, Toby and I had driven
around the island, admiring the seasonal decorations, and we
paused before my old cottage. Someone had put a glowing plastic surfer-themed Santa Claus in the kitchen window. I'd told
Toby stories about growing up. How, for years, my mother had
been the sole seamstress on Cattail, which meant that the wheeze
and chug of sewing machines filled our little home. When I became old enough, my special job was to select pins from the pin-
cushion and insert them into the fabric at precisely the right spot

where she was pointing. I reminisced about slurping ramen noo-
dles by candlelight on the screened-in porch, then taking turns
reading aloud from a clobbered paperback copy of *The Cat Who
Played Post Office*, my favorite cozy mystery, which my mother
had obtained for forty-five cents at the MotherVine . . . "I'm lis-
tening," I said to my uncle. "The cottage on Hyde Road. What
about it?"

"You're bound to find out sooner or later: the new owner rehabbed it and is looking to sign a long-term tenant."

"Wow. You know this from Ronnie?" My uncle's best friend
was more or less retired from real estate, though he still did fa-
vors for family and close friends.

"Rent'll be on the low end, Ronnie reckons. I wouldn't mind
you staying in my loft for the rest of your life. You know that.
But you're itching to get out of here, and it's only natural to want
to get yourself reestablished. Then again, I sure hate to think of
you living on your own with a murderer on the loose." Hudson
wiped his mouth and beard with a paper napkin. "But I could
go with you to have a look at the place. If you like it, I could help
out with the deposit and first and last month's—"

"I'm not taking a dime of your money. I've scraped up enough.
As long as the rent's affordable, I'll be able to handle it."

"But would you be able to—*handle* it?"

I knew what he was getting at. Would the constant remind-
ers of my mother swallow me up? I gave the question a few seconds of serious consideration—and sensed a small smile tugging
at my mouth. The prospect of Adult Me returning to that ram-
shackle cottage and loving it into a proper home? Murderer on
the loose or not, it filled me with poetry.

11

I climbed into my humble sleeping loft. While the space was far from the living arrangement of my wildest dreams, the knowledge that I might soon be leaving it behind gave me a bittersweet sense of gratitude. I yanked down my Murphy bed and flopped onto the mattress. My mind wandered to the murder victim. Seth Goodnow. I wished there was something I could do. Something to help the victim's family or . . . anyone, really.

My phone vibrated. Toby.

"Anything interesting happen to you today?" he asked.

I felt a rush of warmth at the sound of his voice. "Can't think of a thing worth mentioning."

"I got home from the police station a while ago. Threw my ax for a bit. Now I'm just sitting here eating ice cream and watching *Green Hornet* reruns."

We both laughed a bit sadly at the patheticness of that scene. "That doesn't sound like you," I said. "Wallowy."

"I'm not wallowy. Except when I am, I guess. A man was killed, and all I can think about is my own reputation. Word's out, you know. The murder's all over the internet."

"Haven't you heard the expression *There's no such thing as bad press?*"

"Come on, Callie. What parent is going to send their kid to me for karate lessons? What vacationer is going to be like, *You know what? I feel like working out at that place where a dude was strangled to death. Sign me up!*"

"It's not going to come to that," I said. *Not if I can help it.* "Tell me what happened at the station."

"Chief Jurecki questioned me. Detective Fusco too. Asked me about all the same things I'd already told them. It was pretty much just like in the movies, except they offered me a drink."

"Let me guess: orange juice." I told him about Fusco's orange, and we joked about the Cattail police station being a hospitality center. But things felt lighter for only a second or two.

"Jurecki said my alibi is airtight," Toby said.

"He said that? So much for playing his cards close to the vest."

"Fusco, on the other hand, was harder to read." In the background I heard a chorus of frogs croaking. Toby must have wandered out to his side porch. His voice changed then. Got quieter, slower. "About tonight," he said. "It was supposed to be . . ."

"We'll get this all sorted." I didn't really know what I meant. *What* would we get sorted? Our relationship? The murder? Both? Neither?

"He'd just gotten married, you know," he said. "Seth Goodnow. On the beach."

"Yeah." I hadn't known any of Seth's friends or relations who loved him and his new bride, and who'd cared enough to travel here to witness their union. Nonetheless, I felt the loss. The tragedy. An unbidden image popped into my head. Me, driving to that rental property on Love Beach Trail. Knocking on the door and—

"Padget, there's no need to get involved in all this," Toby said, like he knew exactly what I was thinking. "I don't want to be overprotective, but the last thing I need is for you to get hurt."

I wanted to say something reassuring, but I was distracted by a telltale internal vibration, a nervous excitement that could mean only one thing: I was on the verge of full-on sleuth mode.

12

Next morning, it was shaping up to be another beautiful day, with temps in the high seventies. The walk to work took all of six minutes and offered up several gifts for the savoring: a great blue heron flapping high above, casting its shadow on the canal water; delicious fragrances wafting from just about every window—bacon, waffles, home fries.

Between sips of green kale smoothie, I glanced at my phone. The press had gotten ahold of a magazine-worthy Goodnow wedding photograph taken on Love Beach. Naomi and Seth were barefoot, their fingers linked, their foreheads touching. The bride wore a tea-length dress made of shell-pink organdy and a headpiece of hibiscus blossoms. The groom wore khakis, the pant legs rolled up, and a shell-pink collared shirt. The glow of the sand and the rose-tinted waves meant the sun had been setting.

Pity for that carefree couple sliced through me—even as I entertained what this photograph's appearance in the news possibly meant. That Seth's mourners were talking to reporters.

If they were talking to reporters, maybe they were talking to regular folks too.

Folks like me, whose soon-to-be boyfriend's life's work was at risk.

I had time to spare before opening up shop at the Mother-Vine. I kept on walking past it.

Toward Cattail Family Martial Arts.

The place was locked, the blinds pulled. The police had buttoned it up to discourage prying eyes. Yellow tape still made an X over the front door, but no uniformed officer had been stationed there. Even so, I turned down the alley that separated Toby's building from the neighboring one. The rear of the dojo looked like it always did, except that more police tape crisscrossed the back door. There was room enough for a few cars to park in the gravel, though at the moment, no vehicles were present. All the windows were intact, and it didn't appear as though anyone had tampered with anything.

Standing on the back steps, I raked my teeth over my bottom lip. It wasn't like I was expecting to find a bloody handprint or a monogrammed handkerchief. If there'd been any damning evidence left behind—dusty footprints, clothing fibers—the police would have recovered it by now.

I *had* been hoping for a little something to jog my imagination. Something like . . . tiny, dark Addison's Barbershop, which sat across from the dojo's back lot.

My heart thumped as I took in the striped pole and, through the window, the single chair's glinting chrome footrest.

My mind flashed with yesterday morning's ghastly scene. The sand on Seth Goodnow's calves. The trail of sand on the floor.

If Seth's killer had dragged Seth through the dojo's back entrance, anyone near Addison's Barbershop would have had a front-row seat.

I crossed the street and knocked on the door. The silence was no surprise. Barbershops were closed on Mondays. They were closed on Sundays too—the day Seth had been murdered.

I'd encountered old Addison Battle during his regular Sunday morning stint inside the MotherVine, just a couple of hours after Toby and I had stumbled upon the body. He'd seemed off.

Subpar. Subdued. Could that be because he'd recently witnessed someone slinging around a dead, or about-to-be dead, body? If he had, would he then have visited a bookshop? It was possible. If he'd wanted to pretend that nothing crazy had happened. That nothing had disrupted his unassuming Cattail existence.

Then again, old Addison might have been tucked safely inside his home until embarking on his bookshop rendezvous.

I pressed my face to the barbershop window. It was like looking into the past. Rusty mirrors. Checkered floor. The sink faucet dripped, as if keeping time. One sign read, CASH ONLY; another, QUIT CUSSIN'. Sun-faded photographs of Cattail mustangs decorated the walls, showing scenes from before they were corralled, back in the days when the beasts wandered unfenced, as common as backyard squirrels.

A Cattail institution, Addison's Barbershop had occupied this side street for decades. As a teenager, Addison had taken over the business from his father; seventy-some years later, the guy was still cutting hair. Many of the Cattail old-timers had never received a hot shave from anyone else.

I spun away from the window, knowing that sometime very soon, I'd be requesting an audience with the island's legendary barber.

In the meantime, I had ten more minutes to kill before reporting to work—and the tantalizing aroma of deep-fried dough hung in the air, beckoning. I followed my nose one block down, to the Casa Coquina. The turreted Victorian stood out from all the Queen Street brick. Painted purple and cream in honor of the pretty coquina clamshells that dotted Cattail Island beaches, the B and B was like something out of a princess fantasy. Wraparound porches graced two floors, and the third floor had several balconies.

On the side street next to the grand home, a food truck was parked. Both B and B and food truck were owned and operated by Arturo Bravo, voted Cattail's Friendliest Resident ten times over, which was saying something on an island peopled by friendlies.

The truck, Bravo Tacos, served two things: fish tacos and fish taco salads. And on occasional warm-weather mornings, the breakfast crowd could get their hands on green plantain fritters: fist-size deep-fried doughballs of cheese, herbs, and not-quite-ripe plantains. As I was a bit of a health nut, it had been a while since I'd indulged in this particular treat. And if I walked through the MotherVine door bearing green plantain fritters, both Antoinette and Tin Man would do an adorable happy dance.

I happened upon the truck just as the chef, Turo's niece Luzbita, was propping up the canopy. Digging out my anti-wallet—plastic cards and dollar bills held together with a hair elastic—it occurred to me that one of the signers of Toby's sign-in sheet had listed the bed-and-breakfast as her address. Heather Something.

"Buenos dias, cocinera," I said, mentally kicking myself for not paying more attention in Spanish class at Cattail High. I wished I could formulate a few intelligent questions, in Luzbita's native tongue, about Heather Something. Luzbita looked expectantly at me. "Tres buñuelos, por favor," I said. "Is Turo around this morning?" I inserted my credit card into the reader.

Luzbita shook her head.

"How about the police? Have they been around? ¿Policía . . . aquí?"

Another headshake. It was unclear whether she was answering my questions or trying to tell me she didn't want to answer them. Through the window she passed a warm bag. The smells of melted mozzarella and coriander literally made my mouth water. "Gracias," I said. "*Muchas* gracias."

13

My belly pleasantly full, I added two upcoming beach reads to the display window inside the MotherVine Bookshop. It was Monday, which, in the book world, meant the day before release day. Many customers loved being able to snatch up books a day early, if possible. The appearance of these two titles, one by Jennifer Weiner and another by Emily Henry, would excite certain in-the-know readers who happened by.

In the office, I peeled open a can of smoked trout for the mewling Tin Man, who possessed the talent of being able to purr *and* gobble breakfast at the same time. Like my uncle, Tin Man had trimmed down these past few months, sporting a sleek physique thanks to all the beach walks. But the bookshop cat still consumed food faster than any person or animal I'd ever seen.

Next, I harvested some lavender. The plants shot up from pots on every windowsill. Antoinette and I had taken to snipping the buds—strategically. As I was learning, aridity-loving lavender is notoriously difficult to keep alive, especially in an area like the Outer Banks, with its thick humidity. We'd been laying the clippings across the coffee grounds, brewing lavender coffee. It was a big hit. So big that I'd made a sign requesting customers take their coffee either to the back patio or out front to the sidewalk benches. PLEASE DO NOT CROWD THE SELF-SERVE AREA, AND PLEASE DO CLEAN UP ANY SUGAR OR CREAM THAT YOU MIGHT HAVE SPILLED. For the most part, folks complied.

I cued up some beach music on the streaming service. Jack Johnson's strummed ukulele and mellow vocals filled the Mother-Vine as I brewed coffee and filled the carafes—one lavender, one regular, one decaf. I was stocking the self-serve station with sugar, cream, and cinnamon when Antoinette opened up shop, and customers streamed in. A twenty-something woman wearing a mesh cover-up over a bikini entered, followed by a mother and toddler sporting enviable blond waves. The boy peered at me from under his mop of hair. "Hi," he said, extending a chubby hand.

"Welcome to the MotherVine," I replied, giving him a gentle fist bump.

In a matter of seconds, the shop was buzzing.

With gossip.

As I'd noted, Cattailers were rumor-growing experts. They planted a seed, sprinkled it with water, and waited. Other times they employed a more pyrotechnical kind of style—lighted a spark, then backed away as it rocketed upward and exploded.

Of course, vacationers could be just as blabby. They wanted to feel like they lived here, and getting in on the local confabulation was a good way to forget about having to return home.

I overheard a not-so-quiet conversation between two men, both vacationers, glowering near the spinning tower of new releases. "So much for Cattail's reputation as a charming beach destination," one of them said.

"I wouldn't live anywhere else." That voice, surprisingly, was my own. Behind the counter, I was standing tall, my shoulders thrown back, a smile on my face. Sure, this past year had been more murderous than was ideal. But I had faith someone would get to the bottom of things. Preferably Fusco or Jurecki.

Possibly me.

The mom with the pretty hair came to my defense. "This bookshop alone is enough reason to make a permanent move to Cattail Island, as far as I'm concerned," she said. "I'd live here in a heartbeat. If I could only convince my husband." She winked at me kindly before nudging her boy toward the children's area.

A demure octogenarian, her bun like a ball of ice, stepped up to the counter. From the lapel of her couture jacket, a ruby brooch shined, as big and bright as a stoplight. Pearleen Standish—furniture heiress and Cattail's richest businesswoman—slapped a paperback before me. The cover featured a trio of shirtless, burly men wearing kilts, ogling a maiden as she disrobed before a babbling brook. *Three Hot Scots*, the title screamed.

"As far as we Cattailers are concerned, gentlemen," Pearleen enunciated, "if you don't like it here, you can catch the next ferry back to the mainland."

Good-natured laughter rippled through the shop. I grinned. "Shall I put this in a bag for you, Miz Pearleen?" I asked discreetly.

"Oh, Callie." She tucked the bodice ripper under her arm. "I'm afraid I'm far too old to give a hoot."

As she tottered off, I felt grateful for her show of solidarity. But gratitude couldn't keep a dark thought from darting through my mind. Any one of us inside that shop—or outside it—could become the killer's next victim.

14

At closing time, I hopped into my Civic and headed north to Love Beach Trail. Two-thirds up the ocean side of the island, the narrow lane of practically identical cottages led straight to the dunes. And beyond them, to the beach. The cottages huddled so close together, you could hold a conversation with whoever was grilling next door without even raising your voice.

Naomi and Seth Goodnow's friends and relatives had seemingly rented out the entire street. Many vehicles with Massachusetts license plates crowded the driveways. The single car parked before Nine Love Beach Trail, a Volkswagen Beetle, had been decorated. *Just Married* was written on both windshields, along with a phrase that I assumed was in Vietnamese, given the bride's maiden name, Tri. The Beetle had even received the old-fashioned treatment of empty soup cans tied on with string. The license plate was vanity, letters and numbers separated by a colon. A Bible reference, perhaps.

I pulled over.

People of all ages mingled on the small lawns and porches, sipping beers and talking softly. Some of their accents had a singsong lilt, a hint of Carolina mountains, while others bore the dropped *r*'s of New England. I heard clinking—the unmistakable sound of a game of horseshoes. This game lacked any celebratory noises—no happy shouting, no slapping of high fives. It had to be the saddest game of horseshoes ever played on Cattail Island.

Back in my reporting days, I'd have hopped out and intro-duced myself, flashing my press pass like a VIP. Booksellers, how-ever, couldn't get away with that sort of behavior. I'd come off as intrusive at best. At worst, insane.

If I wanted to help—Toby, the widow, the police, *anybody*—I'd have to figure out a way to get in with these people. I was drumming my thumbs on the wheel, thinking, when Detective Fusco emerged from Nine Love Beach Trail. Her badge glinted from her hip, and her hair blazed in the late-afternoon sun.

I sank lower in my seat.

A trim woman strolled next to her. I recognized her from the photographs. The widow, Naomi Goodnow. I strained to hear their conversation, but the clanging horseshoes obscured it.

Fusco was heading for her pickup, which I suddenly recog-nized was parked right in front of me. In a goodbye gesture, she put a hand on Naomi's shoulder—and then her gaze wandered in my direction, and her mouth became a grim line.

"Seriously?" The detective had marched over. She gripped the lip of my open car window.

"I'm paying my respects," I said.

"You know the families?"

"Not yet. Learn anything interesting since yesterday?"

"Did you know I'm the youngest detective in Cattail history? And I'm the first ever—and only—female detective. Actually, I'm the only detective, period. It's Jurecki, then me, then a hand-ful of unis. I'm not about to rejoin their ranks on account of careless mistakes."

"Mistakes?" So there it was. Fusco had come to the official conclusion that putting her trust in me last summer had been reckless.

Maybe she had a point. Maybe her position was a lot more complex than I'd been able to appreciate.

"You have no business being here, bothering this poor family," she said. "Have *you* learned anything interesting since yesterday? That's the only direction information is going to flow." With a fingertip, she drew an invisible line from me to her.

"Do you hate me or something? Because that's what it feels like."

She gave my door a final slap before turning away. "You're parked in a tow zone, A.C."

15

The MotherVine was closed, but Antoinette was inside, running the handheld vacuum over the papasan chairs.

"Say you wanted to give someone a gift," I said, keying in. "Someone who just lost a loved one. A grieving widow, for example. What book would you pick out for her?"

Antoinette hardly batted an eye. She'd been answering random customer questions for forty years. She could do it in her sleep. "This way," she said, tossing aside the vacuum. "Are we talking about the wife of the man who was killed? The Goodnow widow?"

"Thought I'd reach out. Don't you just feel horrible? These kinds of things shouldn't be happening in Cattail. People come here because it's quiet. They come here seeking refuge from the Myrtle Beaches and the Virginia Beaches. They want *less* crazy. Not more. It's usually a safe, gorgeous place. I just think Naomi Goodnow might appreciate hearing from people in this community." I meant that last bit. Yes, I was hoping to gain access to the families and friends. I was hoping to learn . . . well, whatever there was to learn. That didn't mean I had no regard for their grief.

"As usual, you have a point," Antoinette said as we reached the psychology shelves. "And I'm glad you've decided to . . . *reach out*. For religious types, you can't go wrong with C. S. Lewis. For touchy-feely types?" She selected a thin paperback called *I Wasn't Ready to Say Goodbye*.

I had no idea what camp Naomi Goodnow fell into. Was she a pop-psych person, or pious? Couldn't you be both? And what if she practiced some religion other than Christianity?

Selecting a book for a woman I didn't know, who'd been a wife for mere days before becoming a widow, was tricky. She must have had many conflicting feelings coursing through her. I almost chose *I Wasn't Ready to Say Goodbye*. Despite the Van Gogh–esque moonlit ocean on the cover, the whole package seemed to say, *It's okay if you want to give life the middle finger right now*. However, when I remembered the decorated Beetle in the driveway of Nine Love Beach Trail, and the possibly Bible-themed vanity plate, I had a change of heart. "Give me the Lewis," I said, figuring if nothing else, the widow might lean traditional.

"Lewis it is." Antoinette handed me another slender paperback. *A Grief Observed*. The cover showed leaves twisting away from a soon-to-be-nude tree. I tried to take the book from her, but she held on, studying my face. "How are you? Do you need to talk? Discovering a body like you did—"

"That's why I'm reaching out to the widow. Helping others helps me, you know?" Or something like that. I pulled out my makeshift wallet to pay for Naomi's book. Realizing I had no bills, I asked, "Can you dock this from my paycheck?"

"Don't worry about it," Antoinette said. "Tell the poor woman it's a gift from the MotherVine."

"Yes?" Close up, despite eyes puffy from crying, Naomi Goodnow was even prettier than her photograph.

I stood opposite her in the entryway of her rental cottage. A thin chain circled her neck, and a cross hanging from it showed through the fabric of her T-shirt. I was glad I'd gone with the Lewis—until I noticed her bronze cuff bracelet lined with potbellied buddhas in seated meditation.

Introducing myself, I offered the book, which I'd embellished with a raffia ribbon that Antoinette kept in supply boxes behind the checkout counter. I also offered a bag of blueberry muffin tops. I'd stopped at Cattail Café. It had been closed for the night, but I tapped on the window and convinced the owner, whom I'd known since grade school, to let me buy a half dozen of the baked goods she'd been setting aside for tomorrow's bargain day-olds.

"I hope I'm not bothering you," I said now to Naomi. "I'm a local, and a couple of the businesses in town wanted to pass along their condolences."

She inhaled the blueberry aroma, then hugged the bag to her chest. "Cattail Café. My husband got us lattes from there just the other day. He woke up before dawn and pedaled downtown. They make really good lattes. Croissants too."

"They do," I agreed, surprised she could string more than a few words together, considering the tragedy. A rhinestone-studded ohm symbol ring adorned her thumb, and one of her knuckles sported a tattoo of the ancient Egyptian eye of Horus.

"I actually read my fair share of Lewis as an undergraduate," she said. "I'm a professor of religious studies. I never had an occasion to read this one, though."

"Well." Out of habit, I almost piped out *Happy reading* but quickly came to my senses. "I don't want to intrude."

"Wait," she said. "Don't go. Would you like a Huda?"

16

I sure would," I said, having no idea what a Huda was. "Kind of you," I added, as she motioned me inside.

The room had an air of boozy sluggishness, as if the people therein had been drinking the day away, trying to erase reality. They slumped on love seats and easy chairs and floor cushions. Most were bent over phones, drowning their sorrows in digital distractions.

"Wait here," Naomi said before heading into the kitchen.

I felt something nosing my butt cheek and spun around to find a deer-colored greyhound winking up at me.

"Unicorn!" a man scolded. He was sitting on the nearest sofa, a White Claw resting between his splayed legs. Unicorn the greyhound slinked over to him and leaned against his knees. "Sorry," the man said. "It's his only vice."

"No worries," I said. "I like animals."

Several quiet conversations were underway, one in Vietnamese and at least two in New England–accented English. The television was tuned in to local news, the volume low. One woman, perched on an end table, stared at the screen. Seth Goodnow's sister? She had the same copper waves and high hairline as the deceased.

"Cheers." Naomi returned and handed me an ice-cold aluminum can. "It's popular in Vietnam." Her hostessy demeanor was a sure sign of her coping mechanism of choice: denial. The art of acting as if everything was proceeding normally. And when you're on vacation, giving a friendly stranger a beer is normal.

Huda, I was pleased to discover, was crisp and easy. After the warmth of the day, the awkwardness of crowding into a room packed with mourners, and the knowledge that I'd been among the first to come upon the body of the man they'd lost—anyway, I downed half the can.

Naomi glanced around the room. "Seth would love this. *Any excuse for a party.* That was his personal motto. He loved a gathering of any kind. Me too. Extroverts, I guess . . ."

I just listened. What else could I do? Tell her she was in denial? Pepper her with questions? *Can you think of anyone who might have wanted your brand-new husband dead?*

"We'd been having such an amazing week," Naomi said, her eyes glistening. "It was a never-ending celebration, with both our families here, and so many friends too. We rented all the cottages on this adorable street. I just can't believe . . . You know, the police told all the wedding guests to stay put, here on Cattail, until their investigation is concluded. But nobody had any plans to go home anyway. They've all paid in full. Might as well hang around, right? It's what Seth would have wanted. Everybody here, gathered together. Stuck in paradise." She excused herself, leaving me standing there with a beer in hand, looking around. Unicorn's owner was the only person not staring at his phone or engaged in muted chatter.

He stroked the greyhound's long back and said, "We let our daughter name him."

I perched on the sofa cushion, cooing to Unicorn as he licked my fingers, which were damp from the can. I couldn't help but notice that the guy was attractive, with ebony hair and cobalt eyes.

"She was three at the time. Our daughter, I mean." He pulled out his phone and showed me a photograph of a pale girl of nine or ten, her bony arms wrapped about Unicorn's neck. Her eyes were sweet and sad. I could tell by the pic that she was the kind of kid to pour all her affection into the family pet.

A woman sitting on the other side of the sofa leaned over. "That's our Cadence."

The proud father swiped through photos taken on different days. Cadence on a tire swing. Cadence showing off a shiny rock. Cadence with her nose stuck in a book. The girl's mouse-brown hair perked up the same way in every shot, as if styled with industrial-strength fixative. She had one dramatic cowlick.

"She's next door reading *The Mysterious Benedict Society*," the mom said. "She's obsessed. I just checked up on her, asked if she'd be okay reading quietly for another twenty minutes or so, while we finished up here. You know what she said, sweet as pie? 'Mom, could you please stop interrupting me?'"

"We drive eleven hours so she could swim in the ocean," the dad said, chuckling, "and she wants to lie on the floor and read."

"Eleven hours?" I'd assumed Massachusetts was farther.

"Ohio," the woman said. "I'm Ivy O'Neill. This is my husband, Dominick."

"Callie Padget. Local bookseller."

"Oh, Cadence would love that," Ivy said.

We all exchanged handshakes. Ivy had smooth brown hair and expertly applied makeup. She went on to explain that they'd rented the cottage next door. "Dominick used to work with Seth, back in Massachusetts. Then Dominick got transferred to Ohio. I'm a full-time homeschooling mom, so I didn't have to worry about a job when we moved."

"You should have seen the wedding," Dominick said. "Nobody wore shoes. We danced on the beach all night."

"That was one of the reasons Naomi and Seth wanted to get

married here," Ivy said. "A casual, come-as-you-are affair. No bridesmaids, groomsmen, or flower girls. We should have gone that route, babe." She squeezed Dominick's hand. "Their wedding *was* fun. Despite the notary public."

"How do you mean?" I asked.

"The guy who married them had this sourpuss expression on his face the entire time."

"He did set a gloomy tone," Dominick said. "I wonder what his problem was."

"What was his name?" If a notary public had performed the formality, it was likely someone local.

The couple searched each other's faces but came up with nothing. "I don't even know what day of the week it is," she said with a sad laugh. "Vacay brain kicked in fast. On top of that . . ."

"It's inconceivable, what happened," her husband said. "Just last week we chartered a boat to take us out deep-sea fishing. Me, Ivy, Cadence, and Seth."

"Naomi had the good sense to stay behind. It was choppy as *H-E*-double-hockey-sticks. Look at this bruise I got from slamming into the railing of the boat." She held out her arm. A blue-black butterfly-shaped bruise was spread over her elbow. "I've never been so seasick. Dramamine saved the day. I'm not sure it actually cured my motion sickness, but it sure did knock me out. Cadence too."

"Yikes," I said.

"And poor Cadence hated every second of it," she said. "I used an entire bottle of sunscreen on her and she still got burned to a crisp. The curse of the Irish. Babe, show Callie that photo of Cade red as a lobster."

I was treated to another shot of their daughter, positively miserable as she slumped against the seat near the engines—the worst place to park yourself on a boat, in my opinion, because of the fumes. Not being a fan of open-ocean sailing myself, I had a lot of sympathy for the kid. The creeks of Cattail were plenty for me. Even the Pamlico Sound on a gentler day could send a kayak rolling. Plus, who wants their photograph taken when they're seasick? Then again, Cadence and her peers must be used to being models in all kinds of circumstances, thanks to seemingly every parent's addiction to social media.

"What was biting?" I asked.

"Seth was the only lucky one." Dominick swiped to a photo of his friend posing with a stumpy swordfish. "That baby was only forty inches long, so back it went." I studied the photo of Seth, bucket hat shading the broad grin on his face. He grasped the fish near the tail with both hands and hoisted it high. I had the same sobering thought as when I saw the wedding photo. There he was, so alive, so animated—when in reality he was cold as a headstone, lying in the morgue.

As Dominick pocketed his phone, I noticed that the living room was brimming with bric-a-brac. There were stacks of old books, which I definitely would have riffled through if I weren't trying to be unobtrusive. There was a crate of hammered screws. A basket of whelk shells. A doll carriage spilling over with dolls. In fact, now that I looked, well-organized junk was pretty much everywhere, next to little signs saying FREE. Apparently, not many renters had taken advantage of that offer.

"Funky décor, huh," Ivy said. "Our cottage must be owned by the same person, because we've got the same thing going on. In our bedroom, there's a box of old doorknobs, next to another box of old picture frames."

"If you ever find yourself in need of a few hundred balls of yarn, you know where to come knocking," Dominick said. "It's kind of like living in a hoarder's house."

I agreed; the flea market vibe wasn't my jam. I'd feel hemmed in by all the stuff. Also, my allergies would have something to say about the dust.

Dominick drained his White Claw, then crushed the can and placed it on the coffee table. "You with the bride or groom?"

"Sort of both," I said. Although it would have been more accurate to say *neither*. "Did you notice anyone else at the wedding acting—I don't know. Edgy? Confrontational?"

"That describes Cooper," Ivy said. "But he's always like that."

"Cooper Payne?" I asked, remembering the name from Toby's sign-up sheet. The meathead guy who wanted Toby to spar with him.

She nodded, rolling her eyes.

"Cattail police asked us the same thing," Dominick said. "They're systematically interviewing everyone who went to the wedding. It's tempting to write them off as some bumbling, country-bumpkin police force, but they seem really on the ball."

Unicorn rested his chin on my knee, and I gave his neck a few scratches, thinking my expedition to Nine Love Beach Trail had been a success. I was glad to have delivered the book and the muffin tops—*and* to have gathered some intel. The report of a cranky notary public was a lead, for sure. And I got confirmation that this Cooper Payne character was someone to look out for.

I promised myself that somehow, I'd get some more one-on-one time with Naomi Goodnow. There were many things I wanted to know.

For example, her impression of the man who'd officiated their wedding. What his name had been.

What she'd loved about her new husband.

And what she hadn't.

17

Before I began driving, I checked out Naomi Goodnow's Facebook page. There were dozens of beach wedding photos, including one of the bride and groom on either side of a glowering, bespectacled man clasping a faux-leather binder. The sourpuss notary public, I presumed. Another photo showed Seth mashing cake into Naomi's face, which she looked none too pleased about, as if he'd promised not to, then broken that promise. The day after the wedding, they'd evidently taken a trip to Mustang Beach; a selfie showed them on the observation platform, their cheeks smooshed together against a backdrop of glimmering ocean and horses' hindquarters.

Beginnings and endings, I thought, swiping through photo after photo. Everyone's lives were a tangle of beginnings and endings.

Which brought me back to Toby. The past year had been epic. When you take a relationship as molasses-slow as we had been taking ours, things felt super innocent and, at the same time, maddeningly sexy. We spent last summer and early fall frolicking on warm beaches, driving with the windows down while singing and surfing our hands on the wind, like teenagers. We'd spent winter going on runs together and continuing my self-defense lessons. It was all leading up to the day when we could take things to the next level.

But with the occurrence of a corpse, our flirtation had screeched to a halt.

In the weird way of the universe, my phone lit up with a text from the very person I'd been thinking about. Toby.

Come over? So much to tell you.

Toby lived sound side, south of downtown. His home was modest and nestled under live oaks and loblolly pines. I parked in the gravel driveway and immediately heard a repetitive thudding noise, which let me know he was around back. I picked my way over the soft ground, made even softer by fallen pine needles. It was getting dark, but there was still enough light to make out the target nailed to a tree. He was about ten feet from it, poised with the ax above his head, a one-handed grip. I'm sure he knew I had arrived and was now standing there, watching him. My engine produced a distinct noise—whiny with a touch of cough. Plus, I was about as sneaky as a drunken pelican.

After sizing up the bull's-eye, he breathed in, deep and smooth. In a swift motion, he hurled the ax. It spun end over end and *thwack*—struck the target dead center.

"Dang." Whistling, I slow-clapped. "Remind me to never leave a deceased person in your dojo."

"Hey, Padget. You're a sight for sore eyes." He wrapped his arms around me and squeezed, lifting my feet from the ground. It felt good. Reassuring. Like hugs always do when there's anxiety-provoking drama going on. Even though this hug couldn't undo a murder, I felt myself unwinding, just a little, in his arms.

"Seriously, though," I said. "How are you?"

"You just missed your frenemy," he said, gently returning me to the earth.

"Fusco was here?"

"She rifled through my things. Took my nunchucks. They're looking for the murder weapon."

I knew Toby kept three pairs of nunchucks in his home. One pair was wooden, two handles joined by a basic metal chain. Another pair was hard plastic and featured LED lights. One evening not long ago, I had begged Toby for a demonstration. He was reluctant; he wasn't a show-off, and I sensed he was abashed to have even come into the possession of something as gawdy as LED nunchucks, which had been a gift. But the demo he finally agreed to was pretty spectacular. In his dark den, he had whipped them around expertly, making it look like he was steering swirls of green fire. His third pair of nunchucks was the most menacing of all. They were made of aluminum alloy, the sleek handles beveled for grip.

"Hypothetically," I said, "you could strangle someone with a pair of nunchucks. Right?"

"If you know what you're doing? Sure." He worked the ax from the target and passed me the weapon, handle up. "You know I had nothing to do with Seth Goodnow's death, right?"

"What kind of a question is that?" I gripped the ax with both hands, like a tennis racket. For months, under Toby's patient supervision, I'd been practicing ax throwing. But I still wouldn't bet money on my hitting the target. Or even the tree. I positioned myself using the body awareness he'd taught—feet wide, spine tall, arms overhead. I hurled the ax and watched, with fingers crossed, as it nicked the tree. Chips of bark and wood went spinning off. "I'm hopeless."

"No such thing. Your form's perfect—you just need to work on your aim. Which really is another way of saying—*focus, Padget.*" He trotted over and fished the ax from the pine needles. Then he had a throw himself, hitting the bull's-eye.

"Do you remember seeing Addison Battle at any point yesterday morning?" I asked.

"Yesterday? I didn't see him, but I wouldn't expect to. He doesn't come around on Sundays. Or Mondays. The police can't possibly think he's a suspect. He's so frail, he would have a hard time killing a fly."

"He might have seen something, though. Given the barbershop's proximity to the dojo's back door."

"True." He had a few more throws, and I asked him what else he'd done with his day. "I left messages for my students to meet me in the gym at the middle school," he said. "I told them 'We can't work out at the dojo for the time being, but let's have class as usual.' But no one showed up. So I had a nice long solo workout."

"People are freaked out right now, but they won't stay that way. You're not worried, are you?"

"*Worried?*" He retrieved the ax. Handing it to me, he flashed that breezy grin, the one that, for the better part of the past year, had been making my pulse patter. "I'm definitely not worried now that you're here," he said, "mutilating my perfectly innocent tree."

I laughed—but I couldn't shake the weird feeling that there was something he wasn't telling me.

I'd driven halfway to Hudson's when my phone buzzed inside my bag. I wanted more than anything to read the text, or just glance down to see who it was from. But I was strict about never texting while driving, especially on twisty streets and especially at night. So I kept driving. Five more minutes on the road felt like an eternity. On the steering wheel, my fingers were crossed again, but this time I couldn't even say what for. I hoped for a lot of things. But it wasn't like I was going to get a text that said *Seth Goodnow's murderer has been captured*, or *Toby's not hiding anything.*

Only when I'd safely parked in Hudson's driveway did I check out my phone. The text wasn't from any of my usual suspects—these days, Toby, Antoinette, or my uncle. It was from Geri-Lynn Humfeld, head of the Mustang Beach Sanctuary. She must have found my phone number online. If you dug deep enough, you could discover my contact info along with some editorial pieces I'd written for the Charlotte daily, back in my old life. Her text message read:

> Any chance I could get you to come on out to Mustang
> Beach again? The sooner the better.

What was this about? Had the pregnant mare given birth? I'd never been up close and personal with a newborn foal. Was I going to be one of the first humans to lay eyes on Cattail's new horse baby? Did Geri-Lynn want to propose some kind of promotional tie-in with the bookshop? We could brainstorm about it. A naming contest, perhaps! Name the new foal, win some books by local authors. We could even have a signing event . . .

First things first.

Getting to Mustang Beach the following morning wouldn't be a problem. I was sure I could arrange it with Antoinette. I wasn't quite full time, and like a lot of other shop owners in Cattail, she kept sporadic hours. She couldn't exactly demand regularity of her employees when she showed up willy-nilly herself.

Composing a reply, I realized I was eager for this equine distraction. The possibility of new life was like a ray of hope. The pressure inside my chest eased as I composed a quick reply.

Sure. Is there a newborn foal to marvel at???

In the text thread, three dots appeared. They went away, then reappeared. Went away again. Then Geri-Lynn Humfeld sent the following:

See you in the morning.

18

The Tuesday fog dawned brick-thick. I might not have found the way from my car to Sanctuary Bungalow if it weren't for the blossoms dripping from the hibiscus bushes, glowing like beacons through Cattail's version of a whiteout.

Just as I reached the front porch, Geri-Lynn Humfeld emerged. A camera hung from her neck. The lens had to be a foot long. She stuck a sign on the door. BE BACK IN AN HOUR. It didn't announce the time of writing.

"Hell's bells," she said, tossing her wide-brimmed straw hat on the nearest rocker. "I don't need this thing today, do I? Hope you came prepared for a bit of a walk."

"I'm always game for exercise." Which was generally true, even though I was wearing my usual flip-flops. "That's quite the camera."

"My binoculars are clouded over with condensation. This lens works just as well. Ready?" She skipped down the steps and climbed the nearest dune.

I scrambled after her. We descended onto the small portion of Mustang Beach where people were allowed. A breeze dispersed the wall of fog, allowing a glimpse of the bungalow—and a glimpse into Geri-Lynn's personal life. In a second-floor window, I made out the shape of a lava lamp. From another window, a clothesline stretched to the nearest tree, as if delivering T-shirts and denim shorts to the woods.

"This way." She approached a fence, slats wound together

with wire. Except for its extreme height, far above my head, it was a typical Cattail Island dune fence. Closer to the water, it gave way to pilings, which continued straight into the ocean for a quarter mile, so as to discourage anyone who might be tempted to drive or swim around them onto the forbidden portion of Mustang Beach. "As you know," Geri-Lynn said, "it's legal to walk on the north end of Mustang Beach, up to this fence—"

"—as long as the horses are fifty feet away, on the other side of it," I said.

She looked impressed. "That's right. It's unlawful to come within fifty feet of a wild horse. For reference, that's only slightly longer than the length of—"

"—an average school bus."

"I love locals," she said, shaking an approving finger. "Believe me, there is no dearth of humans out there, wanting to blame the horses. *But they came right up to where I was standing!* As if the horses know the fifty-feet rule. It's the human's responsibility to move away. A mustang's only responsibility is to be a mustang."

Following her through a narrow turnstile, I took a tentative step onto the horses-only part of Mustang Beach. I hadn't walked on that sand since I was a child, before it was designated for the horses. Mustang Beach had been my mother's favorite place for sea-glass hunting. She only kept red or blue pieces, which were fairly rare, so we usually made our way back to the car empty-handed . . . "Is this allowed?" I asked, my hand lingering on the turnstile's metal knob, sticky with salt.

"As director of the sanctuary, *I'm* allowed. Along with who-ever else I deem appropriate and/or necessary. Right now, that's you." She took long strides southward, her cowboy boots kicking up sand. Ahead, six horses stood in the fog. They watched us pass, giving no indication that we were bothering them. It was like they were some sort of equine royalty, wordlessly allowing us to traverse their wispy kingdom.

The beach had a wild feeling, mostly thanks to the absence of trash. Relatively speaking, Cattail beaches are clean, but wherever there are people, there's trash. A potato chip bag waltzing in the wind, a left-behind child's pail, a flicked cigarette butt, as if the sand were a gigantic ashtray.

There was none of that nonsense on Mustang Beach. It was pristine.

"Be mindful to keep your distance," Geri-Lynn said over her shoulder. "That stallion's been kicky lately." She pointed to a large white horse who definitely seemed like an alpha male, if that could be said of horses. His ears were extra pointy, his stance fierce, the muscles of his chest rippling. "He and another stallion have been bullying each other lately—and all the other horses too—trying to establish dominance. They both want to be on the top of the pyramid. Herd hierarchy shenanigans."

"What's his name?" I asked.

"Oh no. We don't name them. The moment you give a horse a name, it becomes a pet. These horses aren't pets. They're wild."

It occurred to me that, on Instagram, Geri-Lynn never used names. It was always *this loving mama* or *what a sweet colt*. "So, no names ever?"

"Never."

"What about just in your head? Like, do you have your own secret names for them?"

She didn't answer, but pointed between two breaking waves, where a column of dark water puckered, which meant it was rushing quickly out to sea. "Rip."

Rip currents were common on the Outer Banks. Sadly, every

vacation season, rips claimed several victims, sometimes even experienced swimmers who panicked once caught by their powerful flow.

We headed away from the water, toward the dunes. "How's the pregnant mare?" I asked.

"That makes eleven," Geri-Lynn said, as if to herself.

"Um . . ." Eleven, what? Eleven horses we'd seen since we left the Bungalow? Was I supposed to be counting? *Okay*, I thought. *I'll play along.* "Fourteen?" I pointed a few dune tops down, where three horses were rolling in the sand, scratching their backs, hooves in the air.

"Fourteen so far. Let's keep going." She picked up the pace, heading for the woods.

19

We wound our way through the warm, breezeless forest, using deer trails that the mustangs had hijacked and widened.

Ahead of me, my tour guide slipped into lecture mode, going on about how the life expectancy of a wild horse is twenty years, while domesticated horses typically make it longer, provided they have proper care and conditions; and how, when a mustang is galloping full tilt, it can reach speeds of twenty-five to thirty miles an hour; and how, as recently as a hundred years ago, two million wild horses roamed the United States.

Geri-Lynn and I proceeded slowly, examining our surroundings. Every few paces, she rolled up on her tiptoes, peering through the viewfinder on her camera. Or she crouched behind vegetation so as not to startle any mustangs. When she spotted one, she silently pointed it out.

I kept count.

A few times, I spied the fence demarcating the wood-chip path where Toby and I had gone running. It was hard to believe that was only two mornings ago. I again got that feeling of certainty, a silly notion that he and I were fated for love, because whenever we spent time together, we became better versions of ourselves. Even though Fusco seemed to suspect him of just about the gravest crime a person could commit . . .

The path did an about-face, leading away from the ocean. Rounding the corner, Geri-Lynn touched my arm. "Give him some space," she whispered. I looked around, seeing nothing but trees—until a spindly horse shuffled toward us. He had tassel-like eyelashes and a short tail, and a shaft of sunlight lit him up, giving his fur a beautiful glow. "He's just a yearling," she said.

I wondered if these horses knew Geri-Lynn, and were even attracted to her scent, or her voice, or soothed by her presence.

It was weird to think that by the time this yearling entered his golden years, I'd be pushing sixty years old. Where would I be? Even just a year ago, I might have answered that question with, *I'll be in Charlotte*. Now I felt differently. I'd be right here, in Cattail. For better or worse. Of that, I was sure.

When the yearling moved on, we continued. Deeper in the woods, the mosquitoes became more insistent. As I slapped various body parts—neck, arms, legs—my irritation grew. Why had Geri-Lynn insisted I walk with her? Was *this* what I had passed muster for—following her around, counting horses?

"I forgot to offer you some bug spray," she said. "Sorry about that."

"What's this all about, Geri-Lynn?"

"I was wondering when you would break down and ask. You've certainly earned the right to know. Fact is, you're in a unique position to help me. You're not a cop, you're not a reporter, and you're not a knucklehead."

"Gee, thanks. What do you need help with?"

"If even half the rumors about you are true—"

"Rumors?"

"About your knack for this sort of thing. You know. Puzzle solving."

A *knack*? Great. "Exactly what puzzle are you trying to solve?" I asked. The moment the words left my mouth, the trail underfoot narrowed into no trail at all, and we stood side by side underneath impassably dense trees. Even in the warmth of May, the light had taken on the cool quality of a winter dusk. Before us, two scaly loblolly pines—they must have been hundreds of years old—towered upward, their bristled arms blotting out the sky. The branches of an equally stately live oak tree wrapped around the pines, like it was giving them a hug. Beyond the tree trio, shadows seemed to stretch on forever.

"This is it," Geri-Lynn said. "The farthest reaches of the sanctuary."

I'd have replied, but I felt too enchanted by this spot to utter even the most basic response. How could it be that just a few miles away, the rest of the island was romping in the friskiness of springtime, and meanwhile, by contrast, this hushed corner of the woods held the sanctity of a chapel? The magic of a storybook?

"What is this place?" I asked, finding my voice again.

"Oh, here? It's right appealing, isn't it? I think of it as the Hugging Trees." With the back of her wrist, Geri-Lynn wiped sweat from her forehead. "Two thousand and seventy-one acres. About three and a quarter square miles. All of which we have traversed this morning."

"And why is that?"

"I wanted you to see for yourself: I'm not hiding anything."

"But I didn't think you *were* hiding anything, Geri-Lynn."

"Tell me: What's your final tally?"

"I counted forty-four mustangs total."

"Forty-four. That's what I got too." She heaved a regretful sigh. "Within the confines of this fence, there should be twenty-one stallions and twenty-four mares."

I did a quick calculation. "But—that would make forty-five mustangs total. We only counted—"

"Forty-four."

"One's missing." My eyes got big. "The pregnant mare?"

"I call her Tigress."

20

Tigress.

Geri-Lynn's secret name for the pregnant mare was inspired by the 1500s Spanish shipwreck, *Tigresa*, that sank offshore, fatefully depositing the horses that would make a go of it here on Cattail Island.

"How long has Tigress been missing?" I asked.

"You can't tell anyone. Promise."

"I can't promise. But I can try to keep it to myself."

She pursed her lips, not entirely happy with that response. "Today is day three."

"Maybe she wanted some privacy to give birth. You said that happens."

"I said that. But the truth is, I've been herd manager for ten years, and I've never had a pregnant mare behave that way. Most foaling mamas want their band near them for that moment. Safety in numbers. Herd advantage. That's any prey animal's number one priority."

"When was the last time you saw her?"

She thumbed a few buttons on her camera. The photo she showed me was dated a few days ago. I recognized the horse from Mustang Beach Sanctuary's Instagram account—a rich brown beauty with the unmistakable facial scar. "This was taken about three-quarters of a mile up the beach from the Bungalow," Geri-Lynn said. "She was sunning herself, happy as a clam."

"Could she have escaped?"

"We don't have a Harriet Houdini on our hands. The fence is too tall for these horses to clear it. I've checked the whole perimeter, and there aren't any gaps."

"Then she's got to be around here somewhere. Within sanctuary confines—"

"You're not hearing me. I've scoured every last inch of this preserve. Several times. In the day. In the night. That horse is nowhere. Before you go suggesting that coyotes got her, or that she died of disease or natural causes—then where's the carcass? Where are the buzzards?"

"Could she have drowned?"

"These mustangs only swim when the ocean is calm, and they go in wither-high, no farther. It's more like wading than swimming. But even if she did drown—where's her body? The tides being the way they've been, with all the circular rips horseshoeing back to shore? Not to be gruesome, but all or part of her would have washed up by now."

"You're telling me Tigress has disappeared without a trace."

"Unless an alien spaceship came to Mustang Beach and beamed her up into the sky, there is zero explanation. What I'm telling you is, dead or alive, she's not here."

Back inside Sanctuary Bungalow, Geri-Lynn blasted the air-conditioning. We were alone, so she invited me to stay. "You can understand why I'm so worried, especially now with another murder. I heard you were the one who found the body."

"Me and . . . this guy I know, Toby."

"Toby, huh?" She smirked, which seemed inappropriate, but I chalked it up to her attempt at lightening the heavy atmosphere, or at cutting through her own anxiety. "A *guy you know*," she said. "Okay. Wait here while I get us some bevvies to cool us down. Then we can hash things out."

I sat on the window ledge. Outside, the fog had cleared, and the ocean was a gray blanket.

Our return walk had been uneventful and wordless. She'd wanted to move quietly, so as to get another head count. The second tally was the same as the first. Forty-four, when there should have been forty-five.

Now Geri-Lynn came out of her office carrying a tray. Ice cubes clinked inside two tall glasses of sweet tea. I helped myself, and she sat next to me. Grunting, she yanked off her boots, revealing a pistol inside an ankle holster. From the back pocket of her cutoff jean shorts, she produced a half-pint of bourbon. "It's for emergencies only, so don't go judging me. You want?"

I didn't mind a drop here or there, but it wasn't quite ten thirty in the morning. "No judgment, but how about I join you another time?"

"Fair enough." She tipped a splash into her tea.

"You have a theory, don't you? About what happened to Tigress."

"A theory is a broadly accepted explanation. What I have is a *proposed* explanation, therefore, a hypothesis."

"Enlighten me."

She held up a finger. "Good old-fashioned horse thievery. It's a felony in North Carolina. The sentence is up to two years in prison if convicted."

"Horse thievery?" It sounded so antiquated, I almost laughed. "If we were living a couple hundred years ago, I could see it. But why would anyone want to steal a horse nowadays?"

"Novelty. Cattail mustangs are unique in all the world. Their DNA is different from the mustangs up in Assateague and Chincoteague, and different still from the ones in Corolla and down in Shackleford. In some of those places, foals are auctioned off to the public, and they live out their lives on farms, usually alongside domesticated horses. It's a measure to keep the wild herds manageable, and for the caregivers to stay afloat financially. But Cattail mustangs?" She swept her arm around, indicating the beach and the woods. "Nobody owns these horses. The land belongs to them. They belong to the land, and the land alone."

I sipped my tea, considering. Plenty of people insisted on having special sorts of pets, whether wild or domesticated. Dogs, macaws, whatever. Heck, just last summer I'd encountered a guy who'd snatched a baby alligator from the bayou and raised it in a backyard swimming pool. *Novelty,* Geri-Lynn had said. She was right. To a certain set of animal fancier, a purebred Cattail Island mustang might be irresistibly special.

Okay, so the idea that we needed to track down a horse thief wasn't seeming so far-fetched after all.

"The wheels are turning, aren't they?" she asked. "What are you thinking?"

"That a pregnant horse would be a choice spoil. Two for the price of one."

She held my gaze. "I knew I wouldn't regret confiding in you."

"Could someone be about to extort a ransom payment?"

"I can't imagine anybody actually believing the Mustang Beach Sanctuary could afford ransom. It's not a bad hypothesis, though, Callie Padget. There's no telling what a knucklehead might do."

"What about tracking her by looking for—you know. Her poo."

"Do you know how much manure a single wild horse produces, per day?"

"No. And I'm afraid you're about to tell me."

"Forty to fifty pounds, give or take. Now, a mustang absolutely can tell which of their brethren have passed through, and how long ago, based on droppings. But a person? In the whole world, there might be a handful of highly experienced trackers who could find an individual horse that way." She shook her head. "It's beyond my ken."

"If you really think Tigress was stolen, shouldn't you go to the police?"

"Police means press."

"That's a good thing. Don't you think people would rally around—"

Geri-Lynn's lips pressed together so hard they turned white. "A missing horse would get me fired faster than you can say *banana pudding*. I'd be run off this island on a rail. Don't you know how coveted my job is? I get to live on a beach, rent-free. The salary's a pittance, especially considering the money I've spent for the fancy letters that go after my name. But I get to work with wild horses. You know what else I'm qualified to do? Nothing. Nada. Zilch."

I doubted that. Geri-Lynn was probably adept at a whole host of skills. Deflated, she slumped across from me. Her hair had gone limp, the waves slack against her cheeks. "Do you remember the special selectmen's meeting a few years back?"

"I was living in Charlotte then."

"I was *this* close to receiving funding for wildlife cameras. You see, after balancing the budget, the town had some money left over. I spent hours convincing the board to send those few thousand bucks my way. I even gave them walking tours like the one you just got, so they could see for themselves how the community would benefit from a trail camera system on sanctuary land."

"You'd be able to observe the mustangs twenty-four seven without disturbing them."

"Exactly. I could share footage with the community at large.

I could gather data that might be useful to other biologists. I might even be able to spot an individual horse's transmutable disease early, before it spreads to the whole herd. All that's not even taking the security measure into account. Think about it. If I had some halfway-decent cameras set up on sanctuary land, would I be sitting here wondering what happened to poor mama Tigress?"

"I see your point. *Points.*"

"If I had those cameras, the horse thieves might even be in custody as we speak! I'm winning you over, I can tell. Just like I nearly won over the select board. All I had to do was attend this special meeting and make a final plea, and the money would have gone to the sanctuary."

"I'm guessing things didn't go your way."

"I went to the meeting. I spoke with all the passion I had. Which was a lot, let me tell you. Just as the board was about to officially vote in my favor? In walks one of Cattail's finest. She was armed with a speech about wildlife cams being a waste of taxpayers' money."

"*She?*" It must have been Fusco, the only woman on the Cattail police force.

"In a matter of seconds, that lady cop erased all my stumping. She argued that a nonprofit should raise its own money. That the Mustang Beach Sanctuary had plenty of deep-pocket donors to help me out with—and I quote—'frivolous projects.' She wanted those leftover funds for some youth literacy program. Some deal where cops go into the school and read to kindergarten kiddos."

"She—she did? Really? Fusco?" I was fascinated by this glimpse into my detective frenemy. Was she, at heart, a softie? And a reader to boot?

"Hard to compete with a cause like that," Geri-Lynn was saying. "I have no idea why the police would need extra monies to implement it. But I've got to hand it to her. She beat me out, fair and square." The herd manager took a remorseful swallow of spiked sweet tea. "'Frivolous projects,'" she mumbled.

"As much as I'd like to help you, Geri-Lynn, I'm kind of horse-stupid."

"That's obvious. But it's not an obstacle. You like animals. You admire and appreciate them. You told me so yourself, how you used to hang out with your mom in your old tree house and observe the mustangs whenever they came by."

I smiled despite the sadness that came over me. "My mother told me that someday, they'll all be gone. The mustangs. That was actually the last thing she said to me before she died."

"Your mother was right. Someday they *will* be gone." Geri-Lynn slanted toward me, her eyes flickering. "But not on my watch. Not as long as I have someone on my side who knows about *people*."

I nearly spit out my tea. "That's where I come in? I'm your people expert?" Tigress was really in trouble if that were the case. "What about Animal Control?"

"Animal Control *is* the police," she said with a click of her tongue. "They might be fine for when a raccoon ventures down your chimney in broad daylight. They might be downright heroes when a bat flies into your attic and has a nap while hanging upside down on your curtain rod. But mustangs? I am not about to entrust the well-being of a majestic heirloom thousand-pound wild beast to Animal Control."

"You really went all out," I said, "pumping up this impending birth on social."

"I could kick myself. As far as free publicity goes, you can't

beat a fur baby. I was drumming up the anticipation, trying to get those donations to roll in, trying to seed future generations of donors. It sure did backfire on me. Now I've got thousands of people clamoring for a newborn horse—and no means of delivering one." She grimaced. "I hate it when I accidentally pun."

I chuckled. That got her chuckling. "Cattail Island needs a foal," I said.

"The sanctuary needs it. Tigress needs it. *I* need it—" A cell phone chimed, the digitized version of an old-fashioned telephone ring. "For God's sakes." She yanked her phone from her shirt pocket and, huffing, read the incoming text message. "Freaking Westerly," she said as she punched a reply. "She wants to meet. I don't know how much longer I can put her off."

Westerly . . . Westerly . . . Where had I heard that name?

When it hit me, I sat up straight. The sign-up sheet, the morning we found Seth Goodnow's body. There'd been Seth himself; the mystery initials, D.S.; another name, currently escaping me; and Heather Westerly, local address, the Casa Coquina. "Did you say Westerly?" I asked, as casually as possible.

"Sure did. As in Dr. Heather, the new herd vet. She doesn't start until next month, but she's been asking to get a lay of the land, and I'm running out of excuses. She even showed up here the other day, when I was in the woods. I spied her through my binoculars. She was peeking in the windows—"

"Herd vet? You mean she's a large-animal veterinarian?"

"Equine specialist. A fully funded three-year position, thanks to a grant I received. Until now, the Mustang Beach Sanctuary—in other words, me—has relied on large animal vets willing to work pro bono. They'd ferry over from the mainland whenever we had a problem. Now we won't have to wait until there is a problem. We'll be able to provide the horses preventative care."

"Couldn't Dr. Westerly help you find Tigress?"

"I don't trust her."

"But you hired her."

"Sure. But I don't know her. Never even met her in person. All our interviews were done via Zoom, because she lives ten hours away. Well, she used to. Now she lives here. Just moved."

"You don't know me either, Geri-Lynn."

"I know you love this island. I know you have roots here, on Cattail. The new vet does not. As far as I'm concerned, the verdict's still out on Heather Westerly." Geri-Lynn offered me more tea. I declined. "So, what do you think?" she asked. "Any ideas?"

Ideas? I was too shell-shocked for ideas.

The past forty-eight hours sped through my head. A honeymooner had been strangled inside the business of the man I was falling hard for. Meanwhile, a wild, pregnant horse—for which thousands of people were collectively holding their breath—had up and vanished without a trace.

I didn't have the first clue how to even begin reversing either of those dilemmas. "Geri-Lynn," I said. "The hard truth is, you might not be able to find Tigress *and* keep your job."

"You think I'm being irresponsible."

"No, but, well . . . *are* you?"

"These horses are survivors. They're tougher than turpentine. If Tigress wasn't suffering from pregnancy brain, she'd have outsmarted any horse thief who tried to haul her away."

"The more time you let pass, the harder it's going to be to track her down."

She blew out a breath. "I know."

"I'm trying hard to understand your predicament here. But it can't be in the best interest of Tigress, her baby, or the sanctuary to keep mum any longer. Take it wide. Get help. From people who could really step up and provide some expertise—"

"Just forty-eight more hours. If you and I can't track her down by then, I'll go public."

"I feel strongly that you shouldn't wait."

"I like to try doing things my own way first. I get the impression you're the type of woman who can relate."

She had me there.

21

At any rate, I wasn't going to leave Geri-Lynn Humfeld or Tigress or the future foal in the lurch. As I made my way to my car, wondering what I could do to help in this particular predicament, a grand total of zero ideas presented themselves. The thought that I possessed a special sleuthing talent, a knack for solving puzzles, made me scoff. Was I overpersistent at times? Yes. Might I have been endowed with more stubbornness than two mules fighting over a turnip? Probably. But that was all.

On the bright side—relatively speaking—I did have another intriguing lead. Dr. Heather Westerly, new veterinarian for the famed Cattail Island mustangs—*and* likely one of the last people to see Seth Goodnow alive. One thing needed rectifying: the fact that I hadn't yet conducted an internet hunt for all things Heather Westerly.

Not much came up, aside from a few mentions of her old job in Kentucky. Her sparse and perplexing Instagram profile featured a grand total of ten images, all fantasy illustrations of the sword and sorcery variety. A dragon flapping toward a nightmarish tower. A wizard in a green glade, casting a spell. That sort of thing. Dr. Westerly wrote nothing by way of accompanying captions, except to credit the various websites where the art originally appeared. She followed no one, and had twenty-six followers.

That day at the MotherVine, I was a blur of action. Ringing up sales. Hunting down requested titles. Re-shelving books discarded on window ledges after shoppers succumbed to other books' even more compelling siren songs.

Tuesdays were demanding. Most vacationers arrived on-island on Sunday, which meant that after forty-eight hours of beaching it, they were ready to do something different. Enter: the Queen Street shops. Centrally located. Air-conditioned. Oozing with charm and souvenirs and, at the MotherVine, blessed books.

During the post-lunch lull, I made my way over to the Local Interest section. I wasn't holding my breath for a book about horse thieves to magically appear on the MotherVine shelves. But I'd noticed a title that might illuminate some things for me. *Mustangs of the Outer Banks.*

Flipping through, I learned that wild horses seldom experience deep sleep. Having evolved as prey animals, they're constantly on the alert for predators. The hypervigilance limits them to daytime catnaps, typically while standing up. They do it in shifts.

The cruel irony is, despite chronic sleep deprivation, Cattail Island mustangs have no natural predators. *Humans cause them far more grief than animals*, read one caption.

The hardcover book crackled satisfyingly as I closed it. While it hadn't gotten me any closer to solving the mystery of Tigress, I did feel relieved knowing that she most likely had not fallen victim to a natural predator.

Seth Goodnow certainly had.

Shuddering, I re-shelved *Mustangs* and went out back to wipe down the tables. The repetitive motion, combined with the aromatherapeutic effects of the tea tree oil, cleared my head. When I heard chitchat, I knew that a fresh spate of customers was upon me. Good. Work was a welcome distraction. Something to keep my mind off poor Tigress, possible horse-napping victim, whereabouts unknown.

Feeling calmer in the shade of the mother vine, I plucked a plump Tinnakeet grape and popped it into my mouth. A juicy amuse-bouche to fortify me for the afternoon rush . . .

Someone stepped toward me. I shaded my eyes, squinting against the sun, taking in the figure of a tall man, black T-shirt, fists stuffed into the pockets of his cargo shorts.

Toby, hanging his head like a guilty dog.

At the sight of him, my heart fluttered.

I crossed the patio and gathered him in my arms. He hugged me back. His skin felt warm. Too warm. Sitting-in-a-hot-car-mulling-over-things warm.

"What's up?" I asked, still in his arms. "What's wrong?"

"Antoinette said I could steal you, but only for a few minutes."

"Howdy, folks." A customer carrying a Jimmy Buffett biography and two big coffees, which were apparently both for him, edged around us. Sun-bleached hair exploded from his Life Is Good visor. He pulled out the nearest chair. "Don't mind little ole me!"

Toby whispered in my ear, "Can we go somewhere private?"

22

The second floor of the MotherVine was used as storage space. Whenever a named storm threatened, Antoinette transported to the second floor any and all books displayed below four feet. Queen Street had flooded before, and it would again.

"No one comes up here," I told Toby as we climbed the stairs, avoiding Tin Man's poof bed and the PRIVATE sign. "Except when Antoinette sends me up for decorations or supplies." I ushered him through the door and closed it behind us. Two camp chairs leaned against the wall, on hand for sidewalk sales and other outdoor events. Next to a window overlooking the vine, we set up the chairs so they faced each other.

Toby sneezed a couple times.

"Can you handle the dust?" I knew from our ongoing game of Q and A that, like me, he was allergic to it. Cantaloupe, as well.

"Dust is the least of my worries." He sat forward, elbows on knees, legs bobbing.

"Toby, whatever it is—"

"There was a folded-up slip of paper in Seth Goodnow's pocket."

My scalp tightened.

I'd noticed that slice of paper. I'd forgotten about it. Until now. "What about it?"

He dug into his back pocket. Out came his wallet. My belly buzzed as he tugged out a square, unfolded it, and handed it over.

A receipt. From a gift shop in Emerald, North Carolina, named Dragonfly. *Fine imported goods from Japan* was printed along the bottom.

My mind raced back to Sunday morning, when he and I ran on the Mustang Beach footpath. When everything was hopeful as we answered each other's goofy interview questions. I'd asked about his first job. He replied that he'd worked in his mother's gift shop. Sweeping the floors, keeping the shelves stocked.

Emerald, North Carolina, was the mountain town where he grew up. The tattoo wrapping his forearm—the dragonfly, its wings bejeweled—was the same design decorating the receipt in my hand.

"Why am I looking at this?" My heart rate quickened. "You took this? You took this from Seth Goodnow's pocket? Off the body of a dead—"

"No, no. That receipt is my own. I must have about fifty of them tucked away inside my house. Every time I go home to Emerald to visit my mom, I buy something from her shop. I insist on it."

I nodded, smoothing the receipt against my lap. "But?"

"But I did *examine* the paper in Seth Goodnow's pocket."

"We told Jurecki we didn't touch anything. You tampered with evidence?"

"I put the paper back exactly as it had been. After I came to my senses—"

"Oh, Toby. That looks really, *really* bad." Across from me, he ran a hand over his face, but he couldn't swipe away the expression of remorse that had taken up residence there. I had a feeling even worse news was coming. "Okay," I said. "The piece of paper in Seth's pocket. Was it one of these? A receipt from Dragonfly?"

"From a long time ago. Back when my mom had an old cash register that printed purple ink. I didn't alter the receipt in any way, I swear. I was so careful. I just needed to see what it was. What I *thought* it was—"

"But why would Seth Goodnow have an old receipt from your mom's shop?"

"I gave it to him. We grew up together."

"You—you *knew* him? Like—*really* knew him? From Emerald? You and Seth Goodnow were friends?"

"We definitely weren't friends."

I sat back in the chair. I remembered the Carolina mountain accents when I visited Naomi's rental cottage. They must have been Seth's people, from the Emerald area. Some of them might have even known Toby when he was small. "I'm confused," I said. "Why did you give Seth a receipt?"

"I wrote a message on the back of it." He closed his eyes. *"Dear Seth, Someday, when you least expect it, I'm going to kill you."*

23

W*hat?*" I asked. "You wrote that?"

A shrill wail filled the MotherVine. Downstairs, a child was screaming bloody murder.

I sprinted to the door. "Ant?" I called.

Frazzled, my boss appeared at the foot of the steps. "We've got a bleeder—"

"Oh no—"

"A little boy fell off that darned hobbyhorse."

"Be right down." I turned back to Toby, who had crossed the floor to stand near me. He reached for my hands, but I pulled away.

"There's lots more I need to tell you," he said.

"Tell me. Quickly."

"It's a long story. It's complicated—"

"Then it'll have to wait until later."

The workday flew by thanks to a continual stream of customers, many of whom asked questions. Did we have the latest John Grisham? When was *Where the Crawdads Sing* coming out in paperback? I answered with as much presence of mind as I could muster. Which wasn't much, because all day, I thought about the message Toby had written on the back of the receipt. I knew he didn't kill Seth. I'd been with him for a whole hour before we found that body. Still—the note. The death threat in the pocket of the victim. Penned by Toby himself. He couldn't have harmed Seth. But had Toby somehow been involved in the man's demise?

When my shift was over, I dialed him, but he didn't pick up.

I went for a run on the sanctuary footpath. I tried not to compare it to the last time I'd run there, by Toby's side. All the while, I scanned the trees for a particular missing horse.

One I didn't see hide nor hair of.

On the way home, I popped in at Sanctuary Bungalow. Geri-Lynn was on the porch, looking out over the dunes, when I hopped up the steps. I told her I'd just come from a run on the footpath. "I didn't see Tigress," I quietly reported, so the visitors inside wouldn't hear, "but my thinking cap is dusted off and screwed on tight."

"I appreciate you, Callie. The more thinking caps, the better."

Later that day, I had a house-hunting date with Hudson. The Old Fart Van—OFV for short—was a 1980s Chevrolet with blown shocks. My uncle drove with one hand on the roof, to keep from hitting his head. We bounced down my old street. I braced myself against the dashboard.

"Ronnie said the new owner went all out, redoing the place," my uncle said. "New heat pump, new septic, whitewashed walls . . ." He pulled into the driveway. The cottage I'd grown up in was even smaller than I remembered, and was now an exuberant shade of coral, like the inside of a conch shell. The listing gutters had been straightened. Someone had planted bushes— gardenias, judging by the dark leaves. As I anticipated walking through the front door, I was flooded with memories. Of snuggling with my mother in her bed at night, as she turned the pages of a Mary Higgins Clark novel. Of a younger, thinner Hudson arriving with pizza, and the three of us sitting on the floor, because my mother's sewing projects were draped all over the place, seating areas included.

"It's adorable," I said as I hopped out of the OFV. "Was it always this adorable?"

"It would be a good size for you. And you'd only be about seven blocks from my place."

"I used to live seven *hours* from you," I said, laughing. "For years."

"Exactly."

The live oak sprawling over the property still contained a remnant of my old tree house: a wooden block, clinging just above the grass. How I used to love climbing up there to watch the mustangs mosey through the yard. Maybe, with special permission from the new owner, I could get Hudson to build another tree house. Who said tree houses were for kids only?

In the driveway, Ronnie was waiting next to his car. "There's our girl," he said. He swept his arm before the cottage. "What do you think?"

"I can't wait to go in," I said.

"They installed an outdoor shower around back. Best of all, for you? It's pet-friendly."

"Oh my gosh, really? I'm going to get a kitten. And a puppy. And maybe a baby rabbit—"

"You might want to think that arrangement through," my uncle said as we followed Ronnie up the pathway.

"The rent just posted." Ronnie inserted the key into the lockbox—then quoted a monthly price that made my heart drop down to my feet.

"Seriously," I said. "Don't joke. Tell me what the rent is, for real."

His gaze darted from me to my uncle, then back to me. He hadn't been kidding.

"Ronnie," I said, hanging my head. "It would take me *four* months to earn *one* month's rent. And I wouldn't have any money left over for food." I plucked a leaf off the nearest bush and began shredding it. Antoinette wasn't able to give me any more hours. I could pursue a second job—at another shop downtown, maybe. But in order to afford this tiny home, I'd have to clock ninety or a hundred hours a week. There was always freelance writing, but it would take months to get established—and might not yield a meaningful amount of extra income.

"You said the rent was going to be *low*," Hudson said.

Ronnie threw his arms to the sides. "That is low. This little home's the cheapest there is."

I gaped. "You mean—you don't have anything else you can show me? An apartment, or—"

"There's just nothing out there, Callie. That's the way the market is right now. I'm sorry I wasn't clearer about that. Last year's murders are what did it. It's sick, but—contrary to expectations—the scandals put Cattail on the map. Property values have gone through the roof."

I'd heard rumblings about the housing crisis. About workers on the lower end of the earning scale struggling to secure suitable places to lay their heads at night. It was the kind of story the local paper would have been all over, had it not been on hiatus. Somehow, though—naïvely so—I hadn't predicted the situation would affect me. "But where are all the summer workers going to live?" I asked. "The college kids coming here to lifeguard or wait tables? What can they afford?"

"Not much. They'll have to commute from the mainland, take the ferry over. Or they'll crash on friends' or relatives' couches." He fiddled with the key. "Want to go inside, just for old times' sake?"

I shook my head. At that point, having a look around would have broken my heart.

Ronnie patted my back. "Sure am sorry to disappoint you, kiddo."

"I know it's not ideal," Hudson said, "shacking up with your old geezer uncle, especially after you had your own place in the big city. I don't even have a proper bedroom for you—"

"I appreciate your putting me up." I hugged him. "I'm grateful. You know that."

"Then what's the big deal? Postpone moving out."

Ronnie nodded. "Your uncle's right. See what the housing situation is next spring. You'll have more money saved up then anyway. More money, more options."

"Maybe the real estate market will settle down once this island gets back to normal," Hudson said.

"*Normal?*" I tossed the shredded bits of leaf. What even *was* normal?

24

By dinnertime, I was feeling somewhat wilted. The hot and fruitless run; the housing letdown; the information flying at me from all directions—I needed sustenance. A good meal.

But it would have to wait, because I felt called to do some serious poking around.

Addison's Barbershop was closed for the evening, so I headed back to Hyde Road—not to torture myself by gazing at the sweet cottage that I couldn't afford, but to make a house call. Addison lived on the opposite end of Hyde, where the homes were even older and tinier than the one I grew up in. He lived far enough away that I never got to know the guy super well, especially since I was never a barbershop regular.

I parked behind his classic Ford, which hailed from an era of round headlights and whitewall tires. Should I have been impressed or terrified that Addison still made use of his driver's license?

Getting out of my car, I noticed, across the road, the most vibrant azalea bushes I'd ever seen, awash in pinks and purples like a Cattail sunset. A huge blue ribbon was draped across the central bush. Looked like Addison's neighbor had won first place in the annual azalea contest, which was held rain or shine; this May, of course, it had been mostly shine.

"Don't suppose you've come to cut the grass," said a rickety voice. Addison had come out onto his stoop. His yard was over-grown; a flagless flagpole shot from the center of it like a hyper-kinetic weed.

"I can try and find you someone to cut it," I said.

"A boy comes by. He's been surfing a lot the past few weeks, though."

"The other day, at the MotherVine? You didn't seem like your-self. I just thought I'd stop by and make sure you're okay."

"Oh, just a hitch in my get-along was all." He straightened his bow tie, his fingers trembling. "I'm better now."

He didn't look better. If anything, he looked worse. Like a stiff breeze would knock him over. I decided to get straight to the point. "Did you go to your shop on Sunday morning?"

"That's right—you're like a private investigator now, or some such. When you cut hair on an island for a living, there's no avoid-ing gossip."

"Let's just say, I take a special interest in sordid events that negatively impact Cattail."

"Maybe you shouldn't."

"What's going on? Did something bad happen? You can tell me. I might be able to help—"

"I don't work Sundays. I was here, at home, all morning, until I drove to the MotherVine. Like I always do."

"I noticed your photographs of the mustangs. You know, hanging inside the barbershop? They're nice. Did you take them yourself?"

The subject change seemed to relax him a little. "Time was, I loved to shoot those horses," he said. "Back when cameras re-quired rolls of film. Remember those?"

"Why'd you stop taking pictures?"

"Between you and me, my eyes got old. Oh, they're still good enough to cut hair. Good enough to drive short distances on back roads, ones I know like the back of my hand. But I can't see far off. I think my driving days will soon be over." He gazed across the street at his neighbor's azaleas, as if envying their vitality. To him, they must have looked like pink-streaked blobs. "Take it from me, Callie," he said as he turned to go back inside. "When it comes to—how did you put it? *sordid events?*—better stay away from those."

My next target: the Casa Coquina.

On Queen Street, the setting sun cast an apricot hue on the grand Victorian. I mounted the wide front steps, one hand on the railing, which was sticky with humidity. A few guests—mostly couples—lingered on the porch, sipping cocktails under twirling ceiling fans and hanging ferns. The guests were dressed as formally as you'd ever see on Cattail—khaki shorts and golf shirts for the men, maxi dresses and baubled flip-flops for the women. Was one of them Heather Westerly? If I were a different person—Detective Fusco, for example—I would have had no problem announcing my intentions to those assembled. But it wasn't really my style, or my bailiwick.

Inside the front parlor, an old upright piano anchored the sitting room. Beyond the floral-carpeted staircase, soft Spanish-language music played. I knew it originated from the Andes foothills, where Turo had grown up. A discreet sign hung on a swinging door at the end of the hallway. STAFF ONLY, PLEASE.

"Turo?" I cracked open the door just enough to poke my head into the gleaming chef's kitchen. There was an eight-burner gas Viking range and a Sub-Zero refrigerator big enough to stand inside. Copper pans hung from an overhead rack. One wall held clay ovens and pizza baking stones with long handles. Just thinking about gooey queso, fresh tomatoes, roasted garlic, and Turo's secret dough recipe made my mouth water. The Casa Coquina kitchen was not a bad place to find yourself when you hadn't eaten since lunch.

Turo entered the kitchen through a door that led to the backyard. His hands were covered in dirt; he'd been tending to his vegetable garden. "Callie Padget!" he exclaimed. "¡Entra! I haven't seen you in years. I've been hoping you would stop in and say hello to an old friend." After rinsing off his hands, he scuttled toward me, planting a loud kiss on my forehead. "How's your uncle?" Turo and Hudson knew each other from the farmers market; my uncle used to sell small wooden kitchen creations—cutting boards and salad hands—next to where Turo parked his taco truck. "Have you come for some *ají?*" he asked. "I'm selling it by the pint now. Your first is on the house."

"I'll take it," I said. Hudson loved the smoky, oniony concoction, and it was healthy.

From the fridge, Turo produced a plastic container and wiped it with a dish towel. "I was just about to taste test my latest batch. Join me."

A moment later I had shimmied up to a butcher-block island where he had set a bowl of the salsa along with a second bowl filled with homemade lime-infused plantain chips. *Ají* was a sort of Ecuadorian-style dip he made, using special tomatoes he ordered from a supplier on the mainland. I dipped a chip, crunched into it, and could barely stop my eyes from rolling back into my head. "Outstanding, as usual," I said. Spicy enough to wake up my tongue and clear my sinuses, but not enough to make me gasp for a glass of milk. I dug a tissue out of my bag, blew my nose in as ladylike a way as I could manage, and helped myself to more.

"You didn't come here for *ají*, though, did you?" Across from me, Turo winked. He had copious salt-and-pepper waves, brown eyes tinted with burgundy, and a silvery five-o'clock shadow.

"The lady detective told me that if any civilian were to come around *playing* detective, I wasn't to talk to her."

Fusco! She'd Fuscoed me.

I just couldn't get used to the idea that I had a reputation as a wannabe crime solver. Then again, I wasn't a wannabe. I actually had solved a crime.

Two crimes, as Geri-Lynn had rightly pointed out.

"I know that a veterinary doctor named Heather Westerly is staying here," I said. "And that she's wanted for questioning regarding a murder."

"The murder in the martial arts studio."

"That's where the body was found."

"In that case, I guess I shouldn't tell you that a guest by that name prepaid for two weeks and mentioned she'd probably stay even longer."

"Definitely not. What else shouldn't you tell me?"

"I certainly should not mention anything about her peculiar personality."

"Quite right." I dipped another chip as Turo and I shared a conspiratorial smile. This was not a man freaked out that a possible murder suspect was sleeping under his roof. On the contrary, Turo Bravo seemed delighted by the drama. Either that, or he believed in getting murderers off Cattail Island as soon as possible, and if I was going to put up an assist in that endeavor . . . "Peculiar in what way?" I asked.

"She leaves my housekeeping staff a twenty-dollar bill every morning."

"Really? That's awfully generous."

"And she is a woman of few words. Reticent, as they say. I'm good at small talk, as you know. But I've gotten very few details out of her."

I raised an eyebrow. "There were *some* details?"

"She used to provide veterinary care for wild horses that roam the coal land in eastern Kentucky. She worked for an advocacy group, as I understand."

"You absolutely should not breathe a word about any of the above. You know what else I don't need to hear? What kind of vehicle the lady drives."

Turo punctuated the air with a chip. "A Tesla. One of the bigger ones with the funky doors that open out and up. What do you call them, when they're hinged at the roof like that? Anyway, I just got a charger installed around back, to attract guests who drive electric cars. Heather Westerly is the first guest of mine to actually use it." He went on—the mileage her particular model gets, the cargo space, zero to sixty in less than three seconds, and so on. "I looked up how much those things go for, new. Guess how much."

"Sixty, seventy grand?"

"They start at eighty." He popped the chip, then clapped away the crumbs. "But hers has bells and whistles. Mucho dinero."

I had no idea what kind of salary an equine veterinarian pulled in. Kentucky was a horse-loving state, but I was betting its racehorses enjoyed far cushier conditions than its homeless nags. It was possible, of course, that Heather Westerly had scrimped and saved to buy herself a beautiful car, or been on the receiving end of a plump inheritance, or was the kind of person who lived beyond her means. It was also possible that none of the above was any of my business. "What do you know about horses, Turo?"

"Not much, having grown up in a small city. ¿Por qué?"

"Just thinking about Heather's job, that's all. Back to the woman herself. What about her comings and goings?"

"She's rarely here." He shrugged. "Tell me. If you had six figures to drop, what kind of car would you get?"

Many times, I had fantasized about someday driving a luxurious vehicle. Utilitarian but sexy. Seats that hugged your body. A ride so smooth you felt you were gliding over clouds no matter the road surface.

Fantasies were free, but sweet cars were not. I had no savings. I was living above a woodshop. I was a peddler of books. "Honestly, Turo," I said, accepting the napkin he offered and dabbing it to my lips. "If I had that kind of money, I'd pay off my student loans and invest in a reliable set of wheels. At the end of the day, a car only needs to get you from point A to point B. Am I right? Anything leftover, I'd sock away. Down payment on a starter home."

He mussed my hair. "You've got a good head on your shoulders, Miss Callie."

Maybe he was right.

Now all I needed to do was keep it there.

25

Farther down Queen Street, I made quick note of the shops whose windows offered a good view of Cattail Family Martial Arts. First up was the pottery shop. I greeted the apprentice, a college-aged man whose apron was dabbed with clay. Over the past few weeks, I had seen him many times in the bump-out window, bent over the spinning wheel, a plate or a bud vase forming underneath his slender fingers. I asked if he'd noticed anything weird or out of place on Sunday morning, or anything at all going on across the street at the dojo. "I'll tell you the same thing I told Detective Fusco," he said. "The pottery shop was closed that morning, and I was at home, sleeping."

I checked in with the Pilates studio and, above it, the Yarn Barn. They had both been open on Sunday morning, but no one in either location had anything to share about the dojo.

Catty-corner to Cattail Family Martial Arts: Salty Edward's. I'd saved it for last, since it wouldn't close until after dark.

Raising my voice above the blaring music, I introduced myself to the host, whose face I'd have been hard-pressed to describe, because he never glanced up from his phone. He told me he'd been working the breakfast shift Sunday morning but it had been so busy, he had no idea what was going on outside the restaurant.

Whiffs of cheeseburgers and chicken wings made my stomach rumble. The three plantain chips I'd eaten at the Casa Coquina weren't going to stave off my hunger much longer. Might as well order a meal.

As I made my way deeper into the bar, a commotion got my attention. Cheers of encouragement. Clapping. The rattling of glassware. In the back corner, near the restroom alcove, an arm-wrestling match had just ended. The crowd of onlookers dispersed, revealing the winner. He was straddling a chair backward, counting bills. Though compact, he looked every bit the stereotype of a competitive weight lifter, complete with bloated muscles and a generally dopey expression. His forearms were like tree branches. I put him in his mid-twenties.

"Hey," I asked the teenage host, who made annoyed eye contact with me. "That guy holding court over there," I said. "He's a vacationer?"

The host rolled his eyes. "Cooper Something. Been here every night this week, hustling."

"*Cooper?*" For less than a second, I couldn't pinpoint where I'd recently heard that name. Then it hit me like a dart between the eyes. Cooper Payne, from the sign-up sheet. As a joke, Cooper had listed his local address as Salty Edward's.

This had to be the same dude.

The host shrugged. "He's a savage, but he sounds like a Kennedy when he talks." A large group consisting of several families entered, and the host turned his attention to them.

I elbowed my way closer to the action. Cooper the Yankee Caveman had just made quick work of another opponent, slamming his arm onto the table. They shook hands, a show of good sportsmanship. The loser slapped some bills into Cooper's hand.

How could I get close to him? I didn't want him to think I was trying to pick him up, or on the prowl for a one-night stand.

A shudder of revulsion passed through me at the very prospect. No more guys had lined up to take him on, and he scanned the crowd for his next victim. It was the perfect window.

"Excuse me, sir?" I approached him, saying the first thing that popped into my head. Which was a total lie. "I write for the local paper, and I've heard about your reputation this week, arm-wrestling here at Salty's. Seeing as you keep winning, I thought it would make for a great little piece."

He shook my hand. To his credit, it was not a crushing man-shake to prove how strong he was. *Not* to his credit, his thumb feathered mine, and when I pulled away, he held on and snickered. "*You'd* make for a great little piece. I bet you get that all the time."

"I think I just threw up in my mouth a bit."

His laugh was a high-pitched diminuendo that made me think of a hyena skittering into the shadows. "I like you," he said. "You're fun."

"I'm a little old for you, don't you think?"

"I'm an equal opportunity kind of guy. What are you drinking?"

Oh God. This was quickly getting dangerous. It hadn't been my intention to borderline flirt, but here I was. I needed to get him talking and then get out of there before it went too far. "I'm on the clock."

"You're in a bar, sweetheart. Two more, honey," he said to the long-haired server as she passed. Cooper Payne spread his arms like a throned king granting me an audience. "You're in luck, because my life coach has me looking for opportunities to help people out. What do you want to know?"

"You must be like an East Coast legend in the arm-wrestling circuit."

He squeaked out another retreating-hyena laugh. "Where'd

you get that? I never entered any formal competitions or anything. This is something I do for fun, whenever I travel. Which
isn't often, by the way. I'm too busy training. You're basking in
the presence of a future mixed martial arts superstar, you know."
His accent *was* Kennedy-ish, with dropped *r*'s and a nasally
tinge. "I've got the perfect name for it, don't you think? *Payne?*"

"What motivates you?" I asked.

"How short do you think the shortest fighter in the MMA is?"

"Five-seven?"

"Five-*three*. He's beaten guys who have thirty, forty pounds
on him. I'm five-six."

"Cool." I pretended to take notes on the scratch pad and pen
I always carried around in my bag—old habits die hard. The
server made another circuit and placed two Cattail Island Blondes
on our table. I noticed, at Cooper's feet, a gallon jug filled with
water, next to a backpack.

"Hey, don't you want my picture?" he asked. "For your article."

"Oh, of course. I wasn't about to forget the most important
part." I pretended to aim my camera phone while he flexed his
pecs and pulled a face that could only be described as punchable.
"It's all over the island that you worked out at Cattail Family
Martial Arts this week," I said. "What did you think of the fa-
cilities?"

He scooted his chair closer. He smelled like camphor—prickly,
vaguely mothballish. I leaned away. "Cattail Family Martial
Arts is laughable," he said. "But it's better than nothing."

"Laughable?" Heat crept up my neck, onto my cheeks. I hoped
he didn't notice my defensiveness.

"I usually don't skip workouts. I do two-a-days, sometimes
three-a-days. But that dump, Cattail Family Martial Arts, was
the only place on this island. I was hoping to go to a few classes,
maybe take on the owner, show him a thing or two, but then my

ex-boss had to go and get himself murdered, and the place got temporarily closed down."

"Your ex-boss? You worked for Seth Goodnow?"

"We were in corporate sales together. I was on his team." Cooper's eyes narrowed. "Wait a second. You're not interested in my arm wrestling, are you? You're doing a story on the murder."

"Thanks for your time, Mr. Payne." I pushed away from the table and made my way toward the door.

Behind me came the scrape of chair legs. "I didn't do anything," he boomed, jumping to his feet. "I'm sick of the shade everybody's throwing me. I'm not a bad guy!"

A hush fell over the bar. The Faith Hill song piping through the speakers suddenly stopped.

People stared. At Cooper. At me.

I faced him. He had charged after me and was breathing hard. A vein on his forehead was seconds from bursting.

I felt a flush of embarrassment, quickly followed by boldness. What was he going to do—attack me in front of sixty-odd Salty Edward's patrons? I moved closer and said, "Can I quote you directly?"

As he roared some more, I turned away. The dumbstruck crowd parted, allowing me to duck outside, into the safety of warm, bustling Queen Street.

26

Several people who'd witnessed the encounter followed me outside to make sure I was okay. I thanked them, insisting it had been no big deal. As if I provoked strange guys in bars all the time.

Heart pounding, I marched down the sidewalk, no particular destination in mind. When I reached the cemetery gates, I rested against them, catching my breath. On my phone, I googled Cooper Payne. A Twitter account belonged to someone with that name, and from what I could tell of the tiny photo, it looked like the man I'd just sat with. The profile claimed Massachusetts roots. His most recent Tweet, published last week, read, *Happy Birthday to ME!!!*

I needed to check in with Naomi. What had Cooper and Seth meant to each other? I was formulating a plan—an excuse to visit her again—when my phone vibrated.

Toby.

"I was ten years old when I wrote that note," he said.

"You—*what?*"

"I was a weakling. The puniest kid in Emerald Elementary, and so dorky I had white tape holding my glasses together. Literally."

I couldn't hold back a small laugh. I'd known the receipt itself hailed from many years ago, but somehow, I'd been thinking it was related to a more recent, adult version of Toby. "You were only *ten?*" I asked.

"Please, please, *please* come over."

—

Toby's kitchen counter was strewn with supplies: cream, sugar, gingerroot, chocolate bars, peaches. He had a thing for sweets, and a full-blown ice cream–making operation was underway. He wore an apron askew over his bare chest, a look that was both absurd and undeniably sexy, like I had stepped into a Hallmark movie.

"Nice ensemble," I said.

"I was hot." I could not argue with that. I went to hug him, but his hands were covered in chocolate dust, his apron smeared with peach juice. He gestured to a knife and cutting board. "Can you mince?"

"Oh, I can mince." I set in on the ginger. As the spiky scent filled my nose, I felt thankful for the task. My confrontation with Cooper Payne still had me wired, but as long as my hands were busy, Toby wouldn't notice them quaking. I'd decided not to tell him about Cooper. Toby wasn't a hothead. Far from it. But he was a protector, and I didn't want him heading straight for Salty's without even taking off his apron first. Besides, he had enough going on right now.

"Where were we?" he asked.

"You were a ten-year-old dork."

"Ah, right." He half smiled.

"Seth Goodnow used to pick on you? Is that what this is all about?" I might have half smiled myself had my heart not been flooding with pity at the specter of little-kid Toby, favorite target of a mean kid. I pictured a nerd bullied to his wit's end, scratching out a death threat to his tormentor in handwriting shaky with rage.

"I'll spare you the details, but *picking on me* is a very nice way of summing up the hell Seth Goodnow made my life between the ages of eight and fourteen."

"What happened when you were fourteen?"

He poked a bit of chocolate into my mouth. "Two things. Number one, the most insane growth spurt in the history of adolescence. In just one summer, I shot up almost five inches. But I think number two was more important. I'd spent a couple months studying karate, and I knew he could never beat me up again. On the first day of high school, Seth came charging down the hallway, ready to slam me into the lockers or give me a wedgie or scream in my face or whatever he had planned. But when he realized I stood taller than him by a whole bunch—*and* had a whole lot more confidence—he steered clear. Didn't touch a hair on my head ever again."

I didn't need any more details than that to feel a bit of triumph for fourteen-year-old Toby.

I swept the minced ginger into the tumbler he'd gotten out of the freezer. The other night, when I'd gotten the feeling that Toby wasn't telling me something? Old memories had come to haunt him. Demons from the past could make anyone unsteady. Even a guy like Toby, who was well versed in self-control. It was precisely because he was a warrior that he didn't want his future girlfriend to see him shaken.

Paradoxically, the whole situation was making me even fonder of him. He hadn't let his rough childhood embitter him. Exactly the opposite. He'd spun pain into gold and was now teaching kids that violence was never a go-to option, and that simple, pure preparedness—mental and physical—was the best offense, by virtue of being the best defense.

"Did you tell the police?" I asked. "Did you tell them you looked at the receipt that was inside Seth's pocket?"

"I didn't mention that, no. But they showed it to me. I'd signed my full name to it. You see, way back when, at Emerald Elementary, there were *two* Tobys. Seth bullied both of us because the name Toby, according to Seth, was for sissies. I wanted ten-year-old Seth to know the death threat was from me, so that he wouldn't go after the *other* Toby. Not thinking that he would have known it was me anyway, because everyone in town knew about my mother's store. And not thinking that Seth was going to go after the other Toby anyway. At least at some point.

"When Jurecki brought me into the station Sunday, I came clean about how Seth used to torture me. It was such ancient history. Actually, after high school, he went to college way up in New England. High school graduation was the last time I ever saw the guy."

"Until Sunday morning, when he checked into the dojo."

"When he came to work out. That was freaky. It was like being shot out of a cannon directly into . . ." Toby faltered, waving his chocolate-stained knife. *Into difficult memories I'd rather not relive.*

"Was Seth nice to you? He recognized you, right?"

"He knew who I was. We didn't do the whole *Hey, man, how've you been, haven't seen you in ages* thing. But I could tell by the look in his eyes. He knew me."

"And then when we came back an hour later and found him dead . . ."

"That was even freakier. Despite all my training, I just wasn't present. It was the first time in my life that I ever felt like karate had let me down—or maybe like *I* had let *karate* down."

"Were Jurecki and Fusco understanding? That you didn't fill them in right away on your and Seth's relationship?"

"*Understanding?* That's definitely not the word I would use."

The police had a signed, handwritten note from Toby—vowing not simply vengeance but murder—found inside the victim's pocket.

Someday, when you least expect it, I'm going to kill you.

Granted, Toby had been ten at the time of writing. Wouldn't the twenty-eight years that had intervened count him out as a suspect? And at best, wasn't the receipt circumstantial evidence? I mean, really, how seriously could the police take it?

"You didn't touch a hair on Seth's head," I said. "Anyone who knows you knows you aren't capable."

"I appreciate that, Padget. And I don't feel anger toward Seth Goodnow anymore. I haven't felt that way for years. At one point not long ago, I even considered reaching out to him—to thank him. He was the reason I started studying martial arts in the first place. If he hadn't loomed so large in my life—if he hadn't been such a colossal pain in the ass—I never would have begged my parents for karate lessons. If I never took karate lessons . . ."

"You wouldn't have developed into the peach-ginger-chocolate-chunk ice cream–making stud standing before me." This time, we did share a smile. "All these years," I said, "Seth kept that receipt. Why?"

"Now, that, I just don't get."

"Me neither. One thing that's almost certain, though: He was killed somewhere else and deposited in your dojo."

"What makes you think that?"

"Didn't you notice his legs? They were covered in sand."

"I didn't notice. I must have been too . . ."

"A bully like Seth Goodnow would have collected a lot of enemies, right? You can't be the only person in the world who's felt some animosity toward him."

"*Felt*. As in, past tense. It was a lifetime ago." All the ingredients had gone into the frozen tumbler. Toby fitted it onto the base of the ice cream maker and flipped a switch. The appliance began spinning, emitting a hum. "Not to speak ill of the dead, but Seth Goodnow—may he rest in peace—was a total jerk. A classic bully. He might have done something pretty despicable to provoke an attack on his life. But did he deserve to die? Does anybody deserve to be strangled? This is a heavy conversation . . ."

I was grateful for it, though. Toby's rhetorical questions were getting the gears grinding in my head. Who else had Seth bullied? That was what I needed to find out.

27

The ice cream was delicious, but I couldn't enjoy it. Toby felt the same, I could tell by how he absently twirled his spoon. I considered suggesting a self-defense lesson. He'd been teaching me moves, and I'd actually had the opportunity to use them last summer, on the Smile Beach pier, against the double murderer. But I'd been clumsy. In an ironic twist of fate, it was the pier collapse that saved me. Not my own self-defense skills. I wanted to practice more. Learn more. But tonight, neither my instructor nor I had the heart.

He filled me in on his day. How he'd dropped in on some of his students, assuring whoever came to the door that Cattail Family Martial Arts would be up and running again in no time, and he couldn't wait to get back to work, and he hoped they felt the same.

When yawns overtook Toby and me, we agreed that the best thing for both of us was shut-eye, so I left.

But I didn't end up in my bed.

I ordered takeout at the only bistro still open. Its sea-to-table sensibility meant lighter fare, which I preferred anyway. Ice cream hadn't gone down easily, but maybe a proper dinner would. "A rice bowl with local seared tuna and extra sweet potatoes, please," I said. "Light on the mustard aioli. The appetizer size will be perfect for me."

Food in hand, I headed to the MotherVine. I'd taken to letting myself in after hours. Antoinette was cool with it. It wasn't difficult for her to appreciate the strange succor I found when alone in the darkness with books. *Alone* wasn't the right word, though. Because books were full of people, written by people. Stories and voices seemed to permeate the air inside the Mother-Vine. A bookshop after hours was good company indeed.

I keyed in but didn't flip on the lights. Lights made people think we were open. Antoinette kept a camp lantern in case of power outages, which weren't uncommon during hurricane season. The lantern was collapsible and had a flickering candle setting, much better than my phone's seizure-inducingly-bright flashlight app. I found the lantern in her closet-cum-office and stretched it to its full size. Even though the thing was made of silicon and plastic, and even though I knew every inch of my surroundings, holding the lantern in front of me as I navigated the aisles always made me feel satisfyingly old-fashioned. Like an 1800s lighthouse keeper making a nighttime journey from cottage to beacon. When really, I was making my way from the office to the kids' section.

Lifting the lantern also alerted me to the stress that had taken up residence in my upper back. It felt like a brick or two had been lodged between my shoulder blades. When all this was over, I'd have to ask Toby for a massage. I could return the favor, and one thing would lead to another and—

No.

Now was not the time to make romantic plans. For one thing, my mind was still bouncing with names. Heather Westerly. Cooper Payne.

And a third name, from a couple of centuries ago, which I hadn't forgotten: Rosie Beacon.

On a low shelf, I found a single copy of the middle-grade

book that I'd hand delivered to Geri-Lynn Humfeld, *The Legend of Rosie Beacon*. Lantern light cavorted over the cover, which portrayed a wool-clad, black-haired girl astride a shaggy black stallion. They posed on a dune top underneath a star-sprayed night sky. The girl's nose was red, and the horse's breath wisped from his nostrils.

Yes, this tale was going to provide just the right mix of coziness and adventure.

For the moment, my hunger vanished. I set the tuna bowl in the mini-fridge, in favor of reading.

The kids' corner featured diminutive beanbag chairs. I smooshed three together and made a sort of nest, lying across them with my feet propped on the saddle of the squeaky old rocking horse, which was looking sadder than ever because Antoinette, in the hope of preventing more bloodshed, had duct-taped over its pointiest parts.

On his poof on the stairs, Tin Man was striking a few yoga poses. Antoinette and Hudson must have dropped him off after their beach walk. When he leapt onto my chest with a meowy greeting, I let out an *oof*. He paid no mind, curling up onto the amazing cat bed that apparently was my belly. Within seconds he was purring. Full-on boat-motor mode. I wished, not for the first time, for the ability to produce such a contented sound.

Alone with a book. Finally. A book that might give me some insight into Tigress's whereabouts.

As I opened to page one, someone knocked on the door.

28

Detective Fusco, sporting a sports bra, athletic shorts, and a sheen of sweat, sauntered past me like she owned the place. "Saw you sneaking in. That's something you really like doing, huh? How come you never turn on any lights?"

"Kills the mood."

"Can we talk somewhere?"

"Children's area." I snagged my rice bowl and rejoined Fusco, who was venturing a seat on the ancient rocking horse. When it moaned a bovine-sounding protest, she sprang away.

"Good Lord," she said. "Get this thing some WD-40."

"It's seen better days—but it *is* meant for people who weigh thirty pounds or less." I tossed her a pair of wee beanbag chairs, and she made herself—well, not quite comfortable. The gangly woman was all elbows and knees. "I didn't know you were a runner," I said.

"Walker. Working my way up. Baby steps."

"Nice." Using a plastic spork, I stabbed a few bites of tuna.

"That smells amazing." She outstretched her hand—a request for the spork. I handed it over, wishing I'd gotten the entrée size. I didn't know I'd be sharing my meal with a peckish policewoman. "Dang," she drawled. "That is criminally delicious."

"Cooper Payne worked underneath Seth Goodnow, you know. And he's a total bonehead."

"The Cattail police have already acquired this information."

"Toby's not a suspect, right?"

She eyed me. "We're getting a lot of pressure from the widow. She's heavily scrutinous of Toby Dodge, as is understandable."

Heavily scrutinous. Even when she wasn't on duty, Fusco spoke cop-speak.

So, Naomi thought Toby was worth looking into. I couldn't really blame her. Especially if she knew about the boyhood death threat. "Have you found the murder weapon?" I asked.

"Don't tell me you have," Fusco said wryly.

"Toby's nunchucks were cleared, then? You can't link them to the crime?" She didn't answer, but helped herself to more of my meal. "I know about the receipt in Seth Goodnow's pocket," I said. "I know about the message on the back of the receipt."

"Very intriguing, that slip of paper."

"You must know that it was planted on the body as some kind of lame attempt at a frame-up."

"On the contrary, what we *do* know is that it's a death threat, found on the victim's body, and signed by your boyfriend."

"When he was just a kid. A hurting kid. You also know that I was with him for a whole hour before Seth was found."

"Before you and Toby *found* Seth," she said, curling her fingers at the word *found*.

"Air quotes? Seriously?" I snatched back my spork. "If you want my help—"

"Who says I want your help? Chief thinks you have a special ability relating to this sort of work. He's ready to slap a badge on your chest and deputize you."

"If you don't want to question me, or share information, then what are you doing here? Are you worried I'm going to spook your suspects if I go sleuthing around? Is that it?"

Unfolding herself, she stood and picked up the Rosie Beacon book. As she flipped through it, I suppressed a wave of annoyance. Had she come here to demonstrate proficiency in avoiding direct answers? If so, she was succeeding. "You almost died because of me," she muttered.

My eyes flew wide. "Are you talking about last summer? I *lived* because of you. You saved my life."

"What if I'd arrived at Smile Beach just a few seconds later? What if I didn't see you going under the water?"

"But those things didn't happen."

"If it weren't for our information-sharing arrangement, you wouldn't have been on that pier—alone, with a scumbag—when it collapsed. I was reckless. I'm living with the reality that I came *this* close to having a civilian casualty on my head."

"But you don't have one on your head. You got a promotion."

"You don't think about things from other people's points of view, do you?"

That made me bristle. Defensiveness scratched like a hair shirt. I put myself in other people's shoes all the time, didn't I? I'd mentally revisited the events of last summer again and again and—

—and I always saw them from *my* point of view.

The realization jolted me.

Fusco was right. I hadn't bothered to imagine how other people might have been dealing with the effects of my decisions. I'd never considered that someone else might have been just as traumatized by that night as me.

Namely, Fusco. My rescuer.

"You read kids' books?" she asked, tapping *The Legend of Rosie Beacon* against her palm. "Can't remember the last time I read a book straight through. This any good?"

"Not sure yet. I'll let you know." I was going to bring up the school program she'd fought for. The literacy program, where she went into the kindergarten class and read to the kids. But she'd already switched back to her favorite subject: me minding my own business.

"Listen, A.C.," she said. "Booksellers sell books. Detectives? They . . ."

"Detect."

"Let's just keep it simple like that."

"Simple. Sure," I said. Even though I could have pointed out that once upon a time, she'd blurred the boundary herself.

"You need to stop poking around. Live your life."

Live my life?

I was trying. I really was. But my life contained unprecedented problems. Exhibit A: Fusco. Last summer, she didn't want me playing detective because she feared I would screw up her investigation. Now she didn't want me playing detective because she feared I would hurt myself, or worse—and she would be to blame.

Exhibit B: a boyfriend candidate who'd gotten himself tied up in a murder investigation.

Exhibit C: a missing mustang.

And I hadn't the foggiest idea how to reconcile any of the above.

29

Once again, Tin Man and I had the MotherVine to ourselves. He helped me polish off the last few bites of tuna, and then we nestled down by the lantern.

It took me forty-five minutes to devour the historical middle-grade novel, written in the style of diary entries. The gist: Rosie Beacon had been a reserved thirteen-year-old in the 1700s. Her upbringing, on northern Cattail Island, had been isolated. She was the youngest daughter of English immigrants who occasionally traded oysters—the fattest and tastiest around. Otherwise, the self-sufficient family of seven lived off the land, grew their own vegetables, and raised chickens and pigs.

Back then, Cattail's wild horse herd numbered several hundred. The Beacons made as little impact on their environment as possible—but they did tame a mustang for transportation purposes.

I chuckled, imagining Geri-Lynn's reaction to this detail. She'd probably hurl the book across the room. But three hundred years ago, when the human population of the entire two-hundred-mile stretch of the Outer Banks was a few dozen, issues of overdevelopment, species extinction, and conservation simply didn't exist.

As it turned out, the Beacons' tamed stallion lived with the herd and never saw the inside of a barn. But when Rosie whistled, Roger came running. Rosie and Roger spent many hours exploring their island together. One time they discovered a secret cove, a stretch of tangled shoreline that Rosie believed few people had ever set foot on, except the indigenous tribes who might have once fished that area, or the earliest conquistadors. The cove was hidden by a tucked-away pocket of undergrowth and became Rosie's and Roger's favorite place to gaze at the ocean and marvel at the beauty of their surroundings. *Dense undergrowth hid this magical place from casual passersby. Only my stallion and I knew of its existence.*

Back at home one December evening, visiting relatives brought word of war brewing far away in Boston. Rosie overheard the adults discussing an alarming development: British loyalists were fast approaching, torching homes and slaughtering livestock and Banker horses as they rode. Though the adults were horrified, an impending storm made it impossible for them to travel to the nearest rebel outpost, forty miles inland, to warn the soldiers camped there that an invasion was imminent.

Rosie considered the adults' decision to stay put to be the most cowardly one they could make. In the way of children on the verge of adulthood, she decided to make the impossible, possible. After everyone else in the household fell asleep, she got up, dressed in her warmest clothing, tiptoed outside, and, in the frigid air, whistled for Roger.

Girl and mount swam across the near-frozen Pamlico Sound, then traversed a vast pocosin—wetland wilderness that centuries later would become known as the Alligator River Refuge. *Take heart*, Rosie murmured into Roger's ear. *Take heart, take heart, take heart.* She repeated it over and over, a mantra, as the stalwart Cattail mustang galloped onward, through the night.

Next morning, the pair arrived safely at the revolutionary soldiers' camp. Rosie's dire message was received. The general gathered his troops and advanced—surprising the British loyalist bullies and forcing them to retreat.

—

The Legend of Rosie Beacon had been published twelve years ago by a small independent press. The author, I discovered, had retired after forty years of teaching history in public schools on the mainland, in the same area where the revolutionary soldiers had congregated. I googled her name and discovered she'd passed away years ago.

After closing the book, a feeling like courage blew breezily through my chest. I lay there for a while, stroking Tin Man, who had again curled up on my belly and was serving as a book rest while I'd turned pages. I didn't learn much that might shed light on Tigress. Still, I found myself wishing I'd been taught about Rosie Beacon when I was growing up.

In order to be courageous, you needed fear. It was a symbiotic relationship; one couldn't exist without the other. No fear, no courage.

Rosie Beacon must have been afraid. Of darkness, bears, boars, wolves, men, frostbite, and a hundred other threats. But she rode anyway.

Take heart.

In the bookshop, in the afterglow of a good book, with Tin Man purring so hard my ribs hummed, I let my current emotional reality surface. I was afraid. For Toby. For Tigress and her foal. For my whole island, really.

I had sufficient amounts of the fear side of the equation. I hoped that was a positive sign for things to come, because I had a feeling an immense supply of courage was going to be required.

30

The following morning, I handed Antoinette a steaming mug of coffee. We were just about ready to open the MotherVine for the day, to the delight of eager shoppers waiting on the sidewalk out front. But first, we needed to caffeinate.

"Sometime today," she asked, "do you want to help me make a list of seasonal titles? Customers have been asking for spring-into-summer recommendations."

"I have one in mind for middle-grade readers. *The Legend of Rosie Beacon*."

"Oh, that's a good one," she said, shaking cocoa powder into our coffees. "You know, a portion of the proceeds of every sale go to the Cattail Historical Society. The author wanted it that way. She's since passed on, but I've kept her nice little book in stock all these years."

"*The Legend of Rosie Beacon* is so much more than a *nice little book*, Ant." I bounced on the balls of my feet. Inspired by Rosie, I'd done a bit of research, and I was bursting to share what I'd learned. "Consider Paul Revere. He was no kid when he did his famous midnight ride. He was a grown man. You want to know what else? He only rode fourteen miles."

"Not to be sneezed at," Antoinette said.

"No—but Rosie Beacon rode *forty* miles. Forty! What's more, Paul Revere rode in the springtime. He had buddies with him. Wingmen. They traversed well-defined streets, and other riders joined them as they went along. Rosie? She was all by herself.

Just a teenager and her Banker mustang, navigating swamps, streams, brambles, and forests—in the dead of winter. With a storm approaching. And all that came *after* swimming across the sound from Cattail Island to the mainland. When it was almost frozen."

"But—that's two whole miles. At the sound's narrowest." As the comparison sank in, my boss tapped her fingernails against her mug.

"Rosie's story isn't the only one lost to history," I said. "Around the same era, there was a girl named Betsy Dowdy up in the Currituck area of the Outer Banks. And another girl named Sybil Ludington in New York. They both rode overnight, alone, to warn settlers and militias about oncoming invasions. Over the years, their rides have been dismissed because history books just didn't record the contributions of young girls. When it comes to exactly what happened, what's fact and what's fiction, is anyone's guess. But oral tradition survived. Tales passed down through generations, at bedsides and firesides. There's no doubt those girls did *something*. They risked. They acted. So why isn't Cattail celebrating Rosie Beacon more? We've got a hero in our history." I paused when I realized I'd gotten myself a bit worked up and had banged my palm on the counter, sloshing my coffee. I smoothed my hair, cleared my throat, and calmly added, "My point is, I think we should stock more copies of *The Legend of Rosie Beacon*."

Toasting the idea, Antoinette tapped her mug against mine. "I heartily agree, my dear."

We didn't converse much after that. The morning brought a crush of customers, many of whom made purchases. A few hours later, after the rush had quieted, I was snapping candids of Tin Man curled up next to a lavender pot in a shaft of sunlight, while Antoinette twirled the feather duster over the books. And that was when, outside on Queen Street, a Cadillac coupe glided past. Behind the wheel: Dr. Rasheeda Scarboro, the medical examiner. She steered into a parking spot.

Dr. Scarboro could probably fill in some details about Seth Goodnow's murder, since an autopsy had likely been conducted by now. Considering the recent role I'd played in revealing a killer last summer, I didn't think she'd blink at a bit of nosiness on my part.

Antoinette had also noticed the Cadillac. I turned to her, chewing my bottom lip, giving her my best imploring look.

"Go," she said.

31

Rasheeda Scarboro strode down the tourist-crammed sidewalk. She had a regal quality about her. Straight posture, silver braids piled atop her head, flowing clothing. Her sandals softly slapped her feet. A large tote bag was slung over one shoulder.

I sidled up to her. "Doctor," I said. "Hi."

"Callie!" She put a hand on my arm, and her face lit up. But the warm greeting morphed into concern. "You're not here to make chitchat, are you?"

"I wish."

"I'm running errands. You could walk with me." She paused. "On second thought, our topic of discussion won't be the sort of thing we want overheard."

"It might get grisly."

"Shall we go into the MotherVine? It's on my list anyway."

"It's likely to fill up with people. How about a quieter area?" We took the nearest alley, wanting to get away from the busy sidewalk where children were swinging plastic swords or sucking Popsicles. Only when Dr. Scarboro and I reached a newly planted pear tree did I realize, with a shiver, that we were standing next to Cattail Family Martial Arts.

The sapling was far from a picture of springtime exuberance. Its browned leaves looked like they'd crumble to dust if you breathed on them.

"Heavens, it's been dry," she said. "We really need some rain. And this little buddy needs a drink." She retrieved a water bottle from her tote bag and dumped its contents into the dirt. "Ask away."

Briefly I closed my eyes, centering myself, switching from bookseller who deals in fictional realms to crime solver navigating gritty reality. "The cause of death was strangulation?"

"How graphic do you want me to get?"

"Don't hold back. Former reporter here, remember?"

"The victim died of ligature strangulation, as opposed to manual or suspension strangulation. Meaning the structures of the neck were compressed by a cable-like object, which caused asphyxia and neuronal death."

"The murder weapon is a cable of some sort?"

"The width would be approximately five millimeters," Dr. Scarboro said.

Shuddering, I recalled the bruises purpling Seth Goodnow's neck. "Have you pinpointed the time of death?"

"According to the victim's fitness watch, his heart stopped beating at 9:06 a.m. This concurs with my findings."

I did some quick mental math. By the time Toby and I discovered him lying there, he'd been dead for about ten minutes. "Who did this?" I asked. "Who are we looking for?"

"Someone strong. Goodnow wasn't a big guy, but he wasn't a wimp, either, and he definitely put up a fight. I found his own skin cells underneath his fingernails."

Again I closed my eyes, imagining Seth Goodnow clawing at whatever had been lashed tight around his neck. I steadied myself on the sapling. "What about the cut on his hand?"

"Something jagged and irregular caused it. The wound had been washed. Neosporin was applied."

"Any other forensic evidence?"

"That would be useful, wouldn't it?" She sighed. "I'm afraid not."

When neither of us could think of any other pertinent details to discuss, I thanked her and we exchanged well wishes. Scarboro headed back toward Queen Street—and I stood there trying to come up with things that might involve five-millimeter cables.

Boats and marinas probably made use of them.

Nunchucks came to mind too.

32

Later that day, after my MotherVine shift—if a shift was what my scattered work hours could be called—I'd driven, unannounced, to Mustang Beach. I was doing my intuition's bidding. It told me there was something more to this missing-horse business. Something I wasn't seeing. If I popped in and took Geri-Lynn by surprise, maybe I'd find a puzzle piece, so to speak.

I parked outside Sanctuary Bungalow. The CLOSED sign was flipped, so I climbed the dune and paused at the top like an explorer surveying the bounty. To the north, offshore, a sizeable wave swelled. A group of bronzed surfers spaced themselves apart and rode it in. They must have belonged to the cars and trucks in the lot.

On the south side of the fence, a half dozen horses sunbathed. Every now and then, they swished their tails, stomped their hooves, and tossed their manes. They appeared to shimmer against the turquoise water.

And directly below the dune, halfway to the ocean, crouched Geri-Lynn Humfeld, brushing sand from a segment of cardboard spread on the beach. On top of the cardboard: a black lobster. That was what it looked like, anyway. Until I got closer and recognized what it was.

A drone.

I descended the dune carefully, not wanting to disturb it. When you grow up on Cattail Island, the fragility of dunes and how important they are to beach conservation gets beaten into your DNA. "Hi there, Geri-Lynn," I said over the crashing of the waves. She turned and shaded her eyes as I strode over the warm sand. A gust of wind tried to take her floppy hat. She crammed it in place. Her normally tan face was a shade or two paler than usual and had a raccoonish quality.

Tigress going missing meant the sanctity of her Mustang Beach had been invaded, and it was likely starting to erode her mental health.

"Have you been staying up nights?" I asked.

"I have to," she said. "There's nobody else to share watch with. What do you know about drones?"

"That nothing ruins a fine beach walk more than a low-flying robot spider buzzing around your head." I sat cross-legged beside her. "Other than that, not much. This is the closest I've ever been to one."

"Me too. Only set me back a couple hundred bucks. It's not the trail camera system I've been dreaming about for this land. But in a pinch? I figured, might as well. It's cute, don't you think?"

To each her own, I supposed. As for me, there was something menacing about the propellered thing. Like a miniaturized spy helicopter belonging to a comic book villain. Nonetheless, I could admit to drones' usefulness and appeal. Especially in an area like the Outer Banks, which has an illustrious flight history, thanks to the Wright brothers. More than a hundred years after the first manned aircraft powered through some wind, people were still coming here to pilot things. Kites, hang gliders, ultralights. And more and more, drones. Just a few days ago, as Toby, Antoinette, Hudson, Scupper, Tin Man, and I walked on Starry Beach, we'd seen a wheelchair user pilot a drone carrying baited fishing line. Hovering thirty feet above the water, past the breakers, the drone released the bait. Weights sank down below the waves. The wheelchair user's friend was standing by, ready to help reel in when necessary.

As to what was motivating Geri-Lynn to use a drone, I had a hypothesis. She wanted to take in the mustang's territory from a never-before-seen vantage point, for clues that might have eluded her at ground level. Clues as to where the thief—or thieves— might have taken Tigress.

I scooped some sand and let it sift from my fist. "At my old newspaper job, I was sitting in my cubicle one day when a pair of shoes popped up above the partition. I got up and saw that my coworker was upside down, doing a headstand. She said she needed a change in perspective. Once she was right side up again, she sat at her desk and typed up a two-thousand-word article in sixteen minutes. Our editor didn't change a word. It went straight to ink."

"I take it that's pretty fast."

"Yep." I clapped the sand from my hands. "You think the drone's going to give you a change in perspective?"

"That's the idea. A bird's-eye view. Without standing on my head." She showed me the remote control, all switches and knobs, designed for both hands. Holding her smartphone horizontally, she hooked it up to the remote control so the entire thing resembled a mini-laptop, with the phone as the screen. "It's really not as complicated as it looks. That's what I keep telling myself, anyway. I've been practicing takeoffs and landings with this cool flight-simulator app all morning. I think I'm ready to do it in real life."

"It's not too windy?"

"Not in theory, anyway."

"Have you figured out how to take video?"

She rasped out a laugh. "One step at a time. I haven't even attempted liftoff yet. Technically, I'm not allowed to fly the drone over state-owned land, but Mustang Beach is owned by the sanctuary, and so far, the sanctuary hasn't set up any regulations. Once I get the hang of it, I'll take it low over the tree canopy, if I can."

"What'll the mustangs think?"

"They've survived a few centuries of hurricanes, not to mention biting insects, sandspurs, and other annoyances. Not much fazes them." She paused before adding, "I'd do anything to protect them."

"I believe that," I said. "And I'm happy to be here for the maiden voyage."

"Here's hoping I don't crash and burn."

We got to our feet. Geri-Lynn tapped some buttons. With a hum, the black lobster lifted straight up. "Would you look at that," she said. "Miracles do happen." Quavering, the drone rose two feet, then two more. Our chins lifted as we watched it rise and rise. "Check me out. Not bad for a nature gal, right?"

"I'm impressed."

The drone hovered almost twenty feet above the sand. She tapped the joystick to the right, and the drone obeyed, veering toward the fence. "Piece of cake," she said—just as a gust of wind slammed it downward.

Cursing, Geri-Lynn handed me the remote and trotted over to retrieve the drone. "I think it's okay," she said, blowing sand from the propellers.

A white horse wandered closer to the fence. I backed away. I wanted to coo to the beast, or make a kissy noise or simply say, *Hello, gorgeous.* But I held my tongue, because any of that would be considered enticement, which was a no-no. If staying away from them was a challenge for me, a mere horse admirer, it must have been especially hard for someone like Geri-Lynn, who had such a strong affinity for these animals.

"I call that one Dare," she said, as if offering me a consolation prize for not being able to talk to the pretty white horse.

I grinned. Virginia Dare was the first English child born in the new world, in what became known as the Lost Colony, on Roanoke Island, just north of Cattail. "You have names for all of them, don't you? Come on. I won't tell anyone."

Cradling the drone, Geri-Lynn walked up to me. "The petite bay over there is Echo."

"What's a bay?"

"Dark brown fur with black manes and tails. It's the most common color combo for wild horses."

"That's Tigress's pattern," I said. "Brown with black."

"Tigress's foal will likely be a bay too."

"What do you call the one next to Echo? The silvery, dappled one?"

"Thunder."

It struck me as the perfect name. Dappled silver was exactly what thunder would look like if you could see it clapping across a steely sky. I imagined a freer, wilder world, one in which I could hop onto Thunder's back and sink my fingers into his mane. *Hi-ya!* We'd gallop up the beach, sand flying, salty wind on our tongues . . .

I was going to ask if Geri-Lynn had read the Rosie Beacon book when she tilted her chin toward a reddish-brown mare munching on sea grass. "That's Orla, after my Irish grandmother. Followed by Rivka, after my Jewish grandmother. Closer to the water is Marlin, after the fish, followed by Succotash, after the dish." She squinted toward the nearest dune, atop which posed an all-black mare, her tail blowing in the wind. "That's Starview. Over there's her son, Tundra. After he was born, I couldn't decide on a name. By the time winter rolled around, foaling season was long over, he was already six months old, and I was still calling him 'Hey, You' or 'Starview's Son.' Then one day a migrating tundra swan landed on his back and stayed there, and they walked around like that for hours. Instant interspecies best friends. So I called him Tun—"

An engine roared, cutting her off.

A small fishing boat was cutting fast through the whitecaps, toward the beach. Two men were aboard. One of them jumped out with a splash. He swam through the breakers, heading ashore. Directly toward Tundra.

"Hey!" Geri-Lynn tossed the drone at me and broke for the fence.

Arms outstretched, I dove for the drone—and missed. I landed on my elbows in the sand.

The swimming man appeared to have not heard Geri-Lynn. The wind and the boat's engines must've drowned out her voice. Sopping wet, he emerged from the water and sprinted for Tundra.

The mustang reared up on his hind legs.

"*Hey!*" Geri-Lynn was almost to the fence, but the turnstile was thirty feet away. Too far. She climbed over the fence and dropped to the sand, landing with a grunt on hands and knees. "*Stop!*"

Tundra stomped and whinnied. Even from my vantage point, I could see the whites of his eyes.

Geri-Lynn sprang up and sprinted toward the man. She ran hard, arms pumping, knees practically hitting her chest. The man was mere feet from Tundra when he noticed Geri-Lynn. For a second, he froze, then pivoted and rushed back for the water.

Geri-Lynn bent down and dug something out of her boot. When she straightened back up, she held a small object. She pointed it overhead. A shot cracked the blue sky. Squawking crows lifted from the scrub pines. Tundra galloped for the trees. "Y'all are trespassing!" She fired at the sky a second time.

The man charged into the waves and dove under. Surfacing beyond a breaker, he swam freestyle, haymaker-ing for the boat. He climbed the ladder and hauled it up.

"You came within fifty feet of a wild horse," Geri-Lynn shouted after him. "That's punishable by law and by my boot up your—"

The motors ground full throttle, and the boat sped off, making a wake of frothy aqua that I might have considered beautiful if my heart hadn't been hammering so hard.

33

Do you know what kind of boat that was? Did it have a name?" After holstering her gun, Geri-Lynn had used the turnstile to get back onto the public portion of Mustang Beach. She walked up to me as I tried to gently remove the drone from where it had wedged into the sand.

I wasn't much of a boat person. The watercraft had struck me as a typical small fishing boat, white with a blue Bimini top. In Outer Banks waters, there must have been hundreds just like it. I shook my head. "Couldn't make out the name of it."

"Me neither," she said, still catching her breath. "There was writing on the back of that guy's shirt, but I missed it."

"Everything happened so fast."

"They must be the ones who stole Tigress. And they're coming back for more."

"There's no way they were going to get a horse onto that boat, Geri-Lynn."

"Of course not. They were casing things. They'll be back. In the middle of the night. They'll drive. They'll tow a trailer. They'll snatch another one of my mustangs. Maybe more than one." She headed toward the bungalow, cradling the trashed equipment.

I stared after her, not knowing what to think. On the one hand, that scenario seemed pretty outlandish. On the other hand . . .

No visitors were waiting at Sanctuary Bungalow. A good thing, since Geri-Lynn and I were sweaty and covered in sand. On the porch, we brushed ourselves off the best we could.

"Who do you think they were?" I asked as we went inside.

"You really think they're involved with Tigress's disappearance?"

"Why else would they be on my beach?"

I could think of a number of reasons, just off the top of my head.

A lost bet.

They didn't know any better.

They were hunting for pirates' buried treasure, which believe it or not was a big thing in Cattail, for kids and adults alike.

None of those motives necessarily had anything to do with Tigress and her foal.

But as Geri-Lynn yanked off her boots and let them clatter to the floor, her hands trembling, I kept my mouth shut. I expected the bourbon bottle might make an appearance. No better time than the present for a nerve-soothing splash of alcohol. She didn't reach for it, but instead unbuckled her ankle holster and slapped it on the window ledge. Her pistol was demure, with a mother-of-pearl handle. Patterns of waves and stars were etched into its stumpy barrel. I didn't know guns from Shinola, but I did know that Geri-Lynn's gun was an antique. It looked like something a madam in an Old West swinging-door saloon might whip out from underneath her crinoline.

"Family heirloom," she said. "I could use a pizza and a conversation that has nothing to do with mustangs."

I agreed. After calling in a small pepper and onion, Geri-Lynn procured some sweet tea from the fridge in her office and poured two tall glasses. We sat on the window ledge, gazing out at the waves. "So, what's your story, Callie Padget?" she asked.

I told her a little about myself. How I'd grown up on Cattail, raised by a single mother who'd been a seamstress.

"Did she make your clothes when you were a kid?" Geri-Lynn asked.

"She tried, but I was not the kind of girl to wear a cotton sundress that matched Mommy's."

"You're in a dress now."

"The irony." I told her how my uncle took me in after my mother fell from the top of Cattail lighthouse when I was twelve. I described my adult life, my reporter stint in Charlotte, catching her up to my tumultuous homecoming to Cattail Island. Despite the upsetting subject matter, I got a cozy feeling. I didn't often enjoy talking about myself. Yet there I was, enjoying it. Could it be that I was making a new friend? Not including Toby, a new friend was something I hadn't had in a long time. "What's your story, Geri-Lynn Humfeld?" I asked.

She talked freely too. She grew up in Raleigh, also the daughter of a single mother, who'd since passed away. Her mother, a veterinary technician, introduced her and her older sister to horses when they were just three and six years old. Geri-Lynn herself had been studying to be a vet tech when she visited Cattail Island for the first time, fell in love with the mustangs, and decided to study wildlife biology instead.

"Living here on Mustang Beach is quite the contrast to the urban suburbia where I grew up," she said.

"Who looks after things here when you're away? You must go on vacation, right?"

"Two weeks a year. I have a core group of volunteers. They're devoted. Always on hand to help with the bigger jobs."

"Like what?"

"Just the other day, one of my young mares, Rivka—you met her—got herself hung up on fencing, deep in the woods. Rusted old dune fencing that must have gotten tossed around in a storm and ended up tangled in the brush. After I realized I hadn't seen her in a while, I went out looking for her. I heard her braying and followed the sound and there she was. Unable to move an inch, she was so ensnared. I called in reinforcements. Together we cut her free and cleared the mess out of there."

"Geri-Lynn," I said, setting down my glass. "Do you *know* these people? Your volunteers?"

"I know a few of the major players well enough. There's a larger bunch of them who show up for the less specific jobs. Beach cleanups, that sort of thing." Suddenly getting my meaning, she swung her feet to the floor. "You think—you think—"

"Check all your volunteers' names against the state wildlife commission records," I said. "That way, you can find out if any of them have a motorboat registered."

She opened her mouth to reply, but the front door banged open.

34

Humid air rolled in, invading the small air-conditioned space. Standing in the open doorway, Detective Fusco tensed. Her face bore the usual no-nonsense expression, but something was off. Something had happened.

Her eyes flicked over to me. "What are you doing here?"

"We could ask the same of you, Officer," Geri-Lynn said.

"It's Detective."

Glaring, Geri-Lynn brought her glass to her mouth and swigged. I recalled the long-standing beef between the two women. Fusco had spoken out against town monies going to the sanctuary for a trail camera system. "You just let in a fly," Geri-Lynn said, wiping her mouth with her sleeve. "*Detective.*"

Fusco entered, closing the door behind her. She wore a silk top, the armpits darkened. Dirt spotted her trousers, and her hair clung to her sweaty neck.

"Are you okay?" I asked.

"I've contacted the canine unit," she said. "It's unclear when or if they'll be able to get here. I can't afford to wait."

Canine unit? The tiny hairs on the back of my neck quivered.

"How'd you know about the trespassers?" Geri-Lynn asked.

Fusco's orange eyebrows tilted. "Trespassers?"

"There was just a guy traipsing around on Mustang Beach. He went after one of the horses. His buddy was waiting for him in a boat. They took off when they saw me. Headed south."

This was obviously news to Fusco. She produced her small tablet and stylus and began taking notes. "Can you describe the two men?"

"They were far away," Geri-Lynn said. She and I took turns providing what few details we could. Fusco scowled as she scribbled. She couldn't do much with words like *typical* and *average*. Still, she seemed interested.

She pointed to the drone, which now looked like something picked up at a scratch-n-dent sale. "You have footage?"

"*Footage?* I was lucky to figure out how to turn the thing on."

"Do you have cameras set up anywhere on the sanctuary?"

Geri-Lynn glowered. "Now, wouldn't that be something. Cameras."

"What's going on, Fusco?" I asked.

"Addison Battle."

My tongue suddenly felt like a piece of cardboard in my mouth. "What about him?"

"He was just reported missing by his daughter in Virginia. She couldn't get ahold of him. And a concerned citizen called to report his barbershop wide open, with nobody inside."

"You can't find him?" I said.

"He hasn't used his credit cards or his bank cards. He hasn't bought a ferry ticket. I knew he used to come here a lot, back when he was more mobile, to photograph the mustangs. So I walked the footpath—"

"In those shoes?" Geri-Lynn gestured to the detective's red heels. "Four miles of wood chips? Impressive."

"What happens now?" I asked.

"We search," Fusco said. "Officers are scouring the island. Meanwhile, I'm here to request the cooperation of the Mustang Beach Sanctuary."

Geri-Lynn finally pushed up from the window ledge. Thumbs in her belt loops, she swaggered closer to Fusco. "I've got forty-five wild horses under my protection. Mustangs that are this state's heritage. Rugged descendants of conquistador mounts that have survived on this barrier island for five hundred years. I'm not about to let God knows how many humans go gallivanting all over the place, hollering their heads off, disturbing the peace that those beasts have earned."

"It's not going to be like that," Fusco said. "If there's any risk of Addison being a danger to the public, we're not about to call upon civilians to help search for him."

"But you call upon me?" Geri-Lynn said.

Fusco's jaw clenched. "You know the land."

"Hold up," I said. "Addison Battle, *a danger to the public*? The man's got to weigh less than my left leg. What danger could he possibly pose?"

"We're simply following procedure, in the wake of—"

"Detective," Geri-Lynn butted in. "I don't really have time for . . . *frivolous projects*. That was how you described my efforts to install wildlife cameras around the sanctuary, remember? Wouldn't those come in handy right now."

I got up and stood between them, patting the air. "Let's all take a rational view of things. Geri-Lynn, your job is to protect the mustangs."

"That's goddamn right—"

"*And* a man is missing. A good man. An upstanding member of our community. Do you really want word going around that you got in the way of bringing him safely home? Besides, didn't you say you wanted to see the land from a new perspective?" I gave her a look that said, *Think about it—this is a good opportunity to put in another search for Tigress.* Granted, this search wouldn't be from the air, but it would provide us with additional sets of eyeballs. "I think we can trust Detective Fusco that no members of the search party will come within fifty feet of any of the horses," I said. "As long as it can be helped. Right?"

"The *search party*," Fusco said, air-quoting, "will consist of me and Ms. Humfeld."

"That's *Dr.* Humfeld," Geri-Lynn said.

"And me," I said. "Me too."

"Forget it, A.C.," Fusco said. "You're not coming. *Dr.* Humfeld, we've had our differences. But I believe in letting bygones be bygones. You can help, or you can stay out of the way. But this is happening."

Geri-Lynn slung an arm around my shoulder. "I'll guide you—but Callie comes with. If for no other reason than to keep you and me from killing each other."

35

Outside, the three of us sprayed ourselves down with organic insect repellent. Geri-Lynn had enough bottles of the lemon-scented stuff to coat a small army and make the entire porch smell like a citrus grove. She'd produced a pair of rubber boots and offered them to Fusco, apologizing for not being able to lend her anything more suitable. The detective grimaced as she crammed her feet into them, but she didn't complain. For a beach-and-woods combo walk, tight boots beat out high heels.

Over the dune we went, and then through the turnstile. Geri-Lynn might have wanted to believe Fusco had zero respect for the sanctuary, but I saw the cop's face as she took her first-ever steps onto the forbidden portion of Mustang Beach. She knew it was special. She just didn't have the luxury of savoring the moment.

What she did have was a missing person to find.

We walked the beach three abreast. The mood was solemn. The mustangs that had witnessed Geri-Lynn's earlier drone-flying attempt were nowhere in sight. A larger group of horses frolicked in the surf about three-quarters of a mile away. Too far to count.

We entered the woods on a different path than the one I'd been on before. This one was hillier. Twistier. Geri-Lynn took the lead, with Fusco second and me bringing up the rear. As the sound of pounding waves faded behind us, it was easy to see how someone could get lost here. Even someone familiar with general Cattail Island geography.

Fusco instructed us not to touch or disturb anything. She called out Addison Battle's name. The somber timbre of her voice chilled me.

Geri-Lynn and I added our voices, and we alternated calling out for the old barber. The only sounds we heard were the tapping of a woodpecker high overhead and the occasional buzz of an insect.

At one point, Geri-Lynn stopped short and threw up a hand, signaling for Fusco and me to halt. We tiptoed up beside her. "Movement ahead," she said.

Fusco cupped her hands around her mouth. "Addison!"

A horse lumbered onto the path. The bay mare was too far away to identify any sort of scar between her eyes, and she was probably too scrawny to be carrying a foal, but I glanced hopefully in Geri-Lynn's direction anyway. She gave her blond head a single, furtive shake.

The horse wasn't Tigress.

As the detective took the lead, Geri-Lynn whispered in my ear, "I call that one SOB—short for Southern Belle."

Thirty minutes later, we'd arrived at a landmark I recognized: the Hugging Trees, that enchanted spot where the branches of a live oak wrapped around two loblolly pines. We rested there, chugging from water bottles, wiping the sweat from our necks.

"How're your feet?" Geri-Lynn asked Fusco.

"More blistered than chili peppers in these boots. But I'll survive."

Just then, a hot nip of pain bit my ankle. "Shoot," I said. "I picked up a sandspur." The bean-sized burr had thorned itself deep, needling my skin. Sandspurs grew like weeds in hot, dry weather. The stalks weren't easy to distinguish from regular, harmless grass.

"That sting is like no other," Geri-Lynn said. "It'll stop you in your tracks. Are you okay?"

I picked the thorny ball from my ankle, only to have the spikes nettle into my fingertips. When I finally succeeded in flinging the sticky thing a safe distance away, I said, "All is well."

"Watch your step, ladies," Fusco said. "And let's remember why we're here."

"I'll take us back a different way." Geri-Lynn brought us to yet another trail, this one so narrow, leaves and branches brushed our arms. Along the underbrush, several two-foot-deep holes gaped. "Don't trip," she said over her shoulder. "They've been digging."

"Why?" I asked, imagining mustangs hoofing the soft earth.

"Because it's been so dry. Their usual creeks have shriveled up, so they dig holes in the hope that groundwater will seep in. Smart animals, these horses."

When the trail widened again, Fusco and I fell into step. I asked about Heather Westerly. Didn't Fusco find the woman a bit off?

"Here we go again with the questions," she said. "When's the last time you had your hearing checked? I'm not discussing any details with—"

"What about the initials on the sign-up sheet? *D.S.* Did you figure out what that means?" Her scowl meant she wasn't going to answer. "I *assume* it's someone's initials," I said. "My bet is you've checked out all Cattail residents with the initials D.S. Your next step would be to go through passenger ferry manifests, rental contracts . . . What if it's not even a person? It could be some sort of code, or—"

"A.C., you read too many books." She stopped and pressed a pair of binoculars to her face. We were surrounded by dense trees; there wasn't anything distant she could possibly bring into closer focus. It was a gesture of desperation.

We'd searched the woods and come up empty.

36

Meet me at my uncle's place in 10?

From behind the wheel of my parked Civic, I sent the text to Toby and received an immediate thumbs-up. I almost texted back a smiley face—I couldn't wait to be around him. But I'd be greeting him with the unsettling news of Addison Battle gone missing.

I set aside my phone and began driving, air-conditioning vents aimed directly at my armpits. Full-blast cooldown. The bluegrass failed to calm me. I pumped down my window. Cicadas screeched as I sped by, the Atlantic frothing on my right, Pamlico shimmering on my left. The setting sun washed the sky in a watercolor kind of way, cornflower blue splashing into silvery peach. It was lump-in-your-throat gorgeous.

I white-knuckled the steering wheel.

Toby was waiting outside Hudson's house, leaning on the Wagoneer's back bumper. I told him about Addison being missing, and the wasted search of Mustang Beach.

Toby rubbed his face with both hands. "That doesn't bode well."

I had to agree. "If you're not up for giving me a self-defense lesson, I understand."

"To tell you the truth, it's about the only thing I'm up for."

I glanced over my shoulder. In the woodshop, the lights were blazing. "Could you also be up for a cold beer and some old-guy banter? 'Cause we're going to have to make it past my uncle."

"Addison Battle?" Hudson cracked the caps off three Cattail Island Blondes. "Years ago, that coot burned me in a Hold'em tourney. I lost four bucks in the first ten minutes alone." My uncle seemed confident that the old barber would turn up safe and sound. "Addison might be older than sin," he said, "but he's still got a few tricks up his sleeve."

Bottles in hand, Hudson, Toby, and I followed Scupper across the back lawn. I'd kicked off my flip-flops, and the grass was so dry it felt like tiny blades stabbing the soles of my feet.

"I hope it goes without saying that I want you to be careful, cub," my uncle said. "Proceed with caution."

"You've got nothing to worry about." I pecked him on his whiskered cheek. "I mean, seriously—how much trouble can I get into?"

Toby and Hudson shared a look. We all sat on the dock's edge, our legs dangling, our feet in the water. Scupper trotted to the end of the dock and sat, as still as a ship's figurehead except for the occasional twitch of his pointy ears.

"I don't know about y'all," Hudson said, "but I could go for an old-fashioned thunderstorm."

"So could the grass," I said.

"And just about every plant on this island," Toby said. "There's no rain in the forecast, as far as I've heard."

"We need one of those good surprise Outer Banks rainstorms," my uncle said. "The ones that move so fast they barely have time to show up on the radar."

We sipped our beers and pointed out stars and planets as they blinked into the black sky.

"What are they saying about the new foal?" Hudson asked—
which struck me as random, but I didn't comment.

"It's not quite time yet," I said. "Any day now, though."

"Oh yeah? How do you know so much?"

"Geri-Lynn Humfeld runs the Mustang Beach Sanctuary.
I delivered a book to her, and we're becoming friends." As the
words left my mouth, I was struck by how true they felt. I really
was hoping she and I were becoming friends. I'd never had many
friends. In Charlotte, I got along well with my work colleagues,
but inherent rivalry, however good-natured, prevented any inti-
macy. Since moving back home, there hadn't been many opportunities to make female friends. I'd been spending most of my
downtime with Toby. Or with the MotherVine, after hours.

Groaning, my uncle got to his feet. "Late nights are for the
youths. Good night."

Scupper escorted him to the house.

When we were alone, Toby interlaced his fingers with mine,
brought my hand to his mouth, and brushed his lips along my
knuckles. He smelled good, like that spicy cologne he wore.
Crickets cheeped, frogs gulped, and the cattails were black swords
rising from the canal.

"Favorite constellation?" he asked.

"I don't know that many. But I've made up a few of my own."
I pointed, outlining a curvy string of stars festooning large and
low in the sky, just where the Milky Way brightened, as if it wanted
to drag that spangled band across the sky. "I call that one Cap-
tain Hook."

He chuckled. "I love how imaginative you are. The other night?
For our big date? I was going to cook you a nice meal. Linguine
and clams and oysters and garlic toast."

"My favorite meal. All the quizzing paid off."

"That's not all. I had more surprises planned."

"Surprises, plural?"

"We're going to do them. All of them. When all the craziness dies down."

"Speaking of craziness." I told Toby about my conversation with Scarboro. About the murder weapon being a five-millimeter cable, or something like that.

"That's why the police took my nunchucks."

"Did you notice any signs of someone sneaking into your house?" I asked. Technically, an intruder wouldn't have been breaking in, because Toby didn't lock up his home. Hardly any Cattailers did—even after last summer. If anything, we'd become more adamant about keeping our doors *un*locked. That sort of collective mindset was a big part of what made living on this island so special.

Toby shook his head. "Nothing like that."

"Who knows where you store your nunchucks?" I pictured his duck room, where his collection of antique decoys lined the shelves, floor to ceiling. The only piece of furniture in the room, a small chest, sat underneath a window.

"You," he said. "That's it. Responsible martial artists don't leave weapons lying around, out in the open." He took a defiant swig of beer. "And I'm not going to start securing my house. The day Cattailers begin locking their doors is the day we let the bad guys win."

"Uncle Hudson feels the same way. You're talking like a true non-dingbatter."

We fell silent. There wasn't much else to say about the matter. After a while, Toby helped me to my feet. Right there on the dock, we picked up where we'd left off after our most recent self-defense session: how to break away from an attacker who's got you from behind. I put my back to Toby, and he clamped his arms around me. "If someone grabs you so tight you can't swing your elbow back," he said, "you have other options."

"Like what?" I said, wriggling. "I can't even move."

"Think. Besides elbows, what else is hard?" We both snickered. "That came out wrong," he said. "Get your mind out of the gutter, Padget."

"My skull," I said, recovering. "My skull happens to be very hard."

"Correct. Tip your head back—*slowly*—and see what happens."

"Reverse headbutt?"

"Exactly. In a real-life situation, you'd want to slam your head. As hard as you can."

"Wouldn't that hurt *me*?"

"Not as much as it'd hurt your attacker's mouth or nose."

A few times, we practiced the move in slow motion. Toby clutching me from behind, pinning my arms. Me reverse headbutting his chin and breaking free. Eventually we worked more quickly and added some finishing moves, like pivoting and sprinting away.

When we were warm, sweaty, and bordering on tired, we sat back down, cross-legged this time, facing each other. "The police are going to let me open up shop soon," he said.

"That's great news."

"Want the not-so-great news?"

"Uh-oh."

"Fusco warned me about the mess from the fingerprint dusting. She said the stuff leaves a god-awful residue, and it'll take me hours to clean. Apparently, it's all over the place."

"We'll clean it up together. With two people, the job will go much faster."

He sipped his beer, then asked, "What if no students show up when I reopen? What if I lose everything?"

"They'll come," I said.

"What if they *do* come, and I can't teach? Like—what if I freeze up or something?"

"You just taught me."

"That's different." He shook his head. "Listen to me, being a worrywart."

I noticed fine lines around his eyes. First his childhood nemesis shows up dead in his dojo; then his small-business-owner neighbor becomes an official missing person. The stress had gotten to Toby. Eaten away at the finely honed sheath of calm that martial arts had given him.

"You have your training to fall back on," I said. "Besides— you can't *not* teach. It's what you do. It's who you are. Cattail *needs* you, because it needs to learn to protect itself. Now more than ever."

37

Hudson had a doctor's appointment the following morning, and I'd planned to take him. He was excited to brag about all the kale he'd been consuming, and the poundage he'd lost since his health scare last year.

While he was showering, I did some Cattale Queen maintenance. I could not control the recent murderous proclivities of my island, but I *could* give the patrons of my Little Free Library an orderly book browsing experience. On the bottom shelf, where I kept the hardbacks, a gently used copy of *Tear Me Apart* by J. T. Ellison had appeared, next to *The Thursday Murder Club*. Seeing as it was Thursday, that gave me a chuckle. I also noticed several titles by Sarah Pekkanen, an author whose books I always tore through. I rechecked the alphabetization (authors' last names), spritzed the shelves with my trusty travel-size bottle of bergamot-scented mist, and latched the cattail-shaped handle.

Back inside, my uncle still hadn't emerged. Scupper kept me company while I waited. Loving on a cat or dog soothed me, but even giving Scupper a thorough double ear scratch—his favorite—didn't calm the nervousness swimming in my belly.

And then I remembered Hudson's top secret project, hidden underneath the tarp, right in front of me. The prospect of a solid fact, a straight answer, a mystery solved—how could I resist?

No one was there to tell on me. Except Scupper. "You won't say anything, right, Scup?" Sitting by my feet, he cocked his head, causing his eyebrow to shag over his eye, giving him a mischievous look. "Good boy." I lifted the block of wood that pinned down the tarp.

"You trying to jinx me?" My uncle's voice boomed as he shuffled into the woodshop. "I told you that was a secret."

"So close," I said. "So close."

"I'll be needing your help with it soon enough."

"You're bringing me in?"

"Eventually," he said, twisting on his radio, which twanged out country music. "Doc's office just called. They canceled all their morning appointments. Some sort of personal emergency. Anyway, I'm rescheduled for next week. So you're off the hook." He took the block of wood I was holding. "Now, scram so I can finish this baby. *In private.*"

38

I wasn't due at the MotherVine until later. Might as well try and get in some more face time with a certain tragic widow, I decided.

I pulled up to Nine Love Beach Trail just as Naomi Goodnow was walking down the driveway. Tucked under her arm: something flat and red.

"Hi again," I said. "Just thought I'd stop by and . . ." I trailed off, feeling suddenly gauche.

Naomi, even in her grief, was gracious. "Join me. I was just heading down to the beach. I'm not very good at flying kites. You must be, if you grew up here, right?"

"Not really. I could give it a go, though."

We walked past the cottages. Some of the occupants appeared to be preparing for long drives—they tossed suitcases into hatchbacks, strapped bikes to racks. Apparently, the police had given the wedding guests permission to go home.

"I'm leaving Saturday morning," Naomi told me. "With Seth."

"Oh." Those last two words of hers startled me. She didn't offer any details, and I assumed she meant that Saturday morning was the earliest she would be able to fly back with his body.

"Did you know some mystical traditions teach that in the days after a person dies," she said, "his or her soul is extremely busy? It's meeting all sorts of people from the past. Making amends, visiting, catching up."

"Like a sort of cosmic version of *This Is Your Life*?"

"Exactly. Isn't that reassuring?"

I supposed it was. While back on Earth we're all sad and stupefied, the dearly departed is flying around, too busy to be upset.

Naomi and I trudged into the steady wind. The road narrowed and formed a sandy path. As we climbed the dune, a life-size alligator rippled in the air above our heads. It was joined by a giant skeleton and an enormous monarch butterfly. Kite flying was big on the Outer Banks. Barrier islands got decent wind, with an average velocity of thirteen miles per hour on any given day, any time of the year.

Personally, I hadn't flown a kite since second grade, when Hudson gave me a Kermit the Frog kite for my birthday. He took me and my mom to Wonder Beach, but it turned out to be too gusty there, and after just a minute of watching Kermit's spastic legs climb the sky, the wind chewed him up and spit him out. It was no use trying to dam up my deluge of tears. They streamed down my cheeks. Hudson promised to buy me a replacement but never did, probably because he didn't want to risk retraumatizing me with another uncontrollable nose dive.

On the other side of the dune, Love Beach sloped before us. It was half as crowded as it might have been on a normal May afternoon. The wind whipped the sand into knee-high tornadoes, and only the most determined sunbathers sat in chairs, blocking their faces with opened books, resigning themselves to a good exfoliation.

Naomi and I added our sandals to the pile that had formed at the bottom of the dune and headed for a patch of sand that had the fewest beachgoers. When we were a safe distance from them and the other pilots, she spread her high-quality kite. A bird, fiery plumage flowing from its wingtips. She arranged it so the beak pointed to the sky and the swallow-style tail spilled out over her feet.

"Pretty," I said. "Unique."

"Seth was upset about some flaw in the handle. He wanted to fix it for me, but he never got around to it. I actually don't know if this is going to work." We inspected a dent on the ring that held the wound kite string. Unless Seth had known a lot about kite flying that I didn't, the dent didn't look all that problematic. A dark thought occurred to me—about the murder weapon. Could it have been kite line? No, I told myself; kite line was far thinner than five millimeters, and you'd have to be quite a skilled strangler to actually cut off someone's air supply with something that slippery, if it was even possible at all . . .

"I bet the kite's functional," I said. "Plus, there's so much wind, I don't see how it could fail."

"What do we do?"

"I'm not exactly sure, to be honest. But I've observed a fair amount of people doing this, over the years." Taking the ring, I walked backward, letting out the line as I went. When there was about twenty-five feet between us, I called, "Try lifting it up, and letting it go."

She released it, and the red bird soared. Up and up. "Oh my goodness," she cried, trotting over to me. "First try."

I passed her the ring, shading my eyes as she let out more line. Our necks craned as we squinted upward. The bird ascended.

After a few moments, Naomi said, "I'd like to tell you something," and I got that familiar tingly feeling that came over me whenever someone spoke those words. Back in the city, my newspaper buddies had teased me about this very phenomenon—people I hardly knew randomly opening up to me. It didn't happen a ton, but frequently enough to get noticed. I guess I was the type of person people felt they could trust.

"Go on," I said.

"The night we got engaged, Seth and I drank a lot of champagne in this hotel room we were staying in. He got up to let in room service—more champagne—and left his wallet on the table, and . . . I went through it. I'm not proud of that. In my defense, I was buzzed."

"What did you find?"

"An old note, folded up and tucked away. A receipt, actually. Someone had scribbled on the back of it. A kid, by the looks of it. It said, *Dear Seth, Someday I'm going to kill you.* Something to that effect."

"Wow." I cleared my throat, deciding that playing dumb was the best way forward. "Did you ever ask him about it?"

"Right then and there, as soon as he got back to the couch with more champagne. He was mad at me for going through his wallet, and I can't blame him. He moped for a minute or two. But then he opened up. He admitted that, growing up, he used to give other kids a hard time. That's how he put it. And I realized— I had just said *yes* to a former meanie."

"Did that surprise you?"

"Every now and then, his sarcasm would be . . ."

"Crueler than necessary?"

"Over the line," she said, nodding.

"What do you think made him that way?"

"He didn't tell me much about his past. But I think, growing up, his homelife was . . ." She let the implication linger. For whatever reasons, Seth's upbringing had been rocky. Challenging. I sensed that Naomi and I shared the same attitude: while no excuse for bad behavior, a rough childhood did shine some light on the resulting adult, and cultivate some empathy too. "Anyway," she continued. "That night, he poured us some more champagne and told me he carried the note in his wallet as a reminder to himself to be a better man."

"That sounds like a good thing. Right?"

"Right. Except . . ." She passed me the kite ring and shoved her hands in her pockets.

"Except?"

"The kid who wrote the note grew up to be a martial arts expert, right here in Cattail."

Feigning surprise, I widened my eyes. "You're kidding."

"The day after our wedding, Seth went online to look for places to work out. He'd spent his twenties partying, and now in his thirties, he was dismayed about his paunch. He joked about it—called it his beer baby—but I knew he wanted to get into better shape.

"Seth wasn't looking for a serious gym or anything. He came across the open workout hour at Cattail Family Martial Arts. It sounded low-key. Just what he wanted. And then he recognized the dojo owner's name. He gave it some deep consideration—well, as deep as Seth was capable of. And he decided to go and apologize for his behavior in the past. He told me so that morning, before he left."

Interesting. I believed Naomi. And yet, according to Toby, Seth hadn't apologized. He must have lost his nerve.

Regardless, for all his flaws, adult Seth hadn't been totally unredeemable. Along with that old receipt—a sort of talisman representing the kind of person he no longer wanted to be—he also possessed a measure of regret. "You told the police all this?" I asked Naomi.

"I told the chief, 'What if all these years, while my husband was carrying a note from this kid he used to pick on—what if all that time, that same kid was carrying downright rage?'"

"And what did the chief say?"

"That the dojo owner—Seth's former victim, all grown up—has a rock-solid alibi."

I cleared my throat a second time. If Naomi knew how close

I was with Toby, she'd never be talking to me like this. "Do you know of anyone else Seth had been . . . less than kind to?" I asked.

"I've been thinking about that. The day of the wedding, he snapped at the notary public who married us. This guy Ezra Something."

The notary public. That couple I'd spoken with at Naomi's cottage—we'd sat on the couch together, sipping beers, petting the greyhound, tabbing through photos of their daughter. They mentioned the notary public with the sourpuss face. "Ezra," I repeated. "He must be local, yeah?"

"Yeah. Works at the Cattail Library."

Ezra Something, Cattail Library. Should be easy enough to track him down. "What was their scrap about? Ezra and Seth."

"We hadn't set up any chairs on the sand because the ceremony was going to be short and sweet. Many of our guests drove all the way down from Massachusetts the day before, so we didn't think they'd object to standing for seven or eight minutes on a beautiful beach. Seth was agnostic. I wanted a clergyperson, but it was simpler to just go with a civil ceremony." She took the kite ring back from me. "It was right here, you know. Right about where we're standing is where we tied the knot."

I pictured it. Naomi in her shell-pink dress, Seth in his khakis and pink shirt, and a gathering of barefoot friends and family. Minus this wind, it would have been perfect. The kind of casual, outdoorsy wedding I could see myself having someday.

"Anyway, this Ezra guy muttered a few things about the lack of seating," Naomi said. "And he complained that we hadn't planned a *proper processional*. Seth told him to . . ." She shook her head. "Seth actually told him to shut *the bleep* up."

"Hm. Sounds like Ezra is not the easiest guy to get along with. You weren't paying him to editorialize."

"Maybe he was having a bad day. Like, maybe he had a tooth-

ache, or his pet parakeet died that morning. I get it. Still, you'd
think your few hundred bucks would at least guarantee a pleasant disposition from the person joining you in holy matrimony."
Naomi's voice trembled, and her eyes glistened. "Truthfully, Callie, I've been a mess. I'm so grateful to have all these people around
me. And yet, I kind of just wish I could be alone. Isn't that ter-
rible?"

"I don't think so."

She would be alone, soon enough. She'd go back to Massachusetts and bury her husband, and life would go on.

"Cattail Island is where we met, you know," she said. "I was
here on a bachelorette party. My friends and I were playing beach
volleyball, and it was match point and I dove for it and missed,
and Seth, who just happened to be walking past, dove and hit
the ball before it reached the sand. The ball popped up high, and
I recovered and drilled it over the net." She laughed and wiped
away a tear. "He'd face-planted in the sand at my feet, and he
was looking up at me like a lovestruck puppy. You know what
the first words he ever said to me were? 'Will you marry me?'"

"Love at first sight."

"Do you think they'll catch whoever did this?"

"I know they will."

"It does make me feel better, talking to you." She squinted
upward at the kite, which soared like a winged heart against the
clear blue sky. "How lovely. You know, all the major religions of
the world preach forgiveness. That's tough to ignore."

I was about to agree when, out of my peripheral vision, I saw
a couple with a young girl and a rangy dog climbing over the
dune. The girl raced toward us. "Naomi!" she cried. "I love your
kite!" She had a prominent cowlick, and my heart skipped a beat
at the sweet sadness in her dark eyes. It was the girl from the

smartphone photographs, Cadence O'Neill. Naomi passed her the kite ring, and Cadence's face blossomed. "This is so cool."

Her good-looking parents, Ivy and Dominick, strolled up to us. Between them loped Unicorn, the deerlike greyhound, obviously less than thrilled about the sand lashing his legs. There were hellos all around. Ivy introduced me to her daughter, who smiled shyly. "How's it going, girl?" Ivy asked Naomi, giving her shoulder a rub.

The widow melted at her friend's expression of care. Her face crumpled, but she held back any more tears.

Dominick tipped his head, admiring the strange parade billowing against the sky. Red bird, alligator, skeleton, butterfly. "Last night's sunset was shaping up to be the highlight of our week here," he said. "But the kites right now are pretty cool. What do you think, Cade?"

"Yeah," the girl said. "Totally iconic."

Ivy rolled her eyes. "I don't know where she picked up that expression."

I noticed someone else then—a hydrant-shaped man jogging down the beach, directly toward us. His backpack bounced against his back. He carried a gallon jug like he was going to punch somebody with it.

Cooper Payne, unofficial champion arm wrestler and all-around unsavory character.

39

Thanks for siccing the cops on me, guys." Cooper's pace had been a mere trot, but he was now bent over with hands on knees, sucking air. I was half hoping he wouldn't recognize me as the woman from the bar who'd posed as a nosy reporter. The other half of me didn't really care if he did.

Naomi was visibly trembling. From anger or fear, it was hard to tell.

"No one sicced the cops on you, Cooper," Ivy said, wrapping an arm around Naomi.

Just then a gust of wind yanked the kite from Cadence's hands. The ring drifted over Cooper's big head. "Oh no," Cadence said. "No!"

I leapt, stretching to my full height, swiping the air.

Miss.

I jumped a second time, and my fingertips grazed the plastic ring. It sank just enough for me to grab hold. I landed unevenly, stumbling to my knees as a wind-fueled wave hit me like a piledriver. I slammed into the surf. After a second or two of disorientation, I got to my feet. I was dripping with sea-foam and tiny shell fragments—but I held the ring. "Got it," I said lamely.

But Naomi, the O'Neills, and the still-gasping-for-air Cooper Payne couldn't care less about the kite or me. They were enacting a sort of silent standoff. Evidently, they all had history.

Ivy stepped protectively in front of her daughter, who had

buried her face in Unicorn's fur. "Why don't you just go home, Cooper?" Ivy said.

"I'm going to," he sputtered. "I've hated being stuck in this backwater."

"You're not the victim here," Dominick said.

"Whatever, *Ohio*. Like, who even lives in Ohio?"

"Twelve million people live in Ohio." Cadence O'Neill's tiny voice was barely audible above the surf and wind. She glanced up at her mother and added, "I just read that."

I saw Cooper soften a bit. As if the girl's earnestness and innocence amused him, or made him forget about defending his wounded ego. But then, as if just noticing me, he pointed a beefy finger at my face. "You. I've got a bone to pick with you. You're no reporter."

"That's true." The wind made my teeth chatter.

Naomi, meanwhile, had begun to softly weep, both hands covering her face. Ivy gathered her up and together they headed for the pile of sandals. Cadence and the dog trailed behind. They climbed the dune that would lead them to the road.

"Naomi," Cooper shouted after them. He cupped his hands around his mouth and added, "I'm sorry. I'm so sorry about what happened to Seth."

Naomi didn't respond.

He threw his arms out to the sides. "I'm not a bad guy," he said. "I'm really not." Then he snorted, hocked a phlegm ball in the direction of Dominick's feet, and resumed his steady trot southward, down Love Beach.

40

H ere," said Dominick O'Neill, pulling off his long-sleeved rash guard. He wadded it up and offered it to me. "Use it to dry off."

"Oh, I'm fine."

"Go on. Your teeth are chattering so loud it sounds like a helicopter."

"You really don't have to . . . Well, okay. Thanks." I handed him the kite ring, and he started reeling the bird down from the sky. Using his balled-up shirt, I dried off the best I could, wiping the sand from my cheeks and dress. I picked a few pieces of seagrass out of my hair.

"That was a nice save you had, going after this thing," he said.

"Do I get extra points for style?" I shook out the rash guard, pulled it over my dress, and felt instantly warmer.

"What a tool," Dominick said, spinning the ring, gathering the line. "You've made his acquaintance, I gather?"

"Unfortunately. How do y'all know Cooper?"

"I worked with him, back in Boston. Before we moved to Ohio. Cooper and Seth used to be good friends. Work buddies. Seth fired him. Just a couple weeks ago. Seth was my boss too, before I got transferred. A lot of the wedding guests are work friends. Our company has a very social environment."

"What did Cooper do to get fired?"

"Challenged a coworker to a headbutting contest. The other guy ended up in the ER with a grade three concussion, and the breakroom looked like a butcher shop. I wasn't there, but Seth called and told me all about it. Cooper had to be escorted out of the building by security. He was fighting mad. Screaming and yelling about how he deserved better treatment."

"And he still came to the wedding?"

"He didn't attend the actual ceremony, thank God. But he insisted he wasn't going to lose his deposit since he'd already made plans. So, he came here, to Cattail. He's making people uncomfortable. He lost a lot of allies, you know? I certainly don't want the guy near *my* wife and kid."

"Where's he staying?"

"Within spitting distance, unfortunately. His rental cottage is the next street over."

"Would you mind if I asked—what was Seth like as a boss?"

"I hate to say it, but he could be frustrating. You had to be able to deal with his constant ribbing. I was just barely able to put up with it myself. Although, when it came to firing Cooper, Seth was one hundred percent justified." The kite had finally descended. Dominick brought it gently to the sand. "You know," he said, scooping up the nylon, "I hope Cooper Payne's pipe dream does come true."

"The MMA, you mean?"

"It would be a miracle of miracles, seeing as he's never even won one match."

"Really?"

"Nope. Not a one. But if he did somehow make the pros, I bet he'd get that Napoleon complex beaten right out of him."

Dominick escorted me to the rental cottage that neighbored Naomi's. Outside the back shed, he showed me the garden hose. "Come on in when you're done."

Alone, I sprayed the sand and salt off my arms and legs. There

wasn't much I could do about my damp dress or hair, but as half
the people walking around Cattail Island on any given day were
in various stages of soggy and/or sandy, I didn't worry about it.

I wound the hose back up and placed it on the holder. Even
though Fusco had said it was the super-nice ones who crack—
and Cooper Payne was anything but super-nice—my gut was
telling me to take a serious look at him. After all, he was hitting the opportunity-means-motive trifecta. His name on the
sign-up sheet meant he'd had opportunity. The strength he'd
demonstrated at Salty Edward's meant he had the means. And
thanks to what I'd learned just now on Love Beach, I knew he
had motive.

All that was missing? A pesky little thing called evidence.

Evidence that Cooper had wrapped a cable around the neck
of Seth Goodnow, squeezed, and didn't let up until the deed was
done.

Inside the cottage, Ivy and Dominick were tag-teaming a
pancakes-from-scratch operation. Ivy measured the dry ingredients, while Dominick was in charge of eggs and milk.

"I got everybody calmed down," Ivy said. "Naomi's next door
taking a nap. And check out those two." She pointed her mea-
suring spoon at the front porch, where Cadence sat reading aloud
to Unicorn. Her fingertip feathered along the book's pages. The
dog's chin rested on her lap. It was the sweetest thing I'd seen
since a boy read aloud to Tin Man the other day, in the kids' section. "Stay for breakfast, Callie," Ivy said. "If you've never had
Amish-style pancakes, you're in for a treat."

"I wish I could, but I'd better get going soon. Before I do,
could I ask you something?" I lowered my voice. "What have you
been telling Cadence about . . ."

Ivy got my meaning and lowered her voice too. "What are we going to say? *Listen, sweetie, the guy who was vacationing in the cottage next door to ours—you know, the guy whose wedding we went to the other day, Daddy's old boss? He was strangled. Don't worry, though! Everything's chill.*" She sprinkled cinnamon into the mixing bowl. She had found the time, between the beach and now, to style her hair and touch up her makeup. Her lips shined with freshly applied gloss. "We sat Cadence down and told her something very tragic had happened. That Daddy's friend Seth had passed away. She didn't say much. Her grandfather died last year. Natural causes. Cade probably assumes it's the same sort of situation. And I'm fine letting her keep on assuming that, with all the problems she has."

"Problems?"

Dominick cut in, raising his voice over the whisking he was doing. "We've been on the fence whether to head back home, now that the police have told us it's okay. I mean, our choices are A, mourn the loss of our friend while hanging around our house in Ohio, or B, mourn the loss of our friend while enjoying the ocean, which we only get to see once a year, and while visiting friends we had to leave behind when we moved. Personally, while it might be nice to hang out here a few more days, I think we should head home now. Get back to our routine—"

"And I think we should stay," Ivy said. "Cadence has settled in to Cattail living. She sometimes . . . experiences *big feelings*, according to her therapist. I don't want to do anything to set them off."

Big feelings. I could relate. I'd only been a few years older than Cadence when I lost my mother. For years after, my emotions loomed over me like a hundred-foot wave. Sometimes they still did.

I gave back the rash guard before telling them to enjoy the beach as much as they could. "I'll return Naomi's kite," I said, making my way out. "Nice to see you again."

Cadence and I exchanged greetings as I passed her on the porch.

Next door, I left the kite with one of Naomi's relatives, an older gentleman who bowed slightly and cradled it in his arms. I bowed back and wished him a good morning.

And then I drove directly to Cattail Library.

41

Along the way, I swapped out my usual bluegrass in favor of local news. A press conference peppered through radio static. It sounded like Chief Jurecki was reading a prepared statement, with no hitch in his drawl. *Addison Battle was last seen yesterday afternoon in his barbershop off Queen Street. He is a ninety-year-old white male, approximately five feet seven inches in height. He wears a yellow bow tie. If anyone has any information regarding his whereabouts, please immediately contact Cattail police.*

Reporters fired off questions. *Is the barber's disappearance related to the dojo murder? Is Cattail becoming a hotbed for serious crime?*

Jurecki's answer was as calm as his statement. *Law enforcement is working around the clock to ensure the safety of every soul on this island. Rest assured any and every bad guy will be apprehended—and swiftly, at that. They have nowhere to hide . . .*

The library, off Queen Street, was in the vicinity of the police station and the town hall. It was a newer building decorated to suggest an old-fashioned crab shack, with nets draped over the wood siding and buoys and oars leaning hither and thither. The smell of books greeted me as soon as I got out of my car.

I was all but convinced that Cooper Payne was our guy—but

there was that other weird conflict mentioned by the O'Neills, and Naomi too. Ezra the librarian, who moonlighted as a notary public, was worth further scrutiny.

Inside, the library was chilled to a temperature cold enough to form ice chips in your beverage of choice. The frigidity was intensified by the fact that I was still damp from my impromptu dip. I hugged myself, rubbing the goose bumps off my arms, and headed for the welcome desk.

Behind it hunched a bespectacled man. The same one from Naomi's wedding photographs. He didn't make eye contact as I approached, or when I cleared my throat. Even after I'd ventured a quiet "Excuse me?" he continued to frown at the computer screen.

A name placard had been pushed against the lip of the counter, as if he didn't want anybody to be able to read it. I gave it a few taps until the name became legible. *Ezra Metcalfe.*

"Yeah?" he finally said.

"I was wondering if I could get a library card."

"You live in Cattail?"

"Sure do."

"Then you can get a library card," he said, like I was even stupider than the stupidest patron to ever walk through that door.

"I'm Callie Padget."

"Hold on." Huffing, he tabbed through a few screens, as if I were rushing him rather than simply introducing myself. If he recognized my name from the news stories, he didn't let on.

"You must be Ezra," I said, trying a kill-with-kindness approach. "Nice to meet you. I've recently moved back to Cattail after many years away. I grew up here."

"Address?"

So much for that tactic.

As Ezra Metcalfe angry-typed, I looked around. A senior

citizen squinted at the gardening titles, and another librarian pushed a squeaky-wheeled cart. Even with Ezra grumbling away, the act of requesting a library card had given me a proud sense of civic privilege. I picked up a pamphlet and pretended to flip through it. Really, though, I was checking out Ezra.

A testament to the power of the Cattail Public Library's air-conditioning system, he was bundled in a cable-knit sweater that somehow made me think of oatmeal. His thick blond hair wired out over his ears. His nose was button small, more appropriate for a baby's face than his. In fact, his nose didn't look capable of holding up the chunky black-framed glasses dominating his face.

On a shelf behind him pranced a menagerie of glass figurines. Horses, all of them. The shelf was more suitable to a nine-year-old girl's bedroom than a full-grown man's workstation.

With another grumble, he handed me a plastic card stamped with the image of Cattail Library. "Thank you," I said, tucking it into my makeshift wallet. "Would you happen to know where I could find a notary public?"

This was the first time Ezra Metcalfe made eye contact. He took in my rumpled appearance with the shrewd and glassy eyes of a raven. "What do you need?"

"Oh, nothing at the moment. Just for future reference." My teeth chattered. I clenched them and smiled. I was freezing, yes. I was also creeped out by this guy.

"I'm a notary public," he said, seeming none too happy about it.

"Oh yeah? You must do a lot of weddings this time of year, huh? 'Tis the season, and all of that." Gosh, I could really sound like a dork when I was nervous. Why was I nervous? It must have been the prickly energy he was giving off.

"Are you planning to get married on the beach or something?" he spat, as if the words themselves were bitter tasting.

"Me? Uh—someday, I guess. So, you ride horses, then?" I flashed another smile, but it wasn't enough to keep him from turning away. Giving the figurines a quick glance as he passed, he went into a room labeled EMPLOYEES ONLY and shut the door.

"Yeah," I said. "Me neither."

42

Okay, then. Chipping the ice that encrusted Ezra Metcalfe was going to be a lot more complicated than signing up for a library card. And it was ice that needed chipping. His weirdness on the subject of horses was . . . well, *weird*. He struck me as a generally dour dude. Maybe it wasn't only the nice types who crack. What about the dour ones? Especially after a visiting tourist tells him to shut the bleep up . . .

I put in a few hours at the MotherVine. Per Antoinette's request, I weeded out some of the spring decorations—removing the pinwheels from the lavender pots—to make room for summer gizmos. Little American flags. Napkins decorated with watermelon slices. That was when I noticed a parenting book that had no business being on the floor in the romance section. The book was called *Bullies: How They're Made, How to Defeat Them*. At that moment, I didn't reflect on that particular title seemingly waiting for me in such an unlikely spot. The uncanniness wouldn't occur to me until later.

What I did do was add the book to my armload of pinwheels and scurry upstairs. Tin Man came with, rubbing against my shins as I plopped into a camp chair. I pored over the pages.

As to how bullies are made, the book made a case for inherited trauma, the idea that upsetting experiences can leave a kind of chemical signature on a person's genes, which then gets passed down to future generations. The science was over my head, but the basic theory I grasped: If things like anxiety and depression had genetic underpinnings, then why not the insecurity that leads to bullying behavior? When you get down to it, bullies are all the same, passing along their pain via taunting and shaming tactics—the more publicly, the better, as far as they're concerned. They need someone else to carry their burdens. Which was all well and good, in my humble opinion, except for the fact that plenty of people inherited generational insecurity and *didn't* become bullies.

As to how to defeat them, the book supported tried-and-true schoolyard techniques. Laugh in the bully's face, or stand tall and be confident, or simply walk away. It made me think about Toby. Back in the day, it wasn't until he'd gotten up some guts, some poise, that Seth finally left him alone . . .

Typically, Antoinette called it quits around dinnertime. Tonight, however, was an oysters-and-cocktails night at Salty Edward's, and she was considering staying open for the extra foot traffic, which usually yielded sales.

"Why not, if you've got nothing else to do?" I reasoned. We were unpacking a shipment of books, sorting them into piles. My boss gave me a close-lipped smile. "Oh," I said. "I see. You *do* have something else to do."

"Your uncle and I wanted to get in a beach walk. With Tin Man and Scupper, of course."

I tried not to show too much dismay. I'd really wanted to spend time with Toby—but if I was ever going to get out of my uncle's loft, I needed to beef up my savings. "I know y'all love your beach walks," I said.

"Thank you. Why don't you take a break for now. Come back by six."

Heading outside, I checked my phone and saw a text message from a number I didn't recognize. It had arrived an hour ago, while I'd been working.

> Hola, amiga. Got your number from your uncle. Can you come to the Casa? Our mysterious friend has made a rare appearance.

I beelined it for the Casa Coquina, calling ahead on the way. "Turo? Am I too late?"

"On the contrary. You're right on time."

Strangely, the rockers on the B and B's front porch were empty. I found Turo in the kitchen, a tomato-seed-stained towel tucked into his apron. A pot on the stove emitted the aromas of sautéing peppers and garlic.

"What's going on?" I asked. "Besides your famous spring chili."

He chopped an onion so fast his hand was a blur. "There's an epic game of charades going on in the backyard. Dr. Heather Westerly was partaking, but she's since broken away."

"*Charades?*"

"They've been day drinking." He indicated two empty bottles of tequila on the counter next to a large blender dotted with pink slush. "They requested frozen raspberry margaritas. They're pretty *chumado*."

"Ah." Out back, several couples in their late twenties were gathered. They'd arranged the plastic patio chairs in a semicircle. A man stood before them, hopping on one leg. A woman shouted something, and a cheer went up. She shot from her seat and chest-bumped him.

"I have several couples staying this week," Turo explained. "They came in early from the beach because of the wind." The chopped onion sizzled as he added it to the pot. "Then the wind died down, enough so they could take their margaritas to the backyard, where Dr. Westerly happened to be quietly sitting, reading a book. She took an if-you-can't-beat-them-join-them attitude. That's her." He jutted his chin toward a woman with sunglasses holding back her hair. She sat cross-legged in the grass, some distance away from the others, in the shade of a holly tree. "You should have seen her act out the word *yodel*."

"Huh," I said, feeling a bit like a spy as I observed the elusive Dr. Heather Westerly through the window. Perhaps she was an introvert. The type to warm up slow. Or the type to overheat quickly. It was possible, too, that she was shell-shocked to find herself here, on Cattail Island. I'd never been to Kentucky, but I imagined its landlocked blue hills were a much different place than this whip-thin, wind-battered island off the North Carolina coast.

"Would you like to serve them some water?" Turo asked. "If I don't start the dilution process soon, they'll be too marinated to go to sleep."

"You're awesome," I said.

"Sí."

A minute later I had a two-hand hold on an enormous sweaty pitcher containing ice water, mint leaves, and lemon slices. Turo held open the back door. "Todos," he called. "I'd like you to meet Callie Padget, the daughter of a friend of mine and a true Cattailer." He exchanged a few words with the guests, winked in my direction, and bustled back inside.

The adults gathered around, holding out their wide-rimmed glasses as I poured. "Thanks, water girl!" cried one man with a radish-red nose, the classic indication of too much sun, wind, and alcohol. "Join us!"

I declined as politely as I could, then made my way over to where Heather Westerly sat in the grass, reading. She had a perfectly oval face that somehow make me think of an elf. I estimated she was a few years younger than me. "Water?" I offered.

"Oh, thank you." Heather held out her glass. "You're a local?"

"I'm a bookseller here in town."

"At the bookshop just down the street?"

"That's right. The MotherVine. Cattail's one and only."

"I haven't been yet, but I'm a big reader. Once I get settled . . ."

I crouched closer, balancing the pitcher on my knee. "What do you like to read? I always like to know that about people."

She held up the novel. The cover showed a warrior brandishing a sword at the edge of an evil forest. The image went right along with her high-fantasy-themed Instagram posts.

"I don't read much in the fantasy genre," I said. "I'd love to hear your recommendations, actually."

"Anytime."

"Right now, though, I'd like to ask you a few questions."

"About fantasy books?"

"About real life. Can you tell me anything about your experience Sunday morning at the martial arts dojo? If you're up for it, that is."

Heather frowned down at the book. It seemed as though I'd lost her before I even started. But then she looked me square in the face, her lips pursed determinedly. "Let's go out front," she said.

43

On the porch of the Casa Coquina, palm-leaf ceiling fans stirred the fresh scents of rosebushes. We walked to the far corner, where a small plaque proclaimed, THIS SECTION OF THE PORCH LOVINGLY SUPPORTED BY STANDISH FURNITURE. A few years ago, in order to raise money for mudslide victims back in his hometown, Turo held a naming contest. And rich old Pearleen Standish, unapologetic reader of *Three Hot Scots*, promptly elbowed all other potential sponsors out of the way. She never missed a chance to attach her name to philanthropic causes.

Heather and I selected two high-quality Standish rockers. "How did you know I worked out at the dojo that morning?" she asked as she got settled. "You another detective?"

"Just a concerned citizen. Did you know Seth Goodnow?"

"The dead guy? Oh—" She pressed her fingers to her lips. "You'll have to excuse me. Turo's margaritas really pack a punch."

"It's okay. Seth was murdered Sunday morning, and his body was found in the dojo. Can you describe the scene? What the mood was, who said what to whom, things like that."

"The mood was pretty basic, I guess. One thing stands out. There was kind of a beef-head guy who wanted the guy in charge to spar with him. He wasn't having it, though. He said he needed to supervise."

I leaned toward her. In my mind's eye, I saw Cooper offering Toby a face cage. I saw Toby begging off as kindly as he could. "What was Cooper's reaction?" I asked. "When Toby said no."

"He just went on doing his burpees and his step-ups and his shadowboxing, grunting and groaning the whole while. I was over in the corner, practicing my kata."

Kata, I knew from Toby, was a Japanese term for solo choreographed karate moves. A series or flow you go through, imagining an opponent, in order to build muscle memory. "Who else was there?" I asked.

"The guy that was killed? Seth? He didn't seem like he worked out much. Didn't know what to do. Paced around a lot and occasionally threw down a plank pose."

"Did he and Cooper interact at all?"

"Only to give each other nasty looks."

"And a fifth person was there. Right?"

"The police insisted on a fifth person too. But I swear, it was just the Toby guy, the guy who died, the gym-rat guy, and me."

"And a woman with the initials D.S."

"I told the police and I'll tell you: I don't know anything about a D.S."

"But D.S. signed in just minutes after you. According to the sheet, anyway."

"What do you want me to say?" Heather shrugged.

"But you were seen speaking with another woman. Do you know that lying to police can lead to formal charges?"

"There wasn't anyone else there. Honest. I left first, around seven forty-five. I have no idea what went on inside that building after that."

"Why did you leave before the full hour was up?"

"I had to shower and meet my Realtor. I'm house hunting. I

can't very well live in the Casa Coquina the rest of my life. Too
bad. Turo's cooking is incredible." She fished an ice cube out of
her glass, rubbed it across her forehead, and popped it into her
mouth.

She was lying. She *had* to be. But what about? My pressuring
her hadn't gotten anywhere; might as well go for more of a good-
cop approach. "I was in the market for a new place to live myself," I said, sliding back into the rocker. "But not for very long.
I gave up as soon as I realized how brutal it is out there. Are you
looking to buy or rent?"

"Either. Can you believe the housing situation here on Cattail? At this rate, I'd roll out a sleeping bag on someone's living
room floor."

"You're that desperate, huh."

Glaring, she crunched her ice. "Are we through here?"

Heather excused herself so she could freshen up before Turo
summoned his guests for supper. Only a few moments later, as I
was walking down Queen Street, movement caught my peripheral vision. In the alleyway next to the B and B, the hood of a
parked car had popped open. It was a Tesla, pulled up next to
Turo's new charging station. The sunlight gave the cream paint
job an opalesque sparkle. Under the hood wasn't an engine but
a front trunk. A frunk. While it was big enough to hold several suitcases, the only thing inside this frunk was a standard-
size manila envelope. Heather Westerly approached the Tesla,
carefully picked up the envelope, and pulled out a stiff sheet of
paper. A document? A photograph? She feathered her fingertips
over it, top to bottom. Her expression was that of an adoring
mother to a newborn baby.

I ducked behind a rosebush, using it as camouflage as I tried
to make out what was on the paper. But I couldn't see anything,

so I decided to try a different tack. "Hi again," I said, sidling up to the gate. "What ya got there?"

With cartoonish quickness—I imagined a whooshing noise—Heather hid the paper behind her back. "None of your business," she said.

44

Antoinette dangled Tin Man's red harness. "Walky? Walky-doo with Scuppy-poo?"

Tin Man was nestled in his poof on the stairs of the Mother-Vine. He opened one amber eye, shut it, and curled his tail over his nose.

"Guess he needs a rest day," I said.

In her office, Antoinette swapped out the cat harness for her baseball cap with the MotherVine logo. She crammed the hat over her curls to cute effect. "Be back in an hour, to help you close up," she said.

After she'd gone, I texted Toby.

Can you hang? I'm at the MotherVine for a while, working.
Would love to see you though.

He thumbs-upped my message immediately, so a few minutes later, when the door opened, I expected to see him.

But the two people who came into the bookshop weren't Toby.

Ivy O'Neill patted her daughter Cadence's hair, which had been divvied into two lumpy pigtails. "*Someone* has been begging to come here all day," Ivy said.

"I'm so glad you stopped in," I said.

"Cade saw this place when we drove by earlier, on the way to the doughnut shop. I told her that nice lady we met on the beach this morning was the owner, and she squealed. Didn't you, Cade?"

"Oh, I'm not the owner," I said with a smile. "I just work here."

"Cade, tell Miss Callie where you want to work when you grow up."

Cadence's ears took on a tomato-red hue. She studied her Crocs, which were plastered with book charms.

"She wants to work in a bookshop," Ivy said.

"Fantastic." I crouched down so that I was eye level with the girl. She lifted her chin but didn't quite meet my gaze. Her shyness was palpable. Her goodness too. "What do you like to read, little miss Cade?" I asked.

No answer came, even after Ivy poked her daughter's arm.

A flash of silver poured down the stairs. Tin Man trotted over as if he sensed the need to spring into furry action. He was an eleven-pound superhero crisis counselor. Meowing, he began swiping his chin against the girl's shins. I gritted my teeth—not everybody likes cats, and from what I sensed about Cade, she was the kind of child who might react poorly to surprises.

To my relief, though, she erupted in giggles. Giving Tin Man a few gentle pats, she glanced up at me and said, in a sweet voice just a notch above a whisper, "*The Mysterious Benedict Society.*"

"Right this way," I said. A few days ago, after Ivy had mentioned that book, I made sure Antoinette had the series in stock.

Cade and Tin Man followed me to the children's area. Ivy hung back, flipping through a magazine. I sensed she still had one eye on her daughter and was praying for a positive social encounter.

"So," I asked Cade, "which book do you need?"

"The second one." She buried her face in Tin Man's fur. "We can't have a cat because we have a greyhound and greyhounds chase cats."

"Maybe someday you'll have a cat. You never know. And as long as you're here in Cattail, you can come visit Tin Man anytime."

"Tin Man, like from *The Wizard of Oz?*"

"Just like that. Technically he's called Tinnakeet Man. The grapes growing out back are Tinnakeet grapes, and Tin Man loves them. But grapes are bad for cats, so he's not allowed to eat them. He sneaks one every now and then, though."

"I'm not allowed to eat candy," she whispered. "But I sneak it sometimes."

"I won't tell," I whispered, handing her book two. "What's your favorite thing you've done here on vacation?"

"Crabs."

"You mean looking for them at night? With flashlights?"

"They're totally iconic."

Chasing ghost crabs was a favorite activity of Cadence-aged vacationers. If you shine a light on a crab, it becomes stunned, and you can get a good look at it. I always considered it kind of cruel, but no harm came to the crabs and they resumed their regularly scheduled crustacean activities just as soon as the humans were done harassing them.

A copy of *The Legend of Rosie Beacon* faced outward on a low shelf. Cadence snatched it up. "I want this one too."

"Excellent taste," I said.

Back at the checkout counter, I mentioned Tin Man had an Instagram account. This news delighted both mother and daughter, and within a few seconds, Ivy was a follower. Together they tabbed through Tin Man's most recent posts. Photos I'd taken of books around town, and of Tin Man himself, trying to scratch his chin on a spike of lavender, or striking a sphinx pose in the bay window. "Isn't he just a sweetie pie?" Ivy cooed over Cade's giggles. They were thrilled to pose with him. Cade picked him up and squeezed him and Ivy bent her head to be in the frame. I posted it with the caption, *Greetings, darlings. The MotherVine is the cat's pajamas. Won't you paws in? Free cuddles, free grapes, and the most paw-some selection of new and used books on the Banks.*

"We agreed on just one book, Cade," Ivy said when she noticed her daughter gathering up a few hopefuls. In addition to the mystery and *The Legend of Rosie Beacon*, Cadence had selected *My Awesome Field Guide to Rocks and Minerals*.

She made a whiny noise. "I really, really want all three of them."

"We can't buy every book in sight," Ivy said. I couldn't help but chuckle. My mother had told me the same thing in these very stacks many times.

"Can I get two? Please?"

"*Two*. Not three. Two."

"I want to read this *so bad*," she said, eyeing the Rosie Beacon book. "But I love rocks."

"Do you collect them?" I asked.

"So far, I have thirty-one rocks and minerals. Not with me. They're all at home. Schist, granite, pumice, milky quartz, and gypsum are my favorites. I have a rock tumbler too." She explained the process of placing rocks into a barrel with some special stuff called grit. You switch on the motor and go to bed, and when you wake up the next morning, you have smooth, polished stones.

"Wow," I said. "That sounds super cool."

Cadence skipped off to put the Rosie book back where she'd found it and ended up settling into one of the beanbag chairs.

She was turning the pages of yet another book. Ivy tipped her chin in her daughter's direction. "I told you before that Cade sometimes has a hard time socially. Her therapist wants Dominick and me to encourage her to have new experiences, but it's hard, and—I guess what I'm trying to say is—thank you."

"Oh, I didn't do anything," I said. "Thank the MotherVine. It brings out the best in people. How's Naomi been?"

"A combination of really strong and a complete wreck."

"I can't even imagine," I said. Even though I had been imagining what it must have been like, waking up every morning and having to readjust to the fact that your husband of mere days had been murdered.

"I picked this out for her just now." Ivy showed me a book. I recognized the cover's pointillist ocean-at-night scene. It was the grief book I'd almost selected for Naomi myself. "What do you think?" she asked. "Should I give it to her?"

"Absolutely." I got out some gift-wrapping supplies. "It's very thoughtful of you. Have you had any more drama from Cooper?"

"He's an oaf. But he's harmless. In a way, I feel kinda bad for him. He's been trying to shake the Neanderthal stigma for years."

"Is that so?" I hadn't observed much effort in that vein. But maybe Ivy knew something I didn't.

45

Toby arrived bearing hummus and cheddar wraps he'd made himself, packed with sliced green tomatoes from his garden, still warm from the sun. Paper napkins tucked into our collars, we sat behind the checkout counter, chatting whenever I wasn't ringing up sales. It felt natural and safe. The kind of everyday moment a couple that's been together for decades might share. As if the pall hanging over Cattail had been swept away. For the moment, anyway.

"Favorite color?" Toby asked. "Wait—we've covered this already."

I laughed. "We've covered everything already. We know everything there is to know about each other."

"Your favorite color is blue."

"And yours is black," I said. "Sunrise or sunset?"

"They're both amazing. But if I had a gun to my head?"

"Sunrise?"

"Right on."

"Me too."

"The promise of a fresh new day? Can't beat that."

Laughter drifted in from the back patio. A large party had gathered there, several vacationing families with teenage children. We heard the scraping of iron on pavers—they were returning the chairs and tables to their original spots. Antoinette often commented that the MotherVine had the best customers in the world, and I had to agree.

After they had gone, wishing us a great night as they slipped through the door, a fifty-something woman came over, tumbling an armload of cozy mysteries onto the counter. I recognized the authors' names: Lorna Barrett, Ellery Adams, Amanda Flower . . . "I promised myself I'd stop at one," the woman said.

"I promise you that's a promise you won't regret breaking," I said as I stacked the books inside a large paper bag stamped with the MotherVine logo.

When Toby and I were alone, I plucked an onion slice from the wrap and munched on it. I didn't want to bring up the murder, but I had a positive spin to share. "Guess what I found out today. From Seth Goodnow's widow."

He dabbed his mouth with the napkin. "You talked to her?"

"I did. And she confided in me that Seth kept that old receipt as a reminder of the kind of person he no longer wanted to be."

"Huh."

"It's true. He came here, to Cattail, for his honeymoon, and was surprised to learn that you lived here, that you worked here. And he went to Cattail Family Martial Arts with the intention of apologizing to you."

"Really?"

"For some reason, he must have clammed up. And then . . ."

Toby didn't say anything more on the subject, but something like acceptance flitted across his face. He'd long ago made inner peace with Seth Goodnow. But maybe the knowledge of Seth's regret somehow made Toby's retroactive forgiveness a little easier. As he offered Tin Man a nibble of cheese, the corner of his mouth curled into a sort of grateful half smile.

"What?" I asked.

He leaned in and kissed my cheek. The gesture caught me off guard, and I found myself sitting perfectly still.

As he leaned in again, a tingle zipped up my spine. This was it.

This was going to be our first real kiss. Right here in the Mother-Vine, mutual onion breath and all, Tin Man purring at our elbows.

Just as our lips were about to come together, a loud vibration buzzed. My cell phone rattled against the counter.

Antoinette.

"I should get this," I said.

"Of course."

Answering, I barely got out a hello when I heard my boss's voice. "Have you closed up?"

"What's wrong, Ant?"

"Do you have any shoppers in there with you?"

"It's wound down. Just me, Tinny, and Toby at the moment."

"Good. Your uncle and I are on the way. In the meantime, shut the door. Lock yourselves inside."

46

H ere," Toby said, guiding Antoinette to a papasan chair. "Sit."
Looking pale, Hudson collapsed into the other papasan.
Toby and I exchanged a glance, silently agreeing not to press
them for details. They'd talk when they were ready. Toby filled
a bowl with water and set it down for Scupper, then filled two
mugs with cold water, which he handed to Hudson and Antoinette. I got a small clip fan from the office, attached it to the
magazine rack, and set it to oscillate.

"We found Addison Battle's bow tie," my uncle finally said.

"On Mustang Beach," Antoinette said, as Tin Man jumped
onto her lap and began kneading. "Hud and I had decided to
walk on the footpath. We thought some shade would be nice,
and we could peep for the newborn foal while we were at it. We
got to the turnaround point. You know, the observation platform? The ocean was just beautiful—"

"And then Scupper started barking," Hudson said. "And we
noticed something bright yellow at our feet. Looked like it had
blown up from the sand. We knew what it was—whose it was—
right away. We called the police." He gulped water, then back-
handed the droplets from his beard. "Jurecki was there within
fifteen minutes. He questioned us. *Did we see anyone? Did we see
anything suspicious?* But we hadn't."

"Was Geri-Lynn there?" I asked. "The director of the Mustang Beach Sanctuary."

"That must have been the woman in the big straw hat with the long blond hair," Antoinette said, nodding. "She showed up on the beach after the police arrived."

A while later, as the four of us filed out of the MotherVine, Queen Street was covered by a canopy of winking stars. Intending to take our minds off Cattail's dark happenings, we all ended up at my uncle's house. Ronnie arrived with a cooler of striped bass he'd caught from Smile Beach just that afternoon. Turo came too, bearing fresh *aji* and homemade plantain chips. His niece Luzbita accompanied him. A game of nickel-ante poker got underway. Luzbita was shy with her English, but the language of poker is universal, and she was fluent. After a fast two hours, she'd come out the far-and-away winner, with three dollars and twenty cents more than the rest of us.

Later, after our guests had gone home, I kissed Uncle Hudson good night and climbed the ladder to my loft. As the air-conditioning unit rattled away, I flopped onto my bed. And I wondered about Naomi Goodnow. What was she doing at that very moment? Folding clothes and stacking them inside a suitcase? And what about all the belongings Seth had brought with him on their honeymoon? She would have to pack them up too.

And then there was Geri-Lynn. Tall, strong Geri-Lynn.

I pictured her hat casting shade over Addison Battle's bow tie as police trampled all over her beloved Mustang Beach.

The day before, flying her drone, she'd declared she'd do anything to protect the horses.

I reached for my phone and dialed. She didn't answer, and I didn't leave a message. I wasn't sure what tone to strike. I wanted her to be a friend, but at the same time, doubt nagged. Could I trust her? Should I trust her?

In the end, I decided on a text.

Heard about what was found on Mustang Beach. You okay?
I'm still awake if you want to talk.

I waited a few minutes. She didn't text back.

My yawns became fierce. Exhaustion was like wet cement being poured all over me. I was going to sleep like the dead. *No—* that particular cliché was not one I wanted to evoke. I was going to sleep like I'd run back-to-back ultramarathons in the mountains.

I fluffed my pillow and snuggled into it. Sleep didn't come. But knocking did. A particular knocking I'd know anywhere. Hudson's tough knuckles, rapping a ladder rung.

I got up and drew aside the shower curtain. He was looking up at me with that signature twinkle in his ocean-green eyes, enhanced by the evening's beers. "You ever been to that yarn shop in town?"

I belted my bathrobe and descended, thinking about how I'd visited the Yarn Barn just the other day, when I was asking around about Seth Goodnow's death. Hudson was waiting at his work-table, before his secret project. "Please don't tell me you roused me out of bed at midnight to talk arts and crafts," I said.

"How much scratch do you think some yarn would set me back? I don't need a lot."

"Does this have something to do with your wooden lump of mystery?" I gestured as a massive yawn split my face in two. "You're dying to show me what that thing is. So just show me."

"Guess."

I glared at him.

"Fine, fine. It's not quite finished, understand. For one thing,

I haven't stained it yet. I'm waiting for—well, you'll see." In a magician-like gesture, he whipped away the tarp.

A two-foot-tall model of a horse. An exquisite miniature Cattail Island mustang, sanded smooth, yet rugged and windswept looking. The hooves ended in rockers, and dowl handles stuck from its jaws.

"Oh, Hudson," I said, caressing the strong neck. I'm pretty sure under all those whiskers, my uncle was blushing.

"The MotherVine's hobbyhorse is a lawsuit waiting to happen," he said. "Thought I'd make Ant a replacement."

"It's gorgeous. She'll flip."

"I was on the fence about the yarn. That was why I didn't bring you in sooner. I was thinking about carving the mane and tail. But my whittling skills aren't up to snuff, and I figured yarn would be more practical. Tykes need something to grab on to, right?"

"Definitely. Why stain it? It's beautiful just the way it is."

"Because of the foal."

"You want to match the color?"

"I'm rooting for white. I think a nice washed-out stain would give it a rustic island vibe, you know?" He gave the horse a tap, sending it rocking, smooth and silent. No more squealing, herky-jerky, bloody horseback rides for the MotherVine's youngest patrons.

I knew what he was thinking. That Cattail Island needed that foal now more than ever.

"I hate to burst your bubble," I said, "but the new foal won't be white. It'll probably be bay, which means solid brown with a black mane and tail. It's the most common color pattern for wild horses."

"Listen to you." He chuckled. Without coming right out and saying it, he was asking me to go into the yarn shop for him. He considered himself too manly and unkempt to set foot inside the place. As if they'd turn down any paying customer for not looking the part. "I'm sure the Yarn Barn would be happy to help you pick out just the right yarn," I said.

"That place is too rich for my blood, cub. Too hoity-toity."

"Right," I said with a grin. I helped my uncle drag the tarp back over the rocking horse. "Is there a time constraint?"

"Our one-year dating anniversary is Sunday. It's a small thing, I know. But with all the big things going on . . ."

"Small things are big things. I'll get you some yarn."

47

I woke up to a text response from Geri-Lynn.

> Yesterday was disconcerting. But something good
> happened too. Come see.

A second message, from Antoinette, declared the need for a recharge. She'd closed the shop for the day.

At her request, I stopped by the MotherVine, where I taped an upbeat apology to the red door. I also fed Tin Man, explaining that he'd be flying solo until I checked on him at dinnertime. I let him sweep his velvet cheek against mine three times before locking the door behind me.

When I faced Queen Street, Cooper Payne was waiting, a squat camphor-smelling mound of muscles, backpack over one shoulder, jug of water hooked on his finger. Judging by his pinched expression, he was in the same belligerent mood he'd been in the day before, on Love Beach.

I sighed. My day off was not starting out easy.

"Can we go inside?" he asked.

"No."

"Whatever." He sat on the nearest public bench. "I'm here to say: I'm sorry I came at you in Salty Edward's the other night. That was wrong of me."

"I accept your apology," I said, but my spidey senses tingled. He was angling. "Can I help you?"

"I did some research on you. You're not a reporter anymore. But you used to be."

"Your point?" I lowered one butt cheek onto the opposite side of the bench, as far away from him as possible. We were on Queen Street in broad daylight. I didn't want to be around this guy, but at least I was relatively safe.

"Like I told you, I've been working with a life coach." Cooper took a long drink from his jug. "He's got me doing meditation and Cordyceps mushroom supplements."

"I'm so happy for you. What does that have to do with my previous job?"

"I'm trying to embrace a *balanced lifestyle approach*. That's what my life coach calls it. But that's wicked hard to do when you're a murder suspect."

"You're not a suspect, though. Are you?" I hadn't seen anything in the news, or heard anything on the streets, to that effect.

"Not officially," he said. "But I feel like one. Everywhere I go, that redheaded—*cop*—"

"Fusco. She's a detective."

"Whatever. She's up my— She won't leave me alone. I've done nothing wrong. I'm just a guy on vacation. You get that, right? You can see that. I know you can."

"And assuming I *could* see that?"

"Help clear my name. Write something up about me. Post it on the internet somewhere. Together, we can figure out how to make it go viral. I'll pay you."

"That's not going to work for me, Cooper. But there might be another way you can help yourself." When his eyes brightened, I continued. "Tell me exactly who you saw in Cattail Family Martial Arts that morning."

He leaned in, about to reply—but cut himself off. "I don't think so."

"Why not? You want my help, don't you?"

"On second thought, you lied to me once already. It was stupid of me to come here." He unzipped his backpack, pulled out a protein bar, and took a huge bite.

"That's what you're always carrying around in your backpack? Protein bars?"

"Shakes too. Extra protein promotes muscle gain and improves performance. Want a bite?"

"I'll pass."

Just then a police cruiser slowed to a stop in front of us. Chief Jurecki's head and shoulders appeared over the roof rack of lights. "Everything okay here?"

My bench companion hopped to his feet. "Why wouldn't it be? I'm just a guy sitting on a bench, eating a protein bar. If you don't want people sitting on benches, don't have benches all up and down the street."

Jurecki's face turned redder than the brick buildings all around us. "Come again, son?"

"We're good, Chief," I said. "We appreciate your asking. He didn't mean any of that." I reached over and tugged Cooper's thick wrist, pulling him back down to the bench. "Remember your meditation practice," I whispered. "Your balanced lifestyle approach. You might want to draw on those things right now."

Cooper raised a hand. "What I meant was—namaste, sir."

Jurecki's eyebrows knitted together. "Callie?"

"All is well," I reassured him.

48

Geri-Lynn was on the porch when I pulled up to Sanctuary Bungalow. To my surprise, she greeted me with a quick pump of a hug. We made our way inside the bungalow, where visitors browsed. A family with two small children and a third in a stroller lingered before the main mural. The parents were whispering about the missing barber and his not-missing bow tie. About the honeymooner who was strangled inside the karate dojo.

A petite woman with flyaway auburn hair approached Geri-Lynn. "What can you tell us about the foal?" she asked.

"Oh, we're very excited around here. Mama's doing just fine, and normal birth is expected any day now." Raising her voice, Geri-Lynn addressed the group. "I'll just be in my office if any of y'all need anything."

I followed her into a low-ceilinged room lined with rusting filing cabinets. Diplomas hung crooked on the wall. She had two doctorate degrees, one in education, one in biology. But I noted that on her official correspondence, she went by plain old Geri-Lynn Humfeld, no fancy letters after her name.

"What's going on?" I asked as she shut the door.

Straddling a wheeled stool, she hit a key on a laptop. "This is my old computer. Fusco took my new one."

"Fusco was here again?"

"Called her as soon as I realized what I had. She's all over this thing like a hound on a bone. Look at this."

Before us, the screen blinked on. Photographic details came into focus. A dune fence obscured the sand-level view, but I could clearly make out a man running on a beach. He had a rattail-style ponytail, a necklace of cowrie shells, and a blistering sunburn. Foremost, however, was the white number eleven on the back of his red T-shirt.

"Was this from the other day?" I asked. "When you were testing the drone? And that boat came up, and . . ." I shuddered. Was I looking at the man who'd done something to Tigress— and possibly Addison too? Was this the man who'd murdered Seth Goodnow?

"I was filming the whole time," Geri-Lynn said, "and I didn't even know it. How do you like that? It gets better." She hit a couple more keys, zeroing in on the guy's back, where block letters arched. ZIMMERMAN. "That mean anything to you?"

"Like—what would it mean?"

"I see you and I share a cluelessness when it comes to professional sports. Thank God for the interwebs. Ryan Zimmerman plays for the Washington Nationals."

"Major League Baseball?"

"He's an infielder. Virginia boy. Hometown favorite. Number eleven."

"You do know that's not the real-life, actual Ryan Zimmerman," I said, leaning against the nearest filing cabinet. We both laughed, and a strange kind of relief whizzed through me. "But seriously," I said, "there's got to be millions of red Washington Nationals T-shirts out there, with that name printed on the back."

"Sure. It's reasonable to hypothesize that a few hundred of those shirts made their way to the Outer Banks this spring. Even fewer traveled, on the backs of their owners, all the way to our fair Cattail Island." She zoomed in even closer, this time enlarging the boat. Whitecaps blocked some of the stern, but the words

Cattail Island NC were easy to make out. "That right there," Geri-Lynn said, pointing, "is a Cattail boat. All we need to do is find a guy with a rat tail, a nasty sunburn, a shell choker, and a Zimmerman T-shirt—and we've found ourselves a couple of horse thieves."

"And, potentially, a couple of murderers," I said, high-fiving her offered palm.

49

My hand stung from the high five, reminding me that I didn't quite share Geri-Lynn's confidence. To be sure, this footage seemed like a big break. But it wasn't proof. Of anything.

"Did you tell Fusco about Tigress?" I asked.

"No need to bring that kind of scrutiny down on Mustang Beach Sanctuary," Geri-Lynn said—by which she meant, *on her.* "We're so close to bringing Tigress home, I can feel it."

"I feel it too," I said. And I could feel something, though not the premature sense of triumph Geri-Lynn was exuding. What I felt was the inkling that whatever happened to Tigress wasn't as straightforward as two thieves stealing her. "Your forty-eight hours are up, you know," I said. "You agreed to go public if Tigress hadn't surfaced by now."

"And you agreed to try and help me."

That was all she needed to say; guilt rippled through me like a flag. I'd told her I'd help, yet what had I delivered, besides a book?

She got up to check on the main room, where a new bunch of visitors milled. She fielded some questions, then snapped a photo of a family arranged in front of the shipwreck mural, which struck me as a pretty dismal backdrop, but what did I know?

"I shouldn't have said that," she said when she returned. "I know you've been killing yourself, trying to figure out all kinds of things. For my part, I just need a tiny little bit more time."

I supposed that was fair. "I've got another question for you," I said. "What would happen here, in the case of a wildfire?" The past couple of days, as Cattail grew drier and drier, that scenario had started bothering me.

"A wildfire? On sanctuary land?" She furrowed her brow. Her head was probably filled with visions of mustangs bucking and whinnying as flames and smoke closed in. "I'd open the gates and call to the horses. Hopefully they'd hear me, and trust me, and come running. If there was time, and enough volunteers showed up, we'd try to corral them. Load as many as we could into trailers. Transport them to safety. To horse owners in the area who have extra space and don't mind fostering a mustang or two."

"They couldn't be wild after that."

"No, I don't reckon they could. Has there ever a been a wildfire on Cattail?"

"Not to my knowledge."

She was thoughtful, passing a hand through her hay-colored hair. "Come to think of it, a horse just isn't going to move toward a gate that's normally shut."

"Wouldn't they be smart enough to run to the ocean and wait it out in the surf?"

"Sure. If they didn't panic."

Not for the first time that week, I performed a kind of mental rain dance and said a silent prayer for the wet stuff.

There was a light tap on the door. A familiar, elfish face appeared. Heather Westerly, the new herd veterinarian. She wore a scrub top with a pair of khaki shorts and tennis shoes. "Dr. Humfeld," she said. "You're a hard woman to get ahold of."

An awkward conversation ensued between the two biologists. Geri-Lynn stammered excuses for not returning Heather's repeated attempts at communication. "The days just get away from me, out here on Mustang Beach," she said. "But I agree it's high time we met in person."

"If you have a minute," Heather said, "I wouldn't turn down a chance to get my bearings. You showed me what you could, during our interviews. But that's just not the same as seeing a place in person." Ever so slightly, her eyelid twitched. She must have been thinking she'd made the biggest mistake of her life, moving to a hard-to-access island where vacationers got killed. Not only that, but her future place of work, Mustang Beach, had taken center stage in a missing persons investigation. And her future boss, Geri-Lynn, had been blowing her off.

Geri-Lynn was twitchy too. How much longer could she keep her secret under wraps, especially now, with a fresh hire anxious to roll up her sleeves?

They agreed Heather should have a brief tour. "Inside first," Geri-Lynn said. "Then we'll take it outside. I don't have time to show you the entire property right now."

I excused myself. Heather noticed me for the first time since entering the office and seemed surprised to find me here. Aside from a brief greeting, though, she didn't speak to me.

Outside, her Tesla shined in the sunlight like a gigantic pearl. She'd parked alongside my Civic, which next to her sleek symbol of modernity took on all the sheen of a dull turd. I was just about to get behind my wheel when I remembered the Tesla's frunk, and the mysterious manila envelope stored inside.

I wasn't above going through people's vehicles, provided they were unlocked. One quick peek was all it might take to discover what she'd been so enamored with. That seemingly seductive rectangle of paper.

Inside, Geri-Lynn was showing off Sanctuary Bungalow's main attractions. They lingered before the murals, which Heather admired, nodding as she took in the scenes. As they neared the front door, I saw Geri-Lynn reach for her straw hat. I whipped out my phone, pressed it to my ear, and pretended to be strolling, finishing up a call. The two women descended the porch steps and made their way over the dune, disappearing down the other side.

One more glance through Sanctuary Bungalow's windows assured me that no one was paying much attention to parking lot goings-on.

Again, I went over to the Tesla—and stopped short. The frunk was seamless. There was no latch. No handle. Not even a dimple.

Of course. One doesn't simply manually open a Tesla. All operations are synched to the car's computer, which is synched to the owner's smartphone.

Feeling like a foiled country bumpkin, I returned to my almost-as-old-as-me vehicle and opened the driver's door.

With my hand.

"Don't worry," I said, stroking the worn steering wheel. "I only have eyes for you."

50

I don't know what compelled me to drive past Addison's home. Morbid curiosity? The possibility, however small, of learning something new?

Evidently, Addison's daughter had summoned some off-island family and friends. Cars were parked in the driveway. Someone had pulled a tarp over his Ford, and the grass had been cut.

I learned nothing.

I did, however, notice something odd going on at the house across the street. A man with wiry blond hair was standing before the prizewinning azalea bushes I'd made note of the other day. In his hands: hedge clippers. The blades were open, a menacing V.

Ezra Metcalfe. He had swapped his oatmeal sweater for—could it be? A T-shirt bearing the Mustang Beach Sanctuary logo? Yes, that was indeed what he was wearing. A vehicle—presumably his—was parked with one tire on the grass, as if he'd pulled up in a fury. The name on the mailbox wasn't Metcalfe. I could only assume this wasn't his home, and these weren't his prizewinning azaleas.

Trouble, Padget. This will lead to nothing but trouble. There was scant wisdom in engaging a peeved notary public wielding hedge clippers big enough to decapitate a person. But if I didn't, gorgeous blossoms would be massacred.

I pulled over and got out of my car. "Hey there," I said, approaching cautiously. "Remember me?"

Ezra didn't take his raven eyes off the bushes.

"Yesterday," I said. "You hooked me up with a sweet new library card."

He jabbed his glasses farther up the bridge of his baby nose. "She's not home," he said, his voice whispery with suppressed rage. "I need to *wreck* something. Something that's *hers*."

"Let me guess. We're talking about your ex? This is her house? These are her blue-ribbon azaleas?"

"I was going to ask her to marry me."

I stepped closer as a new narrative for Ezra Metcalfe played out. What if he wasn't a general poopy-pants person, but simply going through a hard time, as Naomi had sensed? I could understand not wanting to marry couple after happy couple if my own pending nuptials had gone splitsville.

"I feel for you," I said. "But you appear to be mere seconds from engaging in criminal activity. Willful destruction of property. Vandalism." I didn't know if those terms would apply specifically to annihilating plants. They were just phrases that had stuck with me from the police reporting I'd done. "Detective Fusco can be a bit of a ballbuster, Ezra," I added. "And she's been in a bad mood this week. I don't think she'd look too kindly on an innocent garden getting trashed."

"Ariel cheated on me. I caught her. In the bookmobile, for crying out loud."

"In the bookmobile? Ugh. Those are for reading. Period."

"Right?" He turned toward me, hedge clippers opened like jaws.

I took a step back. "Be that as it may, you have a public job. You're a civil servant. You don't want to do this."

"Oh, but I do." Ezra's arms were shaking, all the way up to his shoulders.

"Okay. You really, really want to do this. But I don't think you're going to. Because Ezra Metcalfe is a decent person." I had no idea what kind of person he was. I just didn't want to be standing nearby while he had a horticultural spaz attack.

"I'm not a decent person," he said.

"Well, aren't you at least more decent than your ex-girlfriend? My suspicion is that you are an upstanding citizen—with a strong sense of self-preservation. Think about it. You don't want to become known as the town employee who took out the number one most beautiful blossoms in all of Cattail—*during a drought.* On a small island like this, you would *never* live that down. Everywhere you went, people would think poorly of you. Oh, they'd be nice to your face. But underneath their pleasantries, you'd *feel* the disgust." The scenario was a tad overblown, but the man needed to be calmed down, so I laid it on thick. "You *could* come back at night and operate under cover of darkness. But if somebody drove by and caught you in the act, or if Ariel woke up, you'd have a target on your back for the rest of your life."

He winced. "I would?"

"The Cattail Gardening Club, for one, would never forgive you. Neither would the historical society; they keep tabs on town prizewinners. This entire neighborhood would think none too highly of you. And you'd be risking legal trouble, which isn't a good look for anyone, especially for a local librarian and notary public. Of course, it's up to you. Whether you think it's worth it."

Sighing, he tossed the hedge clippers to the grass. "Check this out," he said, extracting his phone.

51

Ariel was a stunner. Glowing skin, toothpaste-commercial smile. "She was way out of my league," Ezra said as he swiped through photographs on his phone. He wasn't exactly a leading man ripped from the pages of a romance novel, and he was well aware.

After ten minutes, I knew more about Ezra's recent personal drama than I ever would have predicted. There were a few base, sympathy-arousing details, but suffice it to say, the day Naomi and Seth got married was the day after Ezra caught his fiancée hopeful, the new children's services librarian, in flagrante delicto inside the bookmobile. With a library patron. During business hours.

"She was just about to hit the Friday Beach section of town," Ezra said, sitting on the curb, his Vans-sneakered feet on the sewer grate. "I went outside to tell her, 'Have a nice drive, honey, be safe, I love you,' blah blah. And there they were. In all their glory."

"Ouch," I said, sitting next to him. I did feel for the guy. Not only was his love life in shambles, but his work and civic life had become unlivable too.

"They broke up. She and the dude. I guess that's good. Although wouldn't it be better if they were in it for the long haul? At least then she wouldn't have cheated on me for a one-off fling." He tabbed through more photographs, including one of Ariel in the library, opening a small gift. The next shot was a selfie—Ezra smooshing his face against Ariel's as she held up a glass figurine.

A tiny red horse.

"That menagerie behind the library welcome desk," I said.

"The horses. Those were all gifts for Ariel?"

"Every one. She loves horses. She was so excited when she found out I'm a volunteer for the Mustang Beach Sanctuary. She wanted to get involved. Now I hope she doesn't."

"You volunteer for the sanctuary? So you know Geri-Lynn?"

"I'm one of the first people she calls when there's a crisis." He kept scrolling, landing on a photo of a mustang in the woods. "Like the other day, for example, when this happened. Poor Rivka."

Filling up the screen was a shot of a speckled mare caught on a tangle of wires, as if she'd tried to leap over it but didn't clear it. Her mournful eyes were like dark wet seeds. My heart ached. This was the incident Geri-Lynn had told me about. The old dune fencing, snagged in the undergrowth. "Lucky Geri-Lynn found her," I said.

"Yeah. We cut her free and gathered up all the junk so it's no longer a hazard."

"That must be really satisfying work." Before I passed back his phone, I made quick note of the date and time the horse rescue photo had been taken. Sunday morning, 9:05 a.m.

Right around the time Ezra Metcalfe was rescuing Rivka the mustang, Seth Goodnow was being strangled.

By someone else.

Which gave me a zip of excitement—until I reminded myself that Ezra wasn't necessarily off the hook for the various other conundrums distressing this island. "Do you own a boat, by any chance?" I asked.

"A boat?" He laughed. "I don't even own a bicycle. So, you said in the library that you grew up here on Cattail?"

Next to him on the curb, I let down my guard and told him a little about my life, including my employment status at the MotherVine.

"You picked quite a time to move back," he said. "With all the murders. You want to know something? The body they found in the dojo? He was one-half of the couple I married last weekend. I can't believe that guy's dead. Strangled. Who would do such a thing?" Ezra ran his fingers through his thick hair. His pallor had become somewhat green. "I was a jerk on their wedding day. I was so— This whole thing with Ariel. That guy's wife— the widow—she must hate me."

"I doubt it. No offense, Ezra, but she's got other things on her mind these days."

"I thought about reaching out to her. What would I say, though? When I marry people, I recite some rehearsed things. Generic things. I'm no good if I don't have a script."

"I think she'd appreciate whatever you might tell her, as long as it's sincere." After a pause, I said, "You must know a fair amount of horse fanciers. You know anybody who would want to steal a horse?"

"Why do that? You can drive down to Mustang Beach any time and observe them."

"Say you really want a horse of your own, but you can't afford one."

"If you can't afford a horse," he said, tossing a pebble into the sewer grate, "then you can't afford to steal one."

"Unless you sell one for a profit."

"What's this all about? Why do you ask?"

"Oh, nothing. Just . . . humor a fellow booklover?"

He thought a moment. "A horse thief for hire? Sounds like a pretty clunky way to make some moolah."

I raspberried my lips. He had a point.

Geri-Lynn's working hypothesis needed some fine-tuning.

52

That night, I trapped my hair in a bandana, donned the faded tank I reserved for scrubbing down the Civic and the OFV, and reported to Cattail Family Martial Arts. Fusco hadn't been kidding about the mess left behind by the fingerprinting process. In the lobby, fine black powder coated everything. Doorknobs, papers on the check-in desk, light switches—even the watercooler spigot.

I found Toby in the big room, kneeling amid rags and spray bottles. Black dust smeared his cheeks and streaked up his forearms. Antoinette had supplied him with extra batches of her special tea-tree solution, and the sharp scent pinched the air. "I'm trying to look on the bright side," he said, wiping his forehead with the hem of a holey Metallica T-shirt. "All this cleaning is a surprisingly good workout. See? Wax on, wax off."

"Let's put on some music. Make a date out of it."

"Music—yes. But under no circumstances are you to think of this catastrophe as our first date."

"You mean cleaning up fingerprint dust wasn't on the list of surprises that you had in store for me?"

"You deserve so much better."

"*Not* a date, then," I said, slipping my phone into the docking station. Bluegrass soared, echoing under the rafters. Three harmonizing voices, crooning about dirt roads and heartache, along with a fiddle and a banjo. Toby was a headbanger, but all year we had been taking turns educating each other on our musical leanings. It was the kind of mutual sharing that made our friendship so fun and satisfying.

He was back at it, scrubbing the mat. I was about to join him when I noticed the foam practice nunchucks in a nearby container. The faux weapon's primary colors—blue, yellow, red—made me think of crayons. They looked as innocuous as preschoolers' toys. I selected a pair, tried flinging it around in the manner Toby had with his LED pair. They slipped from my fingers and went spinning across the room, skidding out at his rag-covered fists.

"Easy, grasshopper." He picked them up and walked over. "You can still give yourself quite a sting with these things."

"They're obviously not made with deadly materials. But sizewise, these practice chucks are the same dimensions as the real thing? The same proportions?"

"As serious nunchucks? Sure. That's the whole point. So you can get the feel of the real deal—*before* you're ready to risk knocking out your own teeth with the real deal."

"Well, then." Foam handle in each hand, I pressed the cord against his throat. "Consider this."

"Whoa. Our not-date takes an unexpectedly kinky turn. I'm into it."

"Seriously. If someone were to be strangled with a pair of nunchucks—think about Seth Goodnow. Think about the bruises under his jaw."

"Where are you going with this?"

"If the murder weapon were nunchucks, wouldn't there have been marks from the handle edges, digging in? Did you notice that kind of bruising on Seth's throat?"

"I didn't notice much else besides the paper sticking out of his pocket. But, come to think of it." Toby closed his eyes, reliving the awful sight. "As far as I could tell, the bruises on his throat were just straight-up lashes. No handle marks."

I tossed the practice chucks back into the container. "The murder weapon wasn't chucks. Not yours. Not anyone's."

"The police have to know that by now."

We held each other's gaze. We were both relieved. But only to a certain extent. Because the fact was, the murder weapon was still out there.

Not to mention the murderer.

For a couple of hours, we scrubbed side by side, until the dojo was looking even more sparkling than before poor Seth Goodnow met his demise. The cleaning itself had a therapeutic effect, heightened by the satisfaction that comes from hard physical work paying off. Goofily tired, we began to crack jokes and spin around with our towels and sing into our spray bottles. We were just starting in on the lobby when Toby's phone rang—the opening guitar riff, accompanied by Axl Rose's howling, of "Welcome to the Jungle." Toby answered, hitting speaker. "Cattail Family Martial Arts," he said cheerily. "Integrity, discipline, courage, respect."

"Oh." A woman's voice faltered. "I was hoping—I mean, it's pretty late, so I was expecting to leave a message."

He grinned. "Is this Abby Tillet? How are you, ma'am? How's Brexley doing?"

There was a heavy pause. "Brexley and I are no longer able to attend your Kids-N-Parents class. I'm so sorry."

"Is Brex okay? Is there anything I can do to help?"

"I—I live next door to the Lowes? And I wanted to pass along that little Archer will no longer be coming to his class, either."

Toby's grin transformed into a frown. "Ma'am, what can I do to change y'all's minds?"

"I just thought we owed you the courtesy of a phone call." Without another word, she hung up.

Toby tossed his phone onto the counter, puffing up a cloud

of black dust. "And so it continues. The downfall of Cattail Family Martial Arts."

"No way." Reaching up, I put my hands on his shoulders. "This is temporary. I know it. That woman—"

"Abby. I've taught every single one of her five kids. Sweet family. Wholesome as can be."

"You know how protective you are? Multiply that by a hundred, and that's how Abby feels about her brood." Not being a mother myself, I had no firsthand knowledge of maternal instinct. But I'd been the daughter of a mother. One who, had she survived, would have kept me secure inside our little home on Hyde Road for as long as she possibly could have. "You can't blame that woman, Toby," I said. "She just wants her babies safe. She's trying to be the best mother she can be. When all this blows over—"

"Yeah. When all this blows over." He sprayed cleaner in a wide arc, then attacked it. Wax on, wax off.

Next to him, I silently did the same.

53

That night, it felt like I'd barely snagged a few hours of sleep when I jolted upright, eyes wide.

Somewhere, Scupper was barking, and Hudson was spewing cusswords the likes of which I hadn't heard since high school, when the Old Fart Van blew a gasket and sheets of blinding smoke nearly sent us careening off the north end of Queen Street and into the Atlantic Ocean.

I jumped out of bed and peered out the window. My uncle—wearing an undershirt and boxer shorts—was loping down the driveway toward a burning blaze. Scupper charged alongside him, his little body quaking with each bark.

My Little Free Library, the Cattale Queen, was on fire. Blue flames licked out into orange. Sparks snaked upward toward the brittle treetops.

Heart pattering, I skidded down the ladder. I ran outside just as my uncle was letting loose with a fire extinguisher, which he'd kept for years in the woodshop. I lunged for Scupper and held him back as white puffs billowed over the flames. When they sputtered out, Hudson sprayed upward into the trees, emptying the contents of the extinguisher.

He turned to me. "You here for the barbecue?"

We linked arms and surveyed the damage. The Cattale Queen was still standing, though the roof was now nonexistent. The paperbacks on the top shelf were a lost cause, singed to illegibility and sopping with carbon dioxide. The hardbacks on the bottom shelf had been spared. Closer inspection was necessary, but as long as I tended to them soon, I could save them.

I directed my attention to the top shelf once again. To a soggy little lump. Sometimes people left pretty stones, seashells, or bracelet charms, but this half-dollar-size object wasn't a trinket on offer. It was a partially burnt book of matches, destroyed except for a sliver of royal-blue ink and what appeared to be the curves of a capital *S*.

Hudson pinched it between his thumb and forefinger and dangled it before my eyes. "You don't need to be a fire marshal to draw some conclusions about what just happened here."

I agreed.

We had stumbled upon the scene of an intentionally set fire.

Up and down the street, there wasn't much action. A bathrobed neighbor had flung open her door and was standing on her porch, blinking at us with a mixture of concern and annoyance. Another neighbor hollered across the street, asking if we needed any help.

"Did you see anyone?" my uncle asked him.

He shrugged.

"What about you?" I asked Hudson. "Did you see anyone?"

"All I know is, I got up to use the commode, and I heard a car peeling out. I shuffled over to the window and saw orange and thankfully woke up enough to realize that orange is not a color I should be seeing at the end of my driveway at four in the morning. I never thought I'd be so glad to be a light sleeper."

Despite the muggy air, I began shivering.

How lucky that no sparks had ignited the treetops, or the gas tanks, or the gutters, which Hudson hadn't cleared out in many months. "At least they didn't target the house," I said. "Or the OFV, or my car, or—"

"The Cattale Queen sparked up faster than a tinderbox. It could have been a disaster."

"But it wasn't. Crisis averted. Thank goodness. Did you get a look at the car?"

He shook his head. "We should call your lady cop friend."

"She's not my friend, and—I don't think so."

"We're dealing with arson here, Callie."

"I know. Which means we're dealing with someone who doesn't have a conscience." Whoever did this wanted to send a message. A warning. I put my hands on my hips, considering. I'd told Geri-Lynn that not alerting the police about her situation was irresponsible. But now I was adopting a similar strategy. Because if I told Fusco someone torched my Little Free Library, the detective would assume I'd provoked the attack by poking around. Which she'd explicitly told me not to do.

No sense getting any higher up on Fusco's blacklist. Not unless it was totally necessary.

"We shouldn't make the person any angrier," I told Hudson. "And bringing in the authorities would definitely make the person angrier."

My uncle didn't appear convinced. He made a slow circle around the Cattale Queen, inspecting the support post and the ground where it met the concrete. He was already strategizing a rebuild. "If they think they're gonna scare me into submission," he said, "they've got another thing coming. This bookshelf on a stick is going to rise like a phoenix from the ashes. It'll be better than ever, faster than you can sneeze. Who would do this? And *why?*"

"Someone who has no qualms with lighting an open flame during a drought. Someone who doesn't care about sending this whole island up in smoke."

54

Back inside, Hudson wanted to officially get his day started by brewing some coffee. I told him it was too early, that if he got up now, he'd be stumbling around and yawning uncontrollably by ten a.m. "Try to go back to sleep," I said.

"I'm too spooked to sleep."

"Whoever did this won't be coming back. They just wanted to scare us. As far as they're concerned, it's mission accomplished."

"I'm not scared. I'm spooked. There's a difference."

"Don't let them win." I scooped up Scupper and delivered him into my uncle's arms. "A few more hours of solid z's will do all of us good."

He muttered something, kissed my forehead, and shuffled down the hall toward his room.

In my Murphy bed, I lay in the darkness, my thoughts running amuck.

Somebody out there didn't want me asking questions. About the mustangs. About Seth's murder, or Addison's disappearance, or about anything that mattered.

It was one thing to put my own life in danger. But my sleuthing had put my uncle's life in jeopardy too. And Scupper's.

And yet, how could I simply . . . *stop*? Seth Goodnow might not have been a wholly stand-up guy, but what happened to him was brutal. Meanwhile, Naomi, an innocent woman, had no answers.

I couldn't stop. I wouldn't.

I got up, got dressed, and stepped outside again, into the steamy darkness.

Walking Queen Street at that hour always felt odd. It felt especially odd that night, so soon after being the victim of a crime. A cowardly crime, at that.

The only signs of activity were a raccoon skittering across the street and moths bumping against a streetlight. I walked swiftly, arms crossed, feeling an odd combination of creeped out and angry.

Angry that someone had destroyed my Cattale Queen. Tried to, anyway. It had been a gift, a handmade welcome-home gift that doubled as a neighborhood enhancer.

I made a mental list of possible culprits. The list didn't amount to much.

Cooper Payne sprang to mind as the most obvious candidate. In the wake of Seth's death, Cooper was the most unlikable person I'd met.

There was also Heather Westerly, who was definitely hiding something.

And let's not forget Ezra Metcalfe. Although, in the ten minutes I'd spent with the guy, I went from thinking he was bad news to thinking he was simply a man in a tough spot. Besides— a librarian, burning books? Then again, I couldn't discount his death grip on the hedge clippers. Could it have been that, every now and then, he dallied in vandalism? Could his sheepish demeanor have been an act? One I'd fallen for?

And what about D.S.?

My head was positively spinning. My pace quickened as I neared the waterfront. The block was still except for a stray food wrapper skipping down the sidewalk. Normally I would have run after it and picked it up; I couldn't stand litter. But I just wanted to get inside the bookshop. Almost there. Keeping my brain occupied, I made another mental list: literary characters who were fire starters. At first, I couldn't dredge up the name of Stephen King's titular antagonist, but then it came to me: Carrie. I also came up with Mrs. Danvers, Montag, and Quasimodo. There were more, of course, but before I knew it, I was keying into the MotherVine.

I locked the door behind me—and drank in the smell of books. A different kind of darkness enveloped me, and I envisioned anger and fear leaving my body. Draining away. Leaking out my fingertips and toes. "Tin Man?" I called.

He meowed several times, an audible breadcrumb trail that I tracked to Antoinette's office. He was batting around the paper foal I had made. The one I'd been saving for the real foal's arrival. "No touchy," I said, easing it from his jaws. I placed it on a high shelf before turning back around. "Did you know that ancient Japanese people believed horses could carry your wishes directly to the gods? I read about that in the kids' origami book I've been consulting. Tinny?"

Silence. He'd taken off.

Then I heard a thud. I quickly turned on the handheld lantern. "Tin?" The floor creaked as I stepped into the aisle, lighting the way with the flickering lantern.

He hadn't gone far. I found him in the children's section. He was sitting on the floor, swishing his tail. Before him lay an open book. *The Legend of Rosie Beacon.*

Everything started tingling. My hands and feet. My scalp. If I'd had whiskers, they'd have been quivering up a storm. I knelt in the aisle as Tin Man headbutted my chin. "Did you pick this out for me?"

It was open to an early page. I reread the first full paragraph, which was about the secret cove Rosie and Roger had discovered. *Dense undergrowth hid this magical place from casual passersby. Only my stallion and I knew of its existence.*

Tigress. Did she have a secret hiding spot? Obviously, it wouldn't be a stretch of shoreline. In all of Cattail, not one inch of beach remained unexplored. But if Tigress had happened upon an obscured corner of Mustang Beach Sanctuary woods and decided it would make an ideal birthing suite . . . Such a spot needn't be far from the footpath or the horse paths. It only needed to be undetectable. Hidden from passing glances.

Geri-Lynn said she looked and looked. She scoured those woods. *There was nowhere to hide,* she'd said.

Rivka, though. That young mare had gotten herself hung up on an old portion of fence. *Geri-Lynn mustn't have realized it was there,* Ezra had told me.

What else didn't we realize was there, hidden in that old wood? What if Tigress was playing—and winning—an epic game of hide-and-seek?

Before I replaced the book, I gave it a kiss. Then I gave Tin Man a good long scratch on the stripy part between his ears. He wasn't some quasi-magical character in a cozy mystery. He was a real live cat. And yet, it wasn't the first time he'd put a weirdly appropriate, eerily synchronistic book in my path. A book that related to a vexing situation. I wondered if he'd had something to do with my finding the book about bullies, as well. "I don't know how you do it," I told him. "Or even if you do it at all. But for what it's worth? Thank you very much."

Without my even noticing, the sun had risen. A silver-coral light crept into the bookshop, brightening things. I no longer needed the lantern, so I turned it off.

As I glanced around, an undeniable love for the MotherVine permeated me through and through. I'd never gallop down the beach bareback, like Rosie Beacon, on a wild horse. I'd never survive alone in the woods for a single night. With help from a humble book, however, I could imagine those things.

And I could imagine Tigress, right at that very moment, nuzzling her newborn amid a secret, foliaged safe haven.

55

It was early when I called Geri-Lynn. Too early. But I was excited.

The call went straight to voicemail. "I have an idea," I said. "Call me."

Antoinette reported to work whistling a tune, leaving no doubt that her day off had been a wise move. Arriving after her, the shoppers generally did not share her improved mood. One young dad demanded to know just when, exactly, Cattail Island had become the "creepo capital" of the South. I sent him and his teenage son to the back patio with some decafs, a stack of books, and my reassurances that a little MotherVine would do them a world of good.

Later, during a lull, I fetched some coffee and delivered it to Antoinette, who was in the office feeding Tin Man. I wanted to make sure she was really okay. That the whistling wasn't an act, or a cover.

"Funny," she said, "I was going to ask you the same thing." She squeezed my arm. "Steady goes it?"

My stomach growled audibly, and I realized I'd forgotten to eat breakfast. "Depends on what you mean by steady."

During my lunch break, eager to fulfill my promise to Hudson, I scooted across the street and climbed the exterior stairs to the Yarn Barn. Inside, the walls were dripping in colors and textures:

ponchos, afghans, leg warmers, even a Scupper-size dog sweater. I marveled that anyone could create such useful beauty using only a stick or two and a bit of twisted fiber.

The Yarn Barn did good business catering to summer's yarnie tourists who couldn't resist a souvenir, and to off-season locals who began shivering as soon as temperatures dipped into the sixties. When they decided a homespun pair of mittens or a lap blanket would be just the thing to make them feel cozy, they climbed on up to the Yarn Barn.

The owner and I exchanged hellos. She rocked a small Afro, ceramic llama earrings, and a sheer-knit bolero shrug over a camisole.

"Did you make all these pretty things?" I asked.

"My partner and I did. Let me know if I can guide you in any way."

The prices were eye-popping.

Hudson was all about reusing materials. Upcycling. Back in the day, the tree house he'd constructed for me was made entirely of recycled wood. I knew that, for any old children's toy, he wouldn't be too happy if I quoted him a price more than his weekly Piggly Wiggly bill. This, however, was to be no ordinary hobbyhorse. It would be a heavily used showpiece. It was also meant for Antoinette.

I went over to a section labeled ART YARN and selected the most expensive black yarn I could find, shiny and silky and fine as cat whiskers between my fingers.

"Tell me about your project," the owner said as I placed a few skeins on the checkout counter.

"It's for a hobbyhorse."

"Ah. So it'll have industrial-strength glue on one end, and little kids' sticky fingers all through the rest." Her eyes flicked from the skeins to my face. "Can I give you some advice?"

"Is it that obvious that I'm out of my element here?"

"You've got a great eye. But this yarn you've picked out might be *too* gorgeous, you know? Get yourself the cheapest yarn you can find. Something sturdy. Cotton will hold up to years of heavy petting. We don't sell that kind of yarn here. It will require a trip to the bigger islands."

I nodded and said, "I owe you one." Even though I couldn't quite see myself taking up knitting or crocheting, I made a mental note to someday figure out a reason to spend some cash in the Yarn Barn.

Back inside the MotherVine, I wandered the aisles, reshelving books and mulling over the yarn situation. Hudson wouldn't want to wait for a shipment of yarn to arrive any more than he would want to wait for me to trek to the bigger islands to get him some. I couldn't shake the feeling that another option was available. Then I remembered—Dominick O'Neill. On the night I stopped at Naomi and Seth Goodnow's rental cottage, the O'Neills had remarked on the boxes of junk all around. *If you ever find yourself in need of a few hundred balls of yarn*, Dominick had said, *you know where to come knocking.*

I didn't know if the yarn in question was a pukey shade of chartreuse, or infused with ancient cigarette smoke, but I decided to at least consider it. The Yarn Barn owner had advised me to go cheap, and it didn't get much cheaper than free.

Since Ivy O'Neill had followed Tin Man on Instagram, I was able to send her a direct message. *Hi there, Callie here from the MotherVine. Your husband mentioned yarn up for grabs. If it's still available, I'm interested! Could you let me know? Thx.* I typed my phone number and hit send—and my phone vibrated.

Geri-Lynn Humfeld was calling.

56

C allie?" Geri-Lynn's voice was gravelly. Quavering.
"What's wrong? You sound off."

"Oh, I'm fine. It's just . . . oh, nothing."

"What? You can tell me."

"Have you ever been so low you couldn't face the day?"

Low? In my life, I had certainly known some low times. "Are you at Sanctuary Bungalow?"

"There was a sweet elderly couple in here. They just left. I'm all alone now."

"Good. Why don't you flip your sign to CLOSED? Maybe just for a half hour or so. You might feel better if you give yourself some time. Brew a cup of tea, or—"

"I could go for a swim. Nothing like a good ocean-water bath to lift your spirits, you know? But the rip currents look bad. There's one that's horseshoeing right back to the beach. At least I wouldn't get swept out to sea—"

"Stay out of the water," I said. This was not the self-possessed Geri-Lynn Humfeld I had come to know. The pressure was just too much. If faced with similar dilemmas—a missing horse, trespassers, and now a missing person linked to the beach that I supervised—I doubt I would have held up so well. "Do you have any friends you can call?" I asked. "Any relatives?" I thought back to the personal conversations we'd had. Geri-Lynn had mentioned a sister in Raleigh, and . . . that was it. There just weren't many people in her life. That was why she'd chosen me to help her out of this low place. I was close by; I'd proven myself trustworthy and maybe even useful, *and* I wasn't in a position to fire her.

"Maybe I could do some target practice," she said. "Fire my gun at some glass bottles or tin cans. That usually makes me feel better."

That didn't strike me as a good idea, either. I pictured visitors and islanders alike, curious about the foal, happening upon the otherwise responsible herd manager who'd had a tough spell and was devoting billable hours to target practice.

Geri-Lynn was a loner, even more so than me. If I believed anything, it was that loners should have each other's backs. Who else was going to make sure she didn't fire her pistol indiscriminately, or strip off all her clothes and dive into a rip current?

"Listen," I said, "just stay put, okay? Don't do anything. Don't talk to anyone. I'll be there in twelve minutes or less. And I have just the thing for you."

Pulling up to Sanctuary Bungalow, I sighed in relief. Geri-Lynn had flipped the sign to CLOSED.

Two other vehicles were parked out front. As I climbed the porch steps, I peered over the dune and saw a few teenagers hanging back a respectable distance from the fence. Several mustangs were on the other side, loping along in the surf.

Another dusty car pulled up, and two gentlemen my uncle's age got out. "Apologies for the inconvenience," I told them. "Sanctuary Bungalow is closed for the time being."

"Because of the pregnant mare?" one guy said. "I heard she was missing."

So the island rumor mill was grinding away. Someone must've finally voiced concern about the pregnant mare being conspicuously absent from social media. Someone else had passed along the sentiment, and it got repeated, embellished, and repeated some more—and the spark ignited into a flame.

"I'm not sure," I told the men. "But I do know that you can walk right over that dune onto the public portion of Mustang Beach, where you can get a nice view of the mustangs. Some are there now."

The man who had spoken grumbled as he lumbered toward the beach. The other one gave me a please-don't-mind-my-grumpy-friend smile before following him.

"Have a good one," I said, before stepping inside.

"Hello?" I called. "Geri-Lynn? You okay? It's Callie."

"You came?" Her voice floated down from the second floor. I moved past her office and made my way upstairs. "You came," she said again as I poked my head through her darkened bedroom doorway. The curtains were closed. The room felt stuffy. It took a moment for my eyes to adjust. She was propped up in bed, fully clothed, a laptop on her thighs.

"Of course I came." I heaved another sigh. This was not going according to plan. I'd wanted to pitch Geri-Lynn my idea about Tigress being in hiding. I'd wanted us to walk the woods together until we found the mother, and hopefully the baby too, safe as could be.

But Geri-Lynn had taken herself out of the equation. Her face was shiny, her eyes red. The eyes of someone who'd been let down by a fair amount people over the years, I guessed. She scooted over and patted the mattress, inviting me to sit, so I did. "There's this video I found online," she said. "Wild horses. Somewhere out west. I can't stop watching it." She hit play. "One of them died? And the others line up to pay their respects. One by one, they make their way over to the deceased, and . . . see?"

Filmed through tall, whispering grass, the video showed exactly what she'd described. The mustangs stood nose to tail. Taking turns, they advanced to hang their heads over the fallen. "Wow," I whispered, watching.

"Elephants do this sort of thing too. They make pilgrimages to the places where their ancestors died. Even after the bones are gone. Buried by the sands of time, or carried off by poachers, or . . . It isn't easy, keeping these horses wild. Keeping them living as they would have a few centuries ago. Interfering as little as possible."

She was making a melancholy sort of sense. I started to believe that, in order to keep Cattail's mustangs wild, Geri-Lynn had to be a bit wild herself. But I hated seeing her so flat, and I didn't think it was good for her to dwell. When she dropped her head onto my shoulder and hit play again, I gently closed the laptop. "How about we give this a rest?" She didn't protest as I eased the machine from her hands.

"I'm embarrassed for you to see me this way," she said. "Sometimes I just get—swallowed up."

"Everyone does."

"I didn't have children, Callie. These horses are the closest I'll ever get to being a mother."

"Everything's going to be okay. Including you."

"Have you locked down your Toby situation yet?"

Surprised, I almost laughed. "What? There is no Toby situation."

"Yeah. Right. When you said his name the other day, you lit up like a firework."

"It's not exactly good timing. Romance-wise, I mean."

"Timing, shmiming. You're perfect for each other."

"What gives you that idea? You've never even met the guy. You've never even seen us together."

She gave a mischievous smile. "I hope you won't think this is creepy. But—that morning you two were on the walking trail? Passing the water bottle back and forth, standing on the observation platform? You were looking this way, at this very cottage. I saw y'all through my camera's zoom lens. I'd been searching for Tigress—but I found you instead. Y'all looked like you'd been together for years."

"It feels that way, sometimes." I smiled. "You *do* have children, Geri-Lynn. You have forty-six children, and they have wonderful, secret names like Starview and Tundra and Succotash, and you're the best and most protective mother they could possibly ask for."

"You're wrong. I only have forty-four children." She held up two fingers. "I lost a couple."

"You don't know that. The story isn't over with Tigress and her unborn foal. That chapter hasn't been written yet—"

"*I'm* a knucklehead. *Me.*"

I went over to the air-conditioning unit and cranked it high. "You said you searched everywhere for Tigress. You scoured the place. And I believe you did. Could you entertain the possibility, though, that you might have left a very small—but imperative— stone unturned? What I mean is—think about Rosie Beacon. You read the book, right?"

"Twice now."

"So you know that she and her wild horse, Roger, spent many hours exploring Cattail Island together. One time they discovered a secret cove, a short stretch of tangled shoreline, obscured by a tucked-away pocket of vegetation."

"Rosie's and Roger's number one place to admire the ocean and soak up all the natural beauty surrounding them," Geri-Lynn said.

"'Dense undergrowth hid this magical place from casual

passersby,'" I quoted from the book. "'Only my stallion and I knew of its existence.'"

"Are you telling me someone stole my horse in order to warn colonists that the British are coming?"

"I'm telling you that there might still be hiding places on Cattail Island. Places so wild, only the mustangs know about them."

"There's one thing you're overlooking, Callie. The book is called *The* Legend *of Rosie Beacon. Legend.* I wasn't a lit major, but doesn't *legend* imply fiction?"

She had a point. While Rosie Beacon had been a real person, history—as I'd so passionately informed Antoinette—was famously incomplete.

Did it matter, though? Mustang Beach was the wildest beach on Cattail. Things were very different now than in Rosie's era, but here on the preserved part of the island, aside from shifting sands, the landscape hadn't much changed . . .

Enough. It wasn't Rosie's musings that ultimately made a difference. It was her actions.

"You scoured this land, Geri-Lynn," I said, chopping my palm. "You investigated one spot, checked it off, then moved on to the next spot. A grid search. But you didn't go about things thinking Tigress might be actively, purposefully hiding. Moving from place to place."

She didn't reply, but she was coming around. I could see it in the stillness of her face.

I pressed. "Think about that old remnant of fencing that Rivka got hung up on. You told me the woods were so dense you didn't even know the fencing was there until you heard Rivka braying."

"I suppose it *is* possible that there are hiding places I don't know about. You think Tigress has been avoiding me? And all the other mustangs?"

"Isn't it possible?"

"It's unlikely."

"So is two men stealing a wild horse, Geri-Lynn. You told me most mares want their band around them when they're ready to give birth. *Most* mares. Not all. Isn't it conceivable—pardon the pun—"

"Nice."

"—that Tigress is different? Maybe she *did* want to be alone. You mentioned a couple stallions have been bullying each other, trying to establish who's boss."

"Johnny Cash and Hot Sauce. They *have* been rambunctious lately."

"What if Tigress, pregnant as a house, just wanted to get away from Johnny Cash's and Hot Sauce's nonsense? Remember the Hugging Trees? The branches of an oak wrapped around two tall pines. It feels like an enchanted spot, like the gateway to a secret hiding place. You took me there when you first told me about Tigress. And we ended up there again, with Fusco, when we were searching for Addison."

"You think Tigress is using that place as a sort of home-base hideaway?" More silence hung between us—but this time, it felt electrified. A crackling energy. Hope, coming back online. "Maybe Tigress is safe after all," she said. "Maybe she's been close by this whole time—and has just been outsmarting us." Geri-Lynn threw off the covers. "We're going there. Right now. You and me."

57

We rushed downstairs—and were surprised to see an octogenarian woman standing before the main mural. Her bun reminded me of a perfectly sculpted lump of ice, and her ruby brooch was the approximate size of a Chips Ahoy! cookie.

"Miz Pearleen?" I crossed the room. Pearleen Standish was the last person I expected to see gracing the dusty hotbox that was Sanctuary Bungalow.

Holding on to her alligator-skin handbag, she air-kissed me. Despite her kitten heels, she still only came up to my nose.

"Sorry, ma'am," Geri-Lynn said, cramming her straw hat onto her head. "Could you come back in an hour or two?"

"I'm afraid not," Pearleen said. "My grandson just informed me that he forgot to call ahead and make an appointment with the general in command here. I do apologize on his behalf." She extended her hand, limp at the wrist. "Dr. Humfeld, I presume?"

"Geri-Lynn," I said, my eyes wide. "This is Miz Pearleen Standish. Of Standish Furniture International."

Geri-Lynn's face blanched. At one point or another, every non-profit on the Outer Banks had courted Miz Pearleen. It was nearly impossible to get a personal audience with her, but judging by Geri-Lynn's gobsmacked expression, she'd addressed her fair share of groveling letters to the infamous furniture heiress.

She gave the tiny woman's hand a polite squeeze.

Pearleen sneezed daintily, then sidestepped the stuffed goose, as if worried its outstretched feet might kick her in the face.

"Let's get right down to brass tacks, shall we, Dr. Humfeld? It has come to my attention that the Mustang Beach Sanctuary is in desperate need of video surveillance. True?"

Geri-Lynn took off her hat and gripped it before her heart. "You must have heard that from Detective Fusco."

"My personal estate is protected by a top-of-the-line state-of-the-art security system."

"Oh, I don't need anything that fancy. I've set my sights on something a lot humbler. They're called trail cameras."

"*Trail* cameras?"

"For recording wildlife? I'd love to tell you all—"

"The Standish Trail Camera System at Mustang Beach Sanctuary. Something along those lines."

"Yes, ma'am. That has a mighty fine ring to it. Care for some sweet tea?" Geri-Lynn got Pearleen settled in her office, then rushed back out to me. She pressed a bottle of insect repellent into my hand. "You go on without me. I've got to seal this deal."

"Don't worry," I said. "I plan on returning with Tigress."

58

On the porch, I sprayed myself down—while cursing myself for having made a declaration like that. Even if I did find Tigress, what was I going to do? Lasso her and drag her back to the bungalow? Poke her with a stick and force her to march?

A Ferrari had joined the parking lot's vehicular riffraff. Behind the wheel sat a large, seersuckered man. Pearleen's grandson and gopher. We exchanged waves; I didn't have time for chitchat.

On the beach, the old men and the teenagers had gotten together to toss around a football. They were all fanned out in a circle, the ball crisscrossing it, sometimes wobbling. Steeling myself, I strode confidently for the fence. The men and teens took a timeout from their throwing to shoot me questioning looks.

"Everything's okay," I called as I pushed through the turnstile. "I have authority."

Honestly. The things that came out of my mouth sometimes.

Setting my jaw, I marched onto the forbidden part of Mustang Beach. I had not envisioned setting out alone. I wasn't afraid of the woods, per se. But I was afraid of getting lost. Of making a problem for everyone.

Though Rosie Beacon hadn't worried about being a problem . . .

Walking, I recalled the first time I'd hiked with Geri-Lynn through these woods. The first time I laid eyes on the live oak wrapping its branches around those two pines that soared upward into a canopy so thick I couldn't see the sky. The spot had seemed so shadowy when contrasted with the bright, warm Cattail Island sunshine.

Enchanted, I'd called it. The Hugging Trees.

That was where I needed to go.

If only I could remember how to reach it.

The twisty paths intersected one another, creating a woodland maze. After twenty minutes of trying to recall which way I'd turned, then backtracking, I recognized a landmark: the fence separating sanctuary land from the footpath. I headed for it, thinking I could rest there, enjoy a few sips of cool water from the bottle I carried, and regain my bearings. But I stopped short when I made out, through the brush, the peak of a dark blue hat.

A police officer had swung by, probably because of Addison's bow tie showing up on Mustang Beach. Undoubtedly, the mustached uni heard me crashing through the woods; he pointed a pair of binoculars in my general direction. I'd been trying to be quiet, so as not to spook any horses, but apparently my best efforts hadn't exactly resulted in stealth.

I dropped to my knees. *Please don't see me. Please don't see me.* That was all I needed. A Cattail police officer hauling me by the collar, delivering me to Fusco.

After sixty seconds of trying not to breathe, I chanced a tip of my head to see if he was still there. Mercifully, he had moved on, out of my line of vision. He must have chalked up my ruckus to a roving gang of hyper squirrels. I heard an engine start and made sure he'd driven off before I straightened back up.

Close call. I blew air through my lips like I was blowing through a straw. I wasn't going to find the Hugging Trees without Gerri-Lynn to guide me. I quick-stepped toward the sound of crashing waves and headed back to the beach.

As gut-wrenching as it was, Tigress would have to wait. If she'd survived a few days on her own, a few more hours wouldn't pose a problem. Hopefully.

Mission: total fail.

59

Any sign of Tigress?" Geri-Lynn ushered me through the bungalow's front door. The cars were all gone, and no one else was inside.

"Sorry." I shook my head. "I got lost. And then a police officer almost bagged me. He's gone now. I heard him drive off."

"Even good girls have to break the rules sometimes. I'm thinking Tigress knows that pretty well."

"How'd you make out with Miz Pearleen?"

A grin overtook Geri-Lynn's face. "I'm gonna get the trail camera system of my wildest dreams. Can you believe Fusco? According to Miz Pearleen, she wanted to make up for the bad blood between us."

"I'm really glad for you." I went to give Geri-Lynn a congrats hug when my gaze floated over toward the main mural. Something caught my eye. Something I hadn't before noticed among the vermillion-tinted spindrift glowing in the setting sun, and the horses' flowing manes and tails. In the bottom corner, near the floor: a slash of salmon pink. The artist's signature. It was thin, elegant, and leaning left, as if it wanted to slide off the painted sand and onto the real sand just outside the window.

I stooped for closer inspection.

D.S. '04

I shot back up.

"What?" Geri-Lynn asked. "You look like someone lit a firecracker under your—"

"D.S. The initials on Toby's sign-up sheet that nobody has been able to make any sense of." Plenty of people had the initials D.S.—but what were the chances that they would appear in the same elegant, left-leaning handwriting? "Who painted these murals?"

"Those things've been here far longer than me. You know, someone else was asking me about them earlier this spring. Wanted to know about the artist."

My heart banged. "Who wanted to know about the artist?"

"Heather Westerly. During one of our Zoom interviews, I showed her the murals, and she loved them. I found some information for her, in the old filing cabinets. The details escape me now. Danielle Something? No, that wasn't it. But— *Oh*. Okay."

I'd flown into Geri-Lynn's office. The filing cabinets were locked but labeled. The drawer I needed—2004—was waist high. My fingertips prickled. A riffle through that drawer was bound to rustle up a record of some kind. A work order, a receipt, correspondence . . .

She had followed me and now handed over a small key. "Try July."

Straddling the wheeled stool, I unlocked the cabinet and set to work, moving front to back through the files, flipping chronologically through every musty sheet of paper in the July folder. And I struck gold.

According to a single sheet that served as a makeshift contract, a Denise Sawicki had been paid eighteen hundred dollars for "art services rendered." Her address was a residence hall at Savannah College of Art and Design. Evidently, she'd been a student. Decorating the walls at Sanctuary Bungalow must have been a summer gig.

"That's it," Geri-Lynn said. "That's the contract I found. Denise Sawicki. You want to tell me what's going on?"

"Ha!" I kissed my fingertips—a chef's kiss—and rolled backward, sending the stool skidding into the wall behind me. "This artist, Denise Sawicki? She's the D.S. who signed into the dojo that morning. It's the same exact penmanship." I typed *Denise Sawicki, artist* into my phone's search window. A listing for an art studio on the mainland popped up.

Several days ago, Denise Sawicki had come to Cattail Island. She'd visited Cattail Family Martial Arts and had evidently balked at the idea of signing herself in.

Fabulous.

Now I needed to figure out why.

"What did Heather Westerly do with this information?" I asked.

"No idea," Geri-Lynn said. "Do you think she wanted to hire Denise for some kind of art project?"

"Maybe as a gift to herself. To celebrate her new job here with Mustang Beach Sanctuary. To mark the occasion of her big move."

"Well, anyway, I found the artist's name for her, passed it along, and that was that. Do you think either of them—Heather Westerly or Denise Sawicki—have anything to do with the murder? The trespassers? Addison? My missing horse?"

"Exactly."

Geri-Lynn got out her phone. "I'm calling Heather right now. I'll see what I can find out."

Meanwhile, on my phone, two red dots caught my attention. Notifications.

Ivy O'Neill had replied to my DM about the yarn. *Sure. You can take as much as you like. Come on over whenever! One of us will be here.*

And a text had come in from my uncle. It said, simply:

Yarn?

I replied:

Coming soon, I promise. Hold your horses. Get it?

I looked back at my search engine results and saw that Denise had a website. I clicked on it.

Since her college days, she'd carved out quite a career for herself. She'd done murals up and down the Virginia and Carolina coasts, including in Charleston, Wilmington, and Norfolk. *If you've got an idea, a vision, I'd love to chat with you and find out if a collaboration is in our mutual future. Contact me using the form below!*

I checked out her headshot, remembering how Toby had described her to Chief Jurecki. Short, tough, and serious. Indeed, she didn't seem to match her stylish signature.

"Heather didn't pick up," Geri-Lynn said. "I'll keep trying."

"Not to judge someone by their photograph, but Denise doesn't look like a let's-sit-down-and-chitchat sort of person," I said. "Let alone like the sort of person to use exclamation points and the word *love* in business dealings." I considered filling out the contact form, but what would I write? *I'm just your average citizen, wondering if you worked out at a martial arts place the morning a man was murdered there. I'd appreciate your getting back to me . . .* That wouldn't fly. One way or another, I was going to risk offending Denise Sawicki. Chances are I'd get more information out of her—and sooner—if I talked to her in person.

"Says here she lives and works on the mainland," Geri-Lynn said. She'd looked up Denise on her phone too. "Owner and operator of Denise Sawicki Arts. Her home studio is just a few blocks from the ferry terminal."

I went to the ferry website and found the schedule. The next departure for Jarvis Harbor was in one hour. I purchased a paperless ticket.

"Who could've predicted this twist?" Geri-Lynn said. "While I'll be out hunting for a horse, you'll be out hunting for an artist."

60

There was just enough time to stop by the O'Neills' cottage and snag the yarn. On the way, I made some calls, with my phone in speaker mode and balanced on the dashboard. When your car harkens from pre-smartphone days, you've got to get creative to be hands-free.

My first call was to Fusco, but she didn't pick up. After that, I tried Chief Jurecki but couldn't get through. Chances were the police might have already figured out who D.S. was. But what if they hadn't? I left messages for each of them, saying I had information pertaining to the murder of Seth Goodnow—and possibly, by extension, the disappearance of Addison Battle too.

Next call: Toby. "Denise Sawicki," I said when he picked up.

There was a beat of silence. I could practically hear the gears turning in his mind. "D.S.?" he said. "From the sign-up sheet?"

"She's a muralist. I know—it sounds totally crazy. Long story. Best told in person—"

"Do the police know about her? How did you figure it out? And does she have something to do with—"

"I'll tell you everything, as soon as I can. Right now, I need to get some more information. What are you up to?"

"At the moment, not much. I've got some time to kill until later tonight, when the dojo officially reopens. I've got a Kids-N-Parents class. That is, if anybody shows up. It's going to be tough teaching at a time like this. But what you said about Cattail needing to protect itself really sunk in. I can't stop thinking that if Seth knew how to defend himself better, then maybe—maybe . . ."

"Want to take a ferry ride with me?"

"Now? Does this have something to do with D.S.?"

"Denise Sawicki. I'm going on a wee fact-finding expedition. I could use a bodyguard. Meet me at the terminal in forty minutes? I've got an errand to run first."

"I'm your man."

61

I was hoping to say goodbye to Naomi, but as I pulled onto Love Beach Trail, I didn't see her out and about. And I didn't have time to ring her bell. The same grandfatherly man who'd taken the kite from me was loading a small suitcase into the back of the VW Bug.

The vehicle had been stripped of its newlywed decorations.

At the O'Neills' cottage, the door was open. Chilled air streamed out into the humidity. "Hello?" I called, stepping inside. "Anyone around?" In the kitchen, a FREE sign topped a folded stack of dish towels, next to a bowl of rubber duckies and a jar of tarnished sundae spoons. I fought the urge to sweep all that random clutter into a trash bag and drop it off at Cattail Thrift. But that decision wasn't up to me—*and* I was about to become the beneficiary of this homeowner's decorating taste, so who was I to judge?

Cadence sat at the table, her back to me. Humming, she kicked the chair legs and leafed through her rock guide. She was so absorbed she hadn't heard me enter. Not wanting to startle her, I cleared my throat.

"Callie!" She jumped up and raced over. She might have had a hard time socially, but she seemed more or less content around me. I was glad for that.

"How are you today?" I asked, just as Dominick shuffled around the corner.

"Hey there." He was pulling a T-shirt over his well-toned torso. His hair was tousled, a just-woke-up-from-a-nap look. "Ivy's down at the beach with Unicorn. She told me you might stop by. Are you, um . . ." He gestured to my forehead.

"Oh." I put my fingertips to my eyebrow. They came back flecked with dried blood. A souvenir from my forest foray. "Just a scratch."

He tore off a paper towel, dampened it in the sink, and handed it to me. "You want Neosporin or something? My wife travels with an entire pharmacy in her purse."

"I carry a lot of things around with me too," I said, laughing and dabbing the cut. "I'm good."

"Well, despite everything, the O'Neill family officially loves your island. Don't we, Cade? The days here on Cattail just go on forever."

I knew what he meant. Even though the days weren't at their longest just yet, sunlight lingered, thanks to the water all around—ocean, sound, canals—bouncing the beams. "How much longer are you here for?" I asked.

"We've started packing, but we'll have one last afternoon on the beach before we head back. We're leaving tomorrow, first thing."

"I don't want to leave," Cadence said, wrapping her arms around her father's waist.

"I don't either, bud. But you have to get back to school with Mommy, and I have to get back to work." When she burrowed her face into his shirt, he added, "You'll survive. I promise. Think of it this way: if we don't leave, we won't be able to come back." Giving her back a few pats, he looked over at me. "Ivy said you need some yarn. It's in great shape. It's seriously like new. Doesn't even smell."

I told him about my uncle's hobbyhorse for the MotherVine,

figuring it was safe to divulge Hudson's secret to a tourist, someone I might not ever see again.

"Sweet," he said. "Cade loves that bookshop. Don't you, Cade? Come on, I'll show you out to the shed."

"I'll take her." Cadence, recovered from her brief mourning of vacation's end, took my hand.

Dominick smiled. "All right, but come straight down to the beach after Miss Callie's gone, okay? I'm headed there now."

"Really?" she said, in a way that made me think her mother would never have granted her that much freedom.

"Really." He planted a loud smack on her cheek, which made her giggle. Then she dragged me toward the back door.

"Thanks, Dominick," I said. "Great meeting you all, despite the sad circumstances. Safe travels tomorrow."

He toasted me with the White Claw he'd cracked open, then closed the front door behind him.

Out back, the shed marked the end of the dirt driveway. Cadence pushed open the door and flipped on the light. We stood there a moment, taking in the overwhelming scent of Pine-Sol permeating the jaw-dropping, orderly jumble of crap. A crate of old padlocks, a hamper full of fabric scraps. The concrete floor was freshly swept and spotless enough to spread out a picnic. In the corner, a decades-old wardrobe shined like it was brand-new. I could practically see my reflection in the wood. "This is the most immaculate shed I've ever seen," I said. "And the most organized."

"How much yarn do you need?" Cadence went over to a table, where skeins of black yarn snuggled inside a wide basket. While I was no textile connoisseur, I recognized what the Yarn Barn owner had been steering me toward. This yarn had the

MotherVine's children's section written all over it. While it was hard-wearing, a far cry from the sleek stuff I'd selected in the shop, it also had some tasteful bling: up close, I saw that bronze, tinsel-like threads were woven in with the black.

"It's perfect," I said. "Exactly the color and style I was hoping for. I have no idea how much I need, to be honest. How much do you think, for a hobbyhorse?"

"Like the one in the bookshop?"

"Just like it. Only, this one's wood. My uncle's making it. Guess what the yarn's for?"

"The tail?"

"That's right. And the mane."

"I wish I could see it when it's all done."

"You'll have to convince your parents to come back to Cattail Island next year. I don't think that'd be too hard. They like it here."

"Me too."

"Me three."

"I wanted to see the baby horse—the real one, on Mustang Beach? But Mom said it's going to be born after we leave."

"Then you'll definitely have to come back sometime."

"Definitely."

I packed five skeins into my bag, figuring that should be more than enough, even if Hudson did somehow screw up early attempts. "This is great," I said. "I appreciate it. Thank you so much."

She beamed. I was sure she'd make an excellent bookshop employee someday. "Can you come to the beach now?" she asked.

"I wish I could, Cadence, but—" *But I'm taking the ferry to the mainland, where I will try and track down a possible murder suspect.* "I'll tell you what. I'll walk you as far as the dune. How would that be?"

Again, she took my hand, and we strolled a hundred feet down Love Beach Trail. She chatted the whole way, mostly about her rock collection. When the ocean got louder and sand took over the road, she let go of my hand and waved.

I waved too, feeling a little sad.

I was going to miss Cadence O'Neill.

62

From behind my Civic's steering wheel, I could see the ferry was about to pull away. Crew members uncoiled thick ropes from the pilings. I stepped on the gas pedal, speeding toward the terminal. Toby, watching anxiously from the ramp, waved as I approached. I parked and ran for it. Laughing, he grabbed my hand and we jumped aboard, spanning the gap over the water just as the boat pushed off.

We sheltered inside the Wagoneer, out of the wind, away from the engine noise and the other passengers milling around. I told Toby just about everything, including the sagas of Tigress and Rosie Beacon and Geri-Lynn. I felt bad, spilling my new friend's secret. But I also felt good. Like iron two-by-fours were being lifted from my shoulders. "So, you and I are going to pay this Denise Sawicki a visit," I said. "See what business she had inside Cattail Family Martial Arts, the same morning we found Seth Goodnow dead."

"You're going to be the kind of girlfriend who keeps me on my toes," Toby said.

"You're just figuring this out now?"

He pointed outside, to a section of boat railing that was unoccupied. "Let's get out there and practice your reverse headbutt."

In Jarvis Harbor, cell reception was notoriously crappy. We couldn't rely on our phones to guide us to Denise Sawicki Arts, so we used a free paper map on which area businesses paid to be featured. Thankfully, Denise had seen the value in that investment. After cruising down a few sunny blocks, we hit the town's so-called arts district: a cluster of antiques stores, a chain-saw sculptor whose wood pelicans graced the sidewalk, and Denise Sawicki's home studio. Painted salmon pink, the beach-box-style home was plastered in collages of sea glass and driftwood.

With Toby standing beside me, I rang the doorbell. The muralist herself answered, cracking the door just wide enough for me to recognize her face from her photo. She was short—no taller than me. Intense yet also soft. She didn't look like a killer. Then again, what did a killer look like? Last summer, I'd bumped into one repeatedly and didn't even know it.

"Hey there." I wished I'd rehearsed what I was going to say. I heard panting and saw, behind the door, a pink tongue and yellow retriever legs.

"Do we have an appointment?" Denise asked. "This isn't a gallery. I don't do tours or anything." She was going to close the door.

I held up a hand. "Please. We don't mean to disturb you."

"We're big fans of your work," Toby put in.

She scowled.

"Would it be possible to have a moment of your time?" I asked.

"You're having it right now."

"The thing is," I said, as she made to close the door again. "The dojo murder," I said.

The dog stopped panting. Underneath a smock dabbed with every color imaginable, Denise Sawicki's shoulders slackened. "I've been wondering when somebody was going to figure that out. Come on in."

63

The artist disappeared inside her home.

I sent up a silent prayer of gratitude that Toby was with me. If Denise came flying around the corner waving a palette knife, he would disarm her. With his warm hand on my shoulder, we edged inside, ducking around a hanging mobile made of oyster shells. The yellow lab was swaybacked and rheumy-eyed and shed dusty fur when I gave him a scratch.

"Hello?" Toby called. "Miss Sawicki?"

"Denise." We followed her voice into the kitchen, where she stood, flyswatter in one hand, bag of microwaved popcorn in the other. "You police?" she asked.

"Far from it." I introduced myself and was grateful she didn't recognize my name. "This is Toby Dodge. He owns Cattail Family Martial Arts."

Denise eyeballed him. "I remember you."

"The police have been stumped by the initials D.S. on the sign-up sheet," I said.

"Not y'all, though."

"Not anymore." I told her about recognizing the pink letters signed to the mural inside Sanctuary Bungalow.

"Sanctuary was one of my first-ever commissions," she said. "Years ago. I was barely drinking age when I decorated those walls. I assumed someone would have painted over those scenes by now. I was pretty tickled to learn they're still there, and that the sunlight hasn't damaged them too much. Beautiful place,

Mustang Beach. Anyway, if the police come knocking, I'll tell them the same thing I'm about to tell you: Heather Westerly owes me money."

"Oh?" I cocked my head. "*Dr.* Heather Westerly, the equine veterinarian?"

"She's been blowing off my calls and texts. That morning—the day they found that guy dead in the dojo—I had taken the ferry over to Cattail Island. Hadn't been in years. My destination was the Casa Coquina. Where Heather was staying."

"She's still there," I said.

"I never made it to the B and B, because I spotted Heather on my way there. She was walking down the street not a half block away. I'd never met her in person, but we'd FaceTimed often enough for me to recognize her. She went into the dojo, so I did too."

"You explained to me that you weren't there for a workout," Toby said. "You only needed a quick word with Heather."

"Which you were fine with," Denise said, nodding. "But you still insisted I sign in. I just scribbled my initials. Figured that'd be good enough."

"And I didn't notice, because that Cooper guy was shoving a pair of gloves in my face, insisting on sparring with me."

Denise lunged for a fly that had landed on the counter, but missed. I noticed a splatter of paint on her chin. "So I went into the big room where Heather was doing karate moves or whatever," she said. "I was only inside the dojo for a minute or so. That's all the time I needed to look her in the eye and let her know, in no uncertain terms, that that if my PayPal account wasn't flush within the next few days, I was taking matters to the good old internet. If my issue went viral, that might inspire her to settle up."

"What did she say?" I asked.

"Nothing."

"Did you notice anything strange or suspicious going on in-side the dojo? A weird vibe, a tense exchange of dialogue—anything?"

Denise thought for a moment before shrugging. "My very presence inside that building was probably the weirdest thing."

"What does Heather owe you money for?" I asked. "A mural?"

"She commissioned a—well, I guess you could call it a self-portrait."

What did that mean? Toby and I shared a glance. "Could we see this self-portrait?" he asked.

"I was hoping you'd say that." She smiled wryly. "It hasn't felt right, keeping it all to myself."

Behind her home, Denise's workspace addition was big enough to shelter a propellor plane or two. The scale of the building, combined with the gigantic canvases it housed, made me feel about the size of a blade of grass. Gargantuan paintings in vari-ous stages of completion adorned the walls. One showed sun-flowers waltzing in the wind, their height towering, their faces bigger than turkey platters. Another painting showed wide-eyed children reading books as rainbows and spacecraft zoomed from the pages.

"Whoa," I said.

"I'm doing that one for the library," she said of the reading-themed one.

Toby and I strolled, spinning around three-sixty, taking in the scenes. At least according to my untrained eye, Denise's art-istry had progressed since her mustang-mural days. These im-ages were more realistic, the colors more vibrant, the overall effect of general wonderment more profound.

And when we came face-to-face with the biggest canvas of all, propped against the far wall, Toby and I gasped.

64

Mm-hmm," Denise said. "That's my reaction whenever I lay eyes on her too, and I made the darn thing."

The canvas itself—much larger than your average garage door—must have cost a pretty penny. It showed a magical night-time beachscape, with purple comets reflected in the water and the moon illuminating sea creatures underneath the waves. The focal point: larger-than-life Heather, about fifteen years younger than she actually was, sitting astride a muscle-strapped warrior horse. Elaborate braids cascaded around her shoulders. Furs made an X across her chest, leaving her muscular midriff bare. Studded leather armbands accentuated dainty but defined biceps and triceps, and her tan, sinewy leg ended in a sexy medieval bootie. In the bottom corner, against moonlit sand, slanted the now-familiar *D.S.*, in Denise's signature salmon pink.

"Oh." I stepped backward and tipped my head up. I noticed a square-jawed merman in the surf, gazing up lustily at warrior-maiden Heather. His eight-pack ab muscles glistened; his tail poked suggestively above a wave. "It's . . ."

"Go ahead. Say whatever you want. I only replicated a print-out Heather Westerly sent in the mail. I don't know where she got it. She must have made it with Photoshop or a meme app or something like that. It was rudimentary, but enough to give me an idea of what she wanted."

On Thursday afternoon, I'd observed a tipsy Heather Westerly lovingly take something out of the frunk of her Tesla. That some-thing bore the same dimensions as a standard sheet of paper.

Had it been a copy of the printout?

"Heather emailed me," Denise said. "We went back and forth. I told her I wasn't a high-fantasy artist. She didn't care. She knew I was competent, she knew I went macro, she knew I could paint horses, she knew I was relatively local. I ticked all her boxes, so she hired me." The artist twisted her hair off her shoulders and pinned it in place with the flyswatter. Her dog had followed us, shuffling inside the workspace. He now lowered himself with a groan to the concrete floor. Denise tossed him a piece of pop-corn. "Everybody's into something funky, or different," she said. "She wanted a portrait of, like, herself as Xena: Warrior Princess or something. Okay. Cool. But I need my money."

"Of course," Toby said. "I get that."

I shifted left, taking in colossal Heather from a patch of sun-light slanting in through a window. The woman was attracted to high fantasy. The books, the art. It was only natural she'd want to put herself inside that world. How heady the prospect must have been, to be portrayed as an object of beauty, imbued with power.

The equine veterinarian's secrecy made sense. If I'd spent—several thousand dollars, I'd guess?—on a portrait of this ilk, I'd want to keep it under wraps too. Hiding a ninety-square-inch sheet of paper was one thing. This?

"Where is she going to put it?" I asked. "She's house hunting in Cattail for a permanent place to live, but most of the homes there don't have that much wall space." Finally able to wrench free of the strange hold the painting had on me, I turned to Denise. "Is that why she's not paying you? Because it's dawning on her that she just won't have the space?"

"It's dawning on her that she doesn't have the money. Last week, I texted her a pic of the finished product, and she hearted it right away. Then she FaceTimed me, boo-hooing about how she'd recently overspent on a car and had underestimated the expenses of moving and buying a home. And now she wasn't sure if she'd even be able to afford rent, never mind a mortgage. She said she'd be paying off student loans for the next twenty-five years. She said she loved my painting but didn't want to dip into her savings, which is pretty skimpy. Then she begged me for a layaway option."

"I'm guessing your answer was no," Toby said.

"Denise Sawicki Arts does *not* do layaway."

I nodded. As I had recently discovered, Cattail Island had become a difficult place for a single person to get established, home-wise. Bargain starter homes—either for sale or lease—were nearly impossible to come by. I felt for Heather, who certainly wasn't alone in having a strained relationship with money. I felt for Denise too, because making a living as an artist wasn't easy.

"Can y'all help me get what I'm owed?" she asked.

"Contact Cattail police," Toby said.

"Ask for Detective Iona Fusco," I said. "Tell her I sent you. Tell her everything."

65

The ferry pushed steadily through the low waves of the Pamlico. Toby had gone for refreshments. I sat in the Wagoneer passenger seat as my stomach pitched. Caressing my aching belly, I considered asking the nice-looking couple in the next car if they had any Dramamine but decided against it. I wasn't suffering from seasickness. I was suffering from dread. Gnawing, nagging unease, twisting my insides into a Gordian knot.

True, the encounter with Denise had been strangely satisfying. Heather Westerly was holding out on Denise. Fusco would set that to rights, I was certain.

But there were other concerns. Bigger ones. A lot of them.

To begin with, as far as I knew, Tigress was still missing.

There'd been no additional headway into the mystery of the man in the Zimmerman T-shirt running on Mustang Beach.

Zero clues had emerged as to who had torched my Little Free Library.

Addison Battle was nowhere to be found.

And the most worrisome tangle of all: Seth Goodnow's murderer was still on the loose.

Fresh air. I needed it like I'd been trapped inside a sauna.

Exiting the Wagoneer, I joined several people at the nearest railing. Something low on the horizon had caught their attention, causing exclamations of awe. I assumed it was a school of dolphins racing alongside the boat, but that wasn't the object of their fascination. Causing the commotion—even inspiring a few people to snap photos—was a cloud. Not counting a couple of foggy dawns, it was the first cloud in weeks to appear in the vicinity of Cattail Island. It looked like a giant had dipped a huge sponge into pink paint and dabbed it onto the sky. As the minutes passed, the cloud morphed from a mammalian shape into something more serpentine.

"Your uncle might get his wish." Toby had found me. He handed over a bottle of water.

"What do you mean?" I asked.

He pointed to the cloud. "A good old-fashioned Outer Banks rain."

"Oh. Yeah. Wouldn't that be nice." I tried to wrangle my thoughts. Toby was right: a cloud bore the possibility of sorely needed rain, of one of those unpredicted storms Hudson had talked about, so fast and localized they don't allow time for preparation. And yet, my mood remained gloomy.

It all came back to the sign-up sheet. Everyone who'd put down their John Hancock had checked out.

Take Heather Westerly. She'd lied about not knowing who D.S. was. She reported having seen only four people that morning in the dojo—when she knew there'd been five, because Denise had confronted her. Heather's lie probably hadn't been to cover up any involvement with Seth's murder. She simply didn't want anybody to know about her commissioned self-portrait. And how she'd stiffed the artist.

Heather Westerly didn't have any reason to kill Seth Goodnow.

Neither, for that matter, did the artist herself, Denise Sawicki. She'd only stopped in at Cattail Family Martial Arts to have a face-to-face with a noncompliant client. Or so she claimed.

"Do you believe her?" I asked Toby. "Denise."

"Every word."

"Me too."

That left Cooper Payne. Frankly, though, the guy didn't come off as smart enough to get away with murder.

Which brought me to my non-sign-up sheet suspect, Ezra Metcalfe. He had seemed genuinely distressed that Seth Goodnow was strangled just a few days after getting hitched to his lovely bride. Ezra had even taken on a greenish hue when speaking about the tragic turn of events.

I was missing something. What?

Cattail Island approached. I saw the smile of beach that was Smile Beach. It looked so much bigger now without the old fishing pier. Farther south, the lighthouse jabbed above the treetops. Mid-island, the masts of the replica pirate ship poked the sky.

My heart swelled. Home.

A home I wanted to protect.

I longed to reconnect with the people there. To tell my uncle I had his yarn. To inform police that D.S. was Denise Sawicki, and that she and Heather Westerly were off the hook.

I got out my phone. No signal. The ferry still hadn't sailed out of the dead zone.

"We should get back to the pride and joy," Toby said, meaning his vehicle.

On the way, we passed the restroom, where a whiff of cleaning solution walloped me. A similar antiseptic odor had hit me in the shed behind Ivy and Dominick's rental cottage.

That shed.

How strange that it had been eat-a-meal-on-the-floor spotless.

During high school and community college, I'd worked as a

cleaner of rental cottages. One thing I was never expected to tackle, ever? Storage sheds.

Even if the owner gave it a regular deep clean, wouldn't the strong disinfectant smell have faded during the O'Neills' stay?

That shed had been cleaned recently. I was sure of it.

Why?

I climbed into the passenger seat, and Toby climbed behind the wheel. The people around us began stirring, jabbing away at their devices.

Service.

I whipped out my phone and could practically feel the dopamine firing through my brain with each notification that popped up. Jurecki had called. Fusco too.

"I got a new recruit," Toby whispered as he listened to his voicemail messages. His eyes sparkled.

"I told you things would get back to normal," I said.

"Mind if I call the parent back?"

"Go for it." I was glad he was distracted. Because I had something urgent to attend to. I googled Dominick O'Neill. The first few relevant hits were work related. An internal corporate newsletter singling him out for outstanding quarterly performance; a conference attendee master list; things like that.

And then something unexpected appeared, from a weekly paper in Massachusetts. It seemed so random, I almost skimmed right over it. A three-year-old news story about a sit-in. *In an effort to raise awareness about bullying, a small group of concerned parents staged a peaceful protest during last night's school board meeting* . . . A color photograph showed solemn-faced twenty- and thirty-somethings lining the walls of a classroom. I easily identified Ivy and Dominick by their striking good looks. Dominick draped an arm over his wife's shoulders as she held up a sign: CHOOSE KINDNESS.

I scanned the article. It appeared the O'Neills hadn't always homeschooled their daughter. I'd put money on the likelihood that once upon a time, back at this school in their former town, Cadence had been the victim of bullying. The incident might have influenced their decision to homeschool—and maybe even to move out of state too. It also occurred to me that the O'Neills did the right thing according to that book I'd come across, *Bullies: How They're Made, How to Defeat Them.* The O'Neills had stood up for themselves.

The ferry sounded its foghorn, and I jumped at the sudden blast. Toby's warm hand rested on my arm. "Hey," he said. "You good?"

I forced a smile. "I should touch base with Fusco. And we need to get you to your Kids-N-Parents class."

"I'll make it. Right on time."

The ferry approached the dock. On deck, there was the usual scramble—the slamming of car doors, the wheezing up of engines. The line wasn't moving yet. I dialed Fusco.

She answered without a hello. "What's the information?"

"Hi to you too. I found out who D.S. is, but she checks out. At first blush, anyway."

"I'll be the judge of that. D.S. is a she?"

"An artist named Denise Sawicki. She lives in Jarvis Harbor." As I explained, the foghorn blasted again.

"Are you on the ferry?"

"That's neither here nor there. Listen, have you come across a wedding guest named Dominick O'Neill? He's renting the cottage next door to Naomi Goodnow. He was a colleague of Seth's. He was transferred out of Seth's office a while back." Dominick's transfer. Was there more to that story? "Some people—including Seth's own widow—had the opinion that Seth was not a very nice person," I added.

"So I understand," Fusco said.

"What if Seth did something to Dominick, and Dominick retaliated?"

"Let me guess. This is all wild conjecture, and you have no proof, and you're just following a hunch."

"I'm not a policewoman, Fusco."

"That's right. You're not."

66

Toby steered into the queue as, one by one, vehicles rolled off the ferry. My bottom lip was becoming shredded as I chewed on it. He reached out and brushed his knuckles against my cheek. "Bad habit," he said. "So—Dominick O'Neill? I knew you had something on your mind. Do you think . . ."

"I don't know what to think," I said, clasping his hand.

"What are you up to tonight?"

"Oh, nothing much. I'll just be chilling with Hudson and Scupper."

"Good. Lay low. Get some rest. That way, I won't have to worry about you."

Get some rest? Not an option.

After Toby drove off, I peeled out of my parking spot, zooming for Love Beach Trail. Balanced on my dashboard with the volume on high, my phone played my messages. The first: Hudson, wondering where I'd been and if I wanted to join him and Antoinette for supper. They were going to hit Bravo Tacos. *And about that* thing, he added, in a way that let me know Antoinette had been right there. He didn't want to give away the surprise of the hobbyhorse but in typical Hudson fashion was being totally obvious. *What's going on with our thing, you know?*

Jurecki had tried getting back to me and urged me to ring again immediately, but I considered that task already accomplished, since I'd just hung up with Fusco.

Before long, I was parking in front of the O'Neills' cottage. It looked so quaint with its porch swing and nodding irises, like it could have been sketched onto a greeting card. Maybe Fusco was right after all—I had read too many books and was letting my imagination get the better of me.

Ivy came to the door wearing one of her husband's T-shirts over a bikini. Despite the casual attire, she looked amazingly well put together, as usual. Not a hair out of place, and makeup so light you'd assume she wasn't wearing any at all. "You're just in time," she said. "Dominick took Cadence down to the beach to hunt ghost crabs. I was just going to join them. Come with us," she said, pulling on a pair of pajama-weight short-shorts.

"Actually." I was disappointed that I'd missed Dominick, but I could play his absence to my advantage by pumping Ivy for information. "I'm here for more yarn."

"Of course. Let's go out back." She flipped on the outside lights, and we headed to the shed. "I can't believe it's our last night here. I'm going to miss this place."

"You'll have to come back sometime." Following her, I thumbed out a text to Fusco.

> Dominick O'Neill is on Love Beach with his young daughter.
> I know you don't believe me but something weird is going on
> here. You said yourself it's the nice ones who crack. This
> Dominick guy is nice, you know? Really nice.

I sent it. Ahead of me, Ivy was tapping away on her phone too.

Once again, I stepped inside the speckless shed. The bare light-bulb buzzed. "Great," I said, reaching into the basket of yarn. I stuffed a skein into my bulging bag. "Thanks."

"You've still got the yarn from before?" she asked.

"I haven't had a chance to drop it off. It's for my uncle, for something he's making, and I just have a feeling he'll need more. In case he messes up the first time."

Ivy's eyes tightened. Tension crept into her face. All week, she'd seemed relaxed. Concerned for others. The day Naomi flew the red bird kite, Ivy had consoled her. Even when Cooper Payne showed up, Ivy had been a rock.

She wasn't a rock right now, though. She was fidgeting. Picking at the hem of her shirt. She moved over to the doorway, blocking it.

"It's so clean in here," I said.

"Right? Yeah. It was like that. The whole cottage was super clean."

"Y'all didn't clean it?"

"The shed?" She barked out a laugh. "Why would we clean the shed?"

"Yeah. I don't know why I said that. Cool old wardrobe, huh?" I smoothed my palm against the polished door.

She put a hand on top of mine. Her fingers were tremoring icicles. She shook her head, just once, a tiny movement, as if to say, *Don't*.

"What?" I asked.

She removed her hand. "Nothing."

67

I pulled open the wardrobe. The shelf at eye level was piled with old matchbooks. They were all the same, blue with big S's. Someone had collected them, or had a bulk amount left over.

Alarm seized me, made me shiver, made my jaw clench. In the past few days, at least one of these very matchbooks had been transported outside this wardrobe. It had arrived at my Little Free Library and been abandoned there on the assumption that the Cattale Queen would burn completely.

I didn't quite understand what I was seeing, other than the possibility—the likelihood?—that the O'Neills had something to do with that fire.

Trying to hide my fear, I fake-coughed, then followed it up with a sound of admiration, as if the contents of the wardrobe were all so quirkily interesting, just like all the other knick-knacks in the shed.

That was when I noticed what occupied the lower shelf. Bungee cords.

My skin cinched. My mouth went dry.

The murder weapon, Dr. Scarboro had told me, was a cable of some sort, approximately five millimeters in diameter.

Five millimeters sounded about the right thickness for a bungee cord.

"You tried to burn down my Little Free Library," I blurted. "It was you."

"I thought it was dramatic enough to get your attention." Ivy's voice sounded so different. Like a frozen blade. "I thought it would make you stay away. You didn't. And you're going to wish you did."

68

The smell of camphor assaulted my nose, and an arm like a tree branch wrapped around my neck and squeezed.

I couldn't breathe.

I slapped the hairy arm. I tried to do the move Toby had showed me, forcing my head back, but I couldn't budge. I was pinned tight.

I scratched, raked, and clawed.

"Ow!" The exclamation was high-pitched, like a hyena's. "Stop struggling," the male voice said. "Nothing bad is going to happen to you. We just need you to go to sleep for a quick sec."

Absolutely not. I needed to stay awake.

I became still, putting all my energy toward keeping my eyes open.

My lungs burned. My knees buckled. Cooper Payne guided me to the floor. The concrete felt warm against my cheek. I saw, sideways, a nail protruding from a baseboard, something fibrous and white stuck to the head. A tiny piece of paper towel.

Someone had cleaned.

Ivy had cleaned. She'd missed a spot. There was a stain on the nail, a tiny, wine-colored slice.

Blood.

Seth Goodnow's blood.

I saw his dead hand, that morning in the dojo. The bandage. The blood seeping through. I blinked, and the image spun into stars.

Scarboro had said that the cut on Seth's hand had been caused by something irregular.

Like an old nailhead.

I kicked, but my feet cycled air. My lungs were blazing.

Keep your eyes open, Padget. Stay here. What could I see right now? The nail sticking out of the baseboard. The speck of dried blood. The paper towel fiber waving in a swirl of air.

Seth Goodnow had been here, in this shed. He had struggled and died here. In this very spot.

Again, I tried to gouge my fingernails into Cooper's arm, but my knuckles went slack.

"Give in to it, Callie," Cooper said. "Make it easy on yourself."

No. I splayed open my eyes.

But they drooped shut.

69

Motion.
  Bumps and turns.
A car window whacking my forehead.
My eyes opened.
I was in the back seat, jostling around. A bungee cord cut into my wrists, squeezing them together. My ankles too.
Trees flew by.
I lunged for the door handle, but Cooper's arm was around me, pulling me to the center of the seat. "Don't struggle," he said as he scooted closer. We hit a pothole and bounced and his stubble scratched my temple.
It was dark, but I recognized the head of smooth brown hair in the driver's seat. Ivy locked eyes with me in the rearview mirror. "This'll all be over soon, Callie."
I tried to snap the mental puzzle pieces into place. Ivy O'Neill? She'd been right under my nose the entire time, and I'd missed her. I still didn't understand exactly what had gone on—but I understood enough to surmise that Cooper was the brawn of this operation, while Ivy was the closest thing it had to brains.
I wanted to yell, *What in the hell is going on here?* but my voice was shot. It hurt to swallow, as if I had a whole apple stuck inside my throat. Cooper had done some sort of choke hold wrestling move on me. Made me pass out. They'd tied me up and stuffed me in this car and now they were taking me to . . .
"Mustang Beach," I croaked.

The other Cattail beaches had people on them. Kids searching for crabs. Lovers gazing upward in hopes of seeing a shooting star. All Mustang Beach had on it was horses. Horses couldn't tell secrets. Ivy would be able to access the parking lot and march me down the footpath. That police officer was long gone; no one would see.

Hot tears tugged at my eyes. I wasn't ready to die. My life was finally making sense in a way it never had back in Charlotte. I had a job that suited me. A guy I was extremely fond of, and the feeling was mutual. The beginnings of a friendship, in Geri-Lynn. I had Hudson, and Antoinette, and Scupper, and Tin Man, and . . .

Someone was sitting in the front passenger seat. On the other side of the headrest, I could make out a thin frame. A frail shoulder. Recognition shuddered up my spine. "Addison?" I kicked the seat. "Mr. Battle? Are you okay?"

"Don't wake him," Ivy said.

"Callie?" came Addison's creaky voice. "Is that you back there?"

An absurd laugh escaped me. I was simultaneously overjoyed that Addison Battle was alive—and horrified by the prospect of Ivy and Cooper holding him captive for the past several days. "Are you hurt?" I asked. "What happened to you?"

"I should have gone straight to the police," he said. "But I just didn't trust my own old eyes."

"What did you see?"

"I brought this all upon myself. And I got *you* wrapped up in it—"

"Oh, Addison, I got myself wrapped up in it. Where've they been keeping you?"

"My rental cottage," Cooper said. "It's a sweet little joint. I gave him the room with the queen-size bed. It's not like he's been chained inside a dungeon."

"They locked me in," Addison said. "Sometimes I was tied up. I think they've been drugging me—"

"You got three square meals a day, old man," Cooper said. "*And* regular protein shakes."

"Laced with something strong enough to take down a Clydesdale, I bet," I said. Poor Addison, slipping in and out of consciousness inside a strange bedroom, too incapacitated to make a run for it. His voice wasn't exactly full-throttled, and even if he did wake up enough to cry for help, who would have heard him over the crashing of the ocean, the blare of portable speakers, the clattering of horseshoes?

So the old barber had lied—he *did* go to the barbershop Sunday morning. "What did you see, Addison?" I asked. "What should you have told the police?"

"Enough chitchat," Ivy said. "Face front, Addison. Close your eyes and let the Dramamine do its job. That reminds me . . ." She tossed something into the back seat. A few packets landed on Cooper's lap. "Dose her," she said.

Dramamine. That was what they'd been using to keep Addison calm and compliant during his captivity. I zeroed in on a recent memory, like twisting the wheel on a pair of binoculars until the fuzzy distant thing you're trying to make out is diamond-sharp. On the couch inside Naomi's cottage, just after I'd introduced myself to Ivy and Dominick O'Neill, they told me about the fishing trip. How seasick Cadence had become. The Dramamine they'd taken. *I'm not sure it actually cured my motion sickness, but it sure did knock me out,* Ivy had said.

"Addison." I gave his seat another kick. "You have to try and stay awake."

"Relax," Cooper said. "We've given him just enough to take the edge off. For now."

"Well, I'm not taking any pills," I said.

"You'll change your mind."

The windows were cracked open, and humid air spurted in. I pulled it deep into my lungs, trying to refresh my brain. "Addison knows you murdered Seth. So you kidnapped the old man. The two of you, working together—"

"There's only one murderer in this car," Ivy said. "And you're sitting right next to him."

I wriggled away from Cooper, again lunging for the door handle. This time, my fingers grazed it, but his arm clamped around me, pulling me to him. "Sorry," he said. "Not happening."

"Dominick doesn't know?" I asked, my voice a bit steadier. The deep breaths were working. "Dominick doesn't know about any of this."

"He can never know," Ivy said. "My daughter can never know. It would kill them. It would kill *me*. You understand that, Callie. You're a reader. Readers are empathic. Like Cadence. She *understands* people. You're like that too, aren't you? That's why Cadence took a shine to you."

"This is all for her," I said. "For Cadence. Did Seth hurt her somehow? And you love her so much, you killed for her—"

"I'm nice and I'm nice and I'm so damn nice. But being nice doesn't inoculate you against bullies. No matter how nice you are, the bullies come out on top. Well, not this time. And let's be crystal clear on who did the killing." In the rearview mirror, Ivy's eyes flicked to Cooper. "Hey," she said, so loud he jumped. "Didn't we talk about stuffing a sock in her mouth? Shut her up, would you?"

There were two sides to every coin—and every person. All week, Ivy had been showing her shiny side. The makeup, the lip gloss, the pancakes from scratch. This version of her? This was the underside, and it was so dark that even Cooper Payne seemed afraid of her.

In front of me, Addison had rested his head against the window, and the slight movement of his shoulder indicated he'd fallen into slow, deep breathing.

"You're taking us to Mustang Beach?" I asked.

"I spoke with a couple surfers earlier," Ivy said. "According to them, the winds and currents have shifted and are really kicking now. Strong rips are forming off the island's southern beaches. And these rips are all outward-flowing. No more horseshoeing back to shore." She signaled for the turn, following the sign for the footpath parking lot.

"The bruise on your arm." Closing my eyes, I could see her, sitting on the couch in Naomi's cottage, the purple bruise butterflying over her elbow. How could I have missed that? "You said you got that bruise when you went deep-sea fishing. But it was too fresh. Too purple to have happened when you said it did. You got that bruise more recently, didn't you? From an altercation you had with Seth. In the shed. He was there for some reason. And something happened. And Cooper showed up and finished the job."

The silence filling the car could only mean I'd gotten it right.

In the rearview, her mouth became tight. She pulled into the parking lot.

Reaching across me, Cooper shoved open the door and shoved me out.

70

I tried to run but crashed, grunting, to the gravel. Sharp stones mashed into my cheek.

The pressure on my ankles released as Cooper whipped off the bungee cord. He hooked his hands under my armpits and set me on my feet like I was lighter than a rag doll.

I held out my bound wrists. He shook his head. "No can do."

Joining us, Ivy hit the lock button on her fob. A blue Nissan Rogue. Ohio plates. Stick-figure decals of two parents, a kid, and a dog.

"Addison's not coming?" I asked.

"He's going to die in his sleep," she said. "They'll find him here in the parking lot, curled up on the gravel. They'll assume he got disoriented, as demented senior citizens do, and—"

"That man is completely with it," I said.

"Lots of old people are. Until they're not."

"Aren't you afraid someone will come along?" I asked—even as I knew that someone showing up at this isolated footpath after dark was about as likely as snowflakes flying. The cops at that moment were likely prioritizing areas where *people*—not horses—congregated.

"We'll deal with the old man later," Cooper said. "First, we need to deal with Little Miss Crime Solver."

I addressed the slightly opened passenger window. "Addison?" I said softly. "I'm going to get you out of this. Don't worry, okay?"

His eyes remained closed, and he mumbled something I couldn't understand.

Fingers clutched my arm. It was Ivy, pulling me in the direction of the path. The same route Toby and I had taken just a few mornings ago. She set a quick pace, grinding her sandals into the wood chips. Cooper followed us.

"Believe it or not, Ivy," I said, "I understand about being nice when you don't want to be. About bottling up your true feelings. I've done that my whole life. I'm an expert at it too. A lot of women are, I think."

As we walked, her eyes searched mine. If I could just get her talking. Get her refocused on what she loved. I forced my voice to mask the panic surging inside me. "You'll feel better if you get it all off your chest. Tell me what happened. Tell me about Cadence."

"Cadence." Her eyes filled up, but she kept on walking. Her hair bounced furiously, and her purse banged against her hip. "It was all because of that day on the boat."

"When you went deep-sea fishing?"

"She hadn't said a word all morning. Seth had been trying to get her to talk, but she wasn't having it. She would just look out over the water whenever he asked her a question. She gets in moods like that, you know? Especially when she's around aggressive people. Like Seth. And then he doubled down. 'Hey Cadence, what are you into besides reading? What about music? No? What about sports? Anything? Nothing? Hello?' He was practically harassing her.

"I was just about to tell her she didn't have to talk if she didn't feel like it. But then she finally got brave and decided to pipe up. She looked at him—I can't tell you how much chutzpah it took for her to simply look at him—and she said, 'Rocks.'"

"She told me about her rock collection," I said. "In the Mother-Vine. How she polishes them and catalogs them."

"Cadence told Seth all about that too."

I trudged along, hands bungeed. My throat was screaming, my head was pounding. Behind me, there was a sloshing noise. Cooper's ever-present gallon of water. It seemed a strange time to bring it along. I heard his backpack rustling against his back too.

As the trees closed in around us, Ivy produced her cell phone, and LED light illuminated the path.

"What happened?" I asked. "What did Seth say to Cadence about her rock collection?"

"He said, 'Rocks? You're into *rocks*? Personality Plus, right here.' Then he patted her head. Cadence doesn't like anyone touching her hair. Some mornings it takes me forty-five minutes just to get it braided—which Seth knew very well, because before we moved to Ohio, Dominick had confided in him about Cadence's challenges. More than once." Ivy stopped. Her hands were tight fists, the knuckles white. "Dominick overheard the whole exchange. He was outraged with Seth. He pulled him aside, and they angry-whispered back and forth. And a minute later Seth came over and apologized. 'Cool kids like rocks,' he said. 'I forgot.' But Cadence is not stupid. She knows when she's being insulted. She knows a hollow apology when she hears one."

I held out my bound hands. "Untie me, and let's talk about all this."

"We are talking about it." She trod ahead.

Cooper gave me a shove. "Keep up."

For several minutes, no one spoke. I thought I could make out the roar of the ocean, but it was hard to tell over the scrunching of wood chips. "Ivy," I said. "Tell me more. Tell me about Naomi."

"I honestly have no idea what she saw in Seth," she said. "They never really seemed to go together. But she insisted he made her happy. She insisted he was good to her. Maybe he was. Maybe he tried hard to be a different person around her. A softer person. Naomi brings out that quality in people."

She did have that effect on me. Even when her own circumstances couldn't get any worse, she had a soothing presence.

"Did you move away from Massachusetts because Cadence was being bullied?"

"The homeschooling took care of the bullying. Dominick requested a transfer because he didn't want to work with Seth anymore. He was *that* annoying."

"Then why go to the wedding?"

"Naomi, of course." Ivy's voice hitched. Tears caught in her throat. "Naomi and I became really good friends. Even after we moved to Ohio, she and I stayed in touch."

"Why was Seth in your shed that morning?"

"He had just gotten back from his workout. He came to the cottage and told me he bought Naomi a kite. There was something wrong with the handle, he said, only he didn't discover the flaw until after he'd already paid for it. He'd poked through all the junk on offer in his own cottage but wasn't satisfied. So he came over wanting to know if I had anything that he might be able to use to fix the kite."

My mind sped back to Thursday morning, kite flying with Naomi. She'd mentioned Seth had wanted to repair the handle but never got around to it.

The truth was, he'd tried. "You invited him in?" I prompted.

"'Why don't you take a look in the shed?' I told him. He followed me through to the back deck. Dominick and Cade were there, reading. Seth waved hello and said some wiseass things to Dominick. They were just trading jabs back and forth, like guys do. Only Seth's jabs were over the top. Over the line. That's the way Seth was. He always took things too far. Anyway, Dominick said something jokey, and Seth replied, *Whatever, bed wetter.* I get that it was guy talk, but that was not the thing you should say in front of a kid. Especially a kid who struggles with that particular issue. It's been going on for years."

"What did Cadence do?" I asked. "When Seth called Dominick that."

"Burst into tears and ran inside the cottage. You see, a couple years ago, Cade slept over at a friend's house. She wet the bed. The next Monday at school, that *friend* told their whole class. And by lunchtime, the entire school was calling her the Bed Wetter. Cade the Bed Wetter O'Neill."

"That's why you started homeschooling," I said.

"I wasn't about to leave her to those evil little jackals. We gave it some time, at first. Dominick and I tried to rally some support. To put an end to the torture. The teachers got behind us, and the administration announced they were going to *take measures.* But weeks went by, and nothing changed. Meanwhile, Cadence got off the bus every afternoon a sobbing wreck. The other kids teased her about her cowlick. They teased her about the way she used to walk with her toes turned in. They teased her about her freckles, and she doesn't even have that many! Yeah, she's quirky. Fair enough. But did they have to make her life unlivable? Was there seriously *nothing more* the adults could have done? Two of her main tormentors were children of school board members. And that was that." Ivy's bitterness was palpable. She and Dominick had fought—and lost. An entire community had let them down.

"Since I started homeschooling Cade," Ivy said, "she's gotten more confident. I think she was starting to put all the agony behind her, and forgive the cruelty. So, when Seth made fun of her on the boat, and then showed up outside our shed slinging around *bed wetter* as an insult—"

"You cracked," I said.

"He's a grown-ass man, for God's sake. Dominick ran inside after our daughter, and Seth just shrugged and went into the shed. Dominick came back out and said he'd convinced Cade to go to the beach. I said I'd join them as soon as I got rid of Seth. I went into the shed. At first, he was just standing there, taking in all the clutter. Surveying it. Then he found the basket of bungees in the wardrobe. He pulled out a cord and was checking it out. Considering it for his kite, I guess. You know what he said? 'You've got a touchy kid, there, don't you?'"

"That was the last straw?" I asked. "The thing that made you snap?"

"I jumped on him. I wasn't thinking. I just—attacked him. I'd never done anything like that before. It was like all this raw emotion just volcanoed up inside of me and erupted. Seth fought back, of course. He pushed me off pretty easily. That's when I got the bruise. And just like that, it was over. It really was."

"And then I showed up," Cooper said. "The couple renting the cottage next door to mine? They're hauling around this trailer, and their bungee crapped out on them. They were worried they wouldn't be able to strap down their big cooler properly, so I told them I'd hook them up."

"Doing your life coach's bidding," I said. "Looking for opportunities to help people."

"That's exactly right. They were going to go to that crappy little island hardware store, but I told them to save their money. Everybody had been talking about all the junk in those rental cottages. I figured I'd see if there were bungee cords. After my workout."

"What a great guy you are," I said.

"I had no idea Seth was planning on stopping by their cottage too. He and I didn't really speak, that morning in the dojo. We were still pretty sore at each other about something that had gone on between us at work."

"What happened when you got to the O'Neills' cottage?"

"No one was there. I went around back and heard a commotion. When I walked into the shed, Seth looked like he was going to attack Ivy. Or like he just *had* attacked her. I didn't know what was going on, but my instincts kicked in. I grabbed the bungee off him and—I was just trying to subdue him, honestly. I figured we'd talk it all out, once everybody got calmed down. I was actually thinking of trying out the conflict resolution techniques my life coach has been teaching me. But Seth was fighting back, hard. Kicking and punching. When I got him down on the floor, he cut his hand pretty bad. I held on to the bungee. His eyes were bulging but he still struggled. 'Calm down, buddy,' I kept telling him. 'Calm down, and I'll let up.' But by the time he started relaxing, that was it. He was gone. I guess I didn't know my own strength. I'd just worked out at Cattail Family Martial Arts, but it was super easy and light, on account of there not being any *real* equipment, so I was feeling a little revved up, and—" Snuffling, Cooper wiped his cheeks.

"So you followed through with the bungee cord favor."

"Later that day, after Ivy and I . . . took care of everything. My neighbors were very grateful."

"Did you give them the *same* bungee cord? The one you used to kill Seth?"

"Of course not. That one's in my backpack." He patted the shoulder strap. "I kept it close, all week. Figured I'd throw it out at a rest stop on the way home. When I'm finally able to leave this pit of an island."

All three of us had stopped walking. I stood there, my jaw

hanging open. Ivy shined her phone light on Cooper, whose breathing was ragged.

"You really are pretty much an idiot, Cooper," she said.

"What a pair you two make," I said. "You are beyond absurd. You are pathetic, atrocious, despicable, and—"

"We had to think fast," she said. "It was such a beautiful, warm day, thank God. It meant just about everybody on the block was down at the water. The first thing that occurred to me was to go through Seth's wallet. I don't know why. I was desperate. Panicked."

"And you found the receipt," I said. From Dragonfly, Toby's mother's store. With the message scrawled on the back.

"It was obviously special to Seth," she said. "At first we didn't know what it was or why he had it—"

"But I put two and two together." Cooper had collected himself. He puffed out his chest, as if bravery was needed to tell this part of the tale. "The guy who owns the dojo? That morning, when I worked out there, I noticed his ink. The dragonfly tattoo on his arm was a fancier version of the one on the receipt in Seth's wallet. The note on the back was signed *Toby Dodge*—and the dojo guy's name is Toby Dodge. It was like a gift. A sign from the universe. *Here's how to cover this up. Here's how to get away with what you've done.*"

"You thought a death threat written by a kid thirty years ago was going to hold water?"

He shrugged. "It worked, didn't it? Threw the police off our scent."

"We moved fast," she said. "I backed my car up to the shed and—"

"I threw him in the back."

That's where the sand on Seth's legs had come from: the floor of the shed. Before she cleaned it so thoroughly.

I fought off a wave of nausea. "You didn't think to take a time-out? To ask yourselves if there was a better way to proceed? Why not call the authorities? Explain the situation—"

"And live out the rest of my days in prison?" she said. "Miss watching my baby girl grow up?"

"I was *not* about to blow a shot at the MMA on account of Seth freaking Goodnow." Cooper poked me in the ribs, and we all continued walking until we reached the ramp to the observation platform. The surf pounded. The moon was high in the sky. I scanned the beach but didn't make out any horses.

"What about the cut on Seth's hand?" I asked. "From the nail in the shed. You washed his wound. Made it look like he'd treated it himself."

"She even put Neosporin on it," he said.

"And then you drove to the dojo?"

"Yeah," he said. "And then things *really* spiraled out of control."

71

Ivy dimmed her flashlight app. Moonlight replaced the artificial glare. The railing stretched before us, guarding a four- or five-foot drop to the sand. She and Cooper surveyed the ocean.

Were they experiencing doubts? I chewed my lip at the prospect of them having a sudden change of heart.

But—no. He swung a leg over the railing and dropped from view, landing with a thud. "Who's next?"

"Now you," she said. "Go."

"Please untie my hands. I promise I won't try any—"

"No way."

"Addison saw you behind the dojo," I said. "When you pulled up." Perhaps he'd forgotten something at his barbershop, or thought to double-check the drippy faucet. Perhaps he'd wanted to peek inside the window like a vacationer might, and marvel at all the blades he'd sharpened; all the conversations he'd had; his long, work-filled life.

Whatever the reason, Addison Battle had shunned routine and reported to his place of business on Sunday morning.

He'd witnessed a loathsome sight—but he didn't believe his own eyes. Even after he heard the news that someone had indeed been murdered, he kept mum. As a weak old man, living alone, he must have feared the same vicious fate would come down upon him if he tattled. Or maybe he simply didn't want to complicate his unassuming existence.

My recent encounters with Addison Battle suddenly clicked.

How, at the MotherVine, he'd asked if my eyes ever played tricks on me. And how, when I dropped by his house, he'd trembled and warned me to stay away.

Sunday morning. If only Toby and I had arrived at the dojo just a few minutes earlier. If only we hadn't lingered so long, right in this very spot on the observation platform. We'd have been too late to save Seth, of course. But if Toby and Addison and I—all three of us, together—had intercepted Cooper and Ivy, the week's events would have been extremely different . . .

"Queen Street was busy," Cooper was saying. "So we investigated the back roads. We found the little lot behind the martial arts place."

I pictured the O'Neills' SUV pulling up to the rear dojo door as the morning sun warmed the gravel and the birds tweeted and flowers scented the breeze. I imagined Ivy and Cooper jumping out, peeking through the dojo windows, actually thinking they might get away with everything.

"The coast was clear," Ivy said. "We opened up the back of my SUV—and a car drove past. An old Ford with fins."

"Addison Battle," I said.

"We didn't know that at the time. We couldn't see who was behind the wheel. The car slowed down, then sped up and drove off, and then the street was quiet again. Empty."

"Addison thought he saw a body in the back of your SUV," I said. "But his vision is going. And he was scared to death— rightly so—of you two wingnuts—"

"Enough talking." She prodded me. "Get over that railing."

Cooper held out his arms, giving me a spot to aim for. The man had more guile than I'd given him credit for. I'd assumed he wasn't smart enough to get away with murder. Evidently, though, when he joined wits with the likes of Ivy O'Neill, he was.

I'd be damned if I was going to end up washed up on a beach where some unsuspecting vacationer would stumble upon my bloated body. If I was going to escape, the time was now. The muscle of this operation was down below, on the other side of the railing. The brainpower stood right beside me. And she was my size.

Granted, my hands were tied. But I was a runner. If I could break past her . . .

"Don't even think about it." She retrieved a bulky object from her bag. It appeared chintzy, like a plastic toy. She pointed it at me, her index finger hugging the trigger.

"Is that a water pistol?" I asked.

"It's a flare gun. Dominick and I keep it in the glove compartment, in case of emergencies."

"You mean that's not even a real gun?"

"A flare gun is a real gun."

"She's right," Cooper said. "I checked it out. That thing fires hollow-tip twelve-gauge cartridges. I don't think that would feel too good, blasting into you at a hundred and twenty-five feet per second. I wouldn't want to get hit with one at close range, I can tell you that."

"Your turn," she said. "Get over that railing."

I obeyed, swinging one leg over, followed by the other. I tumbled awkwardly into Cooper's arms, somehow landing on my feet. Ivy followed suit. Waving her weapon, she made me lead. I stumbled over the sand toward the crashing waves.

Panic coursed through me. *Keep talking, Padget. And keep them talking.* "So neither of you could figure out whose car had driven past," I said. "Is that it? You took care of the Seth situation, but you still had a big problem: what to do about the driver who'd slowed down."

"We figured it was only a matter of time before that person

came forward," Ivy said. "Identified my car, or provided a good enough description of one or both of us."

"Between the two of us, we combed the whole damn island for that Ford," Cooper said. "On foot. By car. Two whole days of searching high and low—"

"The Ford eluded you," I said. "Because for most of that time, it was parked in Addison's driveway on Hyde Road, where the locals live, and where vacationers don't go. You must have finally spotted it in front of the barbershop on Tuesday, when he started his workweek. Why kidnap him, though? Why not just . . ."

"She wanted me to do something permanent," he said. "But I just couldn't bring myself to put any kind of hurt on the old guy. He reminds me so much of my grandfather. She was right about one thing, though: we had to get him off the streets, before he went whispering to anybody sitting in his barber's chair."

"We weren't exactly sure what the endgame was going to be," she said. "We just knew that we needed to buy ourselves some time."

"On Wednesday," he continued, "I stopped by his shop. I waited in my car until a customer left. The old man came outside for some fresh air. I took him by surprise. I felt bad doing the choke hold on him. He dropped like a fly. At least it was painless for him."

I doubted that, judging by the pain still squeezing my own throat. "How have you two been communicating?"

"Extremely carefully coded text messages," she said.

"Everything was her idea, Callie. She's been calling the shots this whole time."

"You killed someone!" Ivy said. "How could I let you call any shots after that?"

"Why come here to Mustang Beach and plant Addison's bow tie?" I asked. "A distraction? A red herring?"

"Something like that," she said. "I'd read about the footpath. It was one of the places Dominick and I had intended to bring Cadence and Unicorn. But we just didn't get around to it."

"How fortunate that you were able to squeeze in a visit here during your vacation," I said.

Cooper got out the packets he'd pocketed. He tore them open and dumped the contents into Ivy's palm.

Dramamine. For me.

We'd reached water's edge. A warm wave crashed around my ankles. I could tell by the extreme tug as it receded—a rip current was sucking it out.

I struggled against the bungee cord but only succeeded in making it slice my wrists. "This is your grand master plan? Bungee me up and force me into a rip?"

She held out a handful of the round white pills. I lunged, chopping my hands, trying to make her spill. He hooked an arm around me and pulled me away.

"You're monsters," I yelled.

"I'm not a monster," she replied. "I've done monstrous things, yes. But at the end of the day, first and foremost, I'm a mother. A really good one."

"All along, you've been acting like nothing hideous has been going on. Playing it completely cool."

"What else could I do?"

"Neither of you could skip town," I said.

"Not even after the police said we could," she said. "Because no one else from the wedding had gone home. They all stuck around—"

"Which meant you had to too," I said. "Otherwise, that would have drawn suspicion." Maybe it was even a clever chess move on Fusco's and Jurecki's parts—telling the guests they were free to leave, then waiting to see who was first to hightail it to the ferry. "*She* is the real bully here, Cooper," I said, twisting out of his grasp. "Can't you see that? She's getting you to do things you don't really want to do." He lifted an eyebrow. I had his attention. "Don't make the same mistake again, Cooper. Don't let Ivy control you like this. Be a man. Be your own man. Be an MMA man—"

"This all got wicked out of control," he said. "I'm just so sorry for everyone involved. One mistake. One moment of underestimating my high level of skill, and my extreme strength, and it led to this . . . this absolute *mess.*"

"You didn't mean to kill Seth. And I don't believe either of you really want to kill Addison Battle. Or me."

"We don't," she said. "But we're out of options."

"What excuse did you give Dominick Sunday morning?" I asked.

"Told him I was out to breakfast with old friends. Other wedding guests. People who'd traveled to Cattail for Naomi and Seth. Dominick didn't question it. At the time, the things Cooper and I did made sense to us. Now, of course, it all seems totally harebrained. But we got away with it. And we're going to get away with it again." She extended the pills toward me. "Bottoms up."

Cooper popped the cap off the jug.

The water was for me. Something to wash down the Dramamine. How considerate.

I reeled backward, toward the footpath. "You're not going to get away with this. Going to jail for killing one person is bad enough. You really want to make it three?"

"I didn't kill anybody!" she cried.

"Exactly. *You* didn't kill anyone. Why make a bad situation worse? Why make it harder on yourself than it already is? You can still choose wisely here, Ivy. Do it for your family. Do it for Cadence. A man is dead. Naomi—*your friend*—lost her husband—"

"And Cattail is going to lose a bookseller," she said. "And its barber. That's just the way it has to be."

"Try to see it from our point of view," he said. "With you and Addison gone, we get away with everything."

"We can go on living our lives. Cooper will go back to Massachusetts and I'll never see his big dumb face ever again. I'll go back to Ohio. With my husband and my sweet little girl—"

"Happily ever after," I said. To them, I was not a person. Not really. All I represented was one more task. Taking away my and Addison's ability to accuse was all that separated them from freedom. "This isn't you, Ivy." I couldn't keep the quake out of my voice. "This isn't either of you—"

"You don't know us." She aimed the flare gun at my face. "You're going into that rip with your hands tied, one way or the other. It's your choice whether you want to be awake or asleep."

Sniveling, Cooper swiped his wet cheeks. "Just take the pills. You'll go right to sleep—"

"If you think I'm taking *any* of those, you can forget about it." I glanced past Ivy, past the gun, at the ocean. A vast blanket, glistening under moonlight. My knees quivered. My mouth became drier than Mustang Beach sand.

Here I was again, smack dab in the very scenario I'd vowed to avoid: drowning. Only, this time, there were twice as many people trying to kill me—and no one racing to my rescue.

I'd put forth my very best. My most valiant efforts. I was sure Addison had too. As much as he could, in his diminished state.

But it was time to face reality. Ivy and Cooper had beaten us. They'd won.

I held out my trembling hands. She dumped a few pills into them. I hesitated. Should I? Wouldn't it be more heroic to face the rip current stone-cold sober? But when I looked out over the seething sea, and the black channel that had formed, rushing out . . .

I placed the pills on my tongue.

"Wash them down." He held the jug to my mouth. I squirmed—an automatic reaction—but he steadied my head. "Drink."

The water tasted like plastic, but it was cool, a gift after all that walking through the thick night air. I gulped it down.

She transferred another pile of pills into my hand. They tapped my skin, feeling so small and inconsequential—I gasped. What was I doing? Giving in? Giving up? This wasn't me. I'd let fear take me over. But fear and courage went hand in hand. Flip sides of the same coin. To defeat fear, immense courage was needed.

"Take them," she said. "Hurry up."

I tossed the pills in her face. Her eyes flashed with fury, then became resolute. Composed. "Suit yourself." She clutched my arm, and he clutched the other, and together they dragged me toward the churning ocean.

Toby and I had not rehearsed what to do in this situation. How to fend off two attackers. While my hands were bound. While fog clouded my peripheral vision. The fog wasn't real. It was the Dramamine. I'd swallowed four or five pills—enough to make things wacky.

Then came a spotlight, piercing the fog. Not an actual spotlight, but an intense inner knowing that, drugged or not, Callie Padget does not go down without a fight.

"Wait," I said, as a wave receded. "Can you give me a moment? Please. Just one moment. I'll be fast. I promise. I just need to—say goodbye."

He released his grip. She did too. I knelt, bowing my head like I was offering up a final prayer.

And I was praying—for my idea to work. *For once in my life, let my aim be true.*

I sank both hands into the wet sand and filled them with as many grains as I could grab. Spinning upward, I flung one fistful into Ivy's face and hit Cooper's ugly mug with the second.

My captors sputtered and swore.

I bolted.

My tied hands made my balance wonky. The Dramamine made my feet feel like they were moving through wet cement. I was halfway up the dune when big arms seized me. Lifted me. My legs bicycled. I inhaled huge and slammed my head back with all my might and—*whiffed*. Nothing but air. Cooper had a losing record, but enough fighting experience to know when a reverse headbutt was coming his way.

"Nice move," he said. And then he dropped me. "That stings!" he howled. "What is that?"

A half dozen sandspurs were sticking out of his ankle. He'd barreled through a whole tangle of them. When he brushed them off, they transferred to his hand, the tips biting deep. "Get these off me!"

I took off, stumbled, kept on climbing. Behind me, Cooper tumbled down the dune in a slurry of sand and hyena-pitched curse words.

I scrambled to the top. The nearest tree had bumpy bark, rough like alligator hide. I had only a few seconds to get this bungee cord off, and that tree could be my savior. It looked like it could hold up to some serious friction. I ran for it—but then I heard a pop and a whistle, and a hot slice ripped my calf. Gasping, I crashed into the ground. A mouthful of dirt. A nose full of sulfur. I touched my leg. My fingers came away bloody.

She'd shot me. A graze, but enough to shred my skin. Enough to make me think a burning-hot poker had impaled my leg.

I got up and reeled, hands outstretched, for the tree.

Another pop. Another whistle.

Just a few feet in front of me, the tree exploded into a crackling column of fire.

72

Within minutes, the trees all around would be blazing.

Footsteps sounded behind me. Someone—Cooper? Ivy?—crested the dune.

I veered left. Charged into the woods. Ran, slipped, crawled, got back up and ran. The movement was likely speeding up the Dramamine, pumping it through my bloodstream at a faster rate, making my limbs into two-by-fours, making my brain feel like it was being ground through a sieve. What I really needed to do was bring up the drug. Stop and jam my fingers down my throat. But there wasn't any time. The footsteps were right behind me.

I chanced a glance over my shoulder. Ivy.

I ducked my head and pushed my legs with all my might, but they didn't move any faster. Behind me came a leafy crash, followed by a thud and a string of profanity. When I turned around, Ivy was splayed on the ground in front of a gaping hole.

A watering hole, dug by a thirsty mustang.

Cursing, she got to her feet.

I kept running. Time became blobby; since the second flare had struck the tree, I didn't know whether five minutes or five hours had passed. The woods thickened into a soupy wall of leaves. Branches scratched my cheeks. Roots snatched my feet. Multiple trails crisscrossed these woods, I knew—but I couldn't seem to pick up a single one.

Just when the trees seemed darkest, someone clutched my

arm. I spun around, my elbow flying up. I caught something hard. Heard a grunt. "Callie?" a female voice said. "What on God's green earth—"

"Get away—"

"Callie, it's Geri-Lynn. Are you okay? What's wrong?"

"Geri-Lynn?" My eyes blurred on the face. The straw-bale hair. Her hand held over one eye, where my elbow had made contact.

"What in the—hold still, girlfriend." She untied my wrists. As the cords eased their bite, relief in the form of crazy laughter streamed out of me. "What's going on with you?" Geri-Lynn asked, brushing the hair from my face.

She didn't have any way of knowing there was a good amount of antihistamine gushing through me. And I didn't have any way of telling her, because my tongue felt about as useful as a spoiled oyster. "Murderers. I swallowed—"

"Okay, okay."

Then and there, as Geri-Lynn held back my hair, I expelled the Dramamine—with little effort on my own behalf, thanks to all the water I had chugged. "Geri-Lynn's here, don't you worry," she said when it was over. She guided me over the pine-needle-softened ground, eased me to the earth, and propped me against something hard. A tree or a rock. "What did you go and get yourself into?"

"We need to hide. *Now*—"

"Hush, hush. We are hiding. Don't you recognize where we are? You stumbled right into it."

73

Before us, moonlight shined down on two side-by-side lob-lolly pines, and the branches of a live oak, squatter but just as mighty, embracing them.

The Hugging Trees.

We were on the other side of them, in a clearing. A secret oasis.

"Don't talk," Geri-Lynn said. "What happened? Don't answer that. Hell's bells, are you bleeding? Don't say anything. You just rest."

The tearing of fabric.

Pressure on my calf, where the flare cartridge had blazed.

She spoke in soothing tones. I couldn't focus on her words. I wanted to scream, *The people who murdered Seth and kidnapped Addison tried to murder me. They're after me. The woods are about to burn down. Us with it . . .*

My ears began ringing. Faintly at first, like the tinkle when you enter a Queen Street shop. Then deafening, like I was high in a belfry next to a few hundred-pound bells gonging away. Either I hadn't gotten all the poison out of me, or my body was rebelling against it having been ingested in the first place.

"I don't know what to do here," Geri-Lynn was saying, alarm fraying her voice. Her arm encircled me. My head rested on her shoulder. She stroked my forehead. "Obviously I need to get you help. But I can't get a signal, and you can't walk, and—" She held her breath.

What's wrong? I tried to ask. It came out as a whimper.

Rustling. Footfalls. Had Cooper arrived? Had Ivy tracked us? Was it the fire, coming to consume us?

"Shh," Geri-Lynn whispered. "Look who's here." She lifted my head, straightened it.

A strange odor hit my nose. Earthy and warm, like the scents of tall grass and animal breath. My vision was blurry, but I could make out, on the opposite side of the clearing, two pairs of wide-set eyes gleaming in the darkness.

Two mustangs approached. A little wobbly one, followed by a bigger, darker one, scar zigzagging between her eyes. Mama scratched her neck against a tree trunk, while baby scratched her neck against mama.

I outstretched a hand, even though I knew I couldn't touch them, and even if I could, they were too far away. As a kid, I'd spent hours gazing down on the mustangs from my tree house. Now I was on the ground, gazing up.

"Callie, can you hear me?" Geri-Lynn whispered. "Are you in there? Stay with me. I think the foal's only a half day old, but she's already got her legs underneath her. Tigress has been hanging around this spot, for a bit of privacy, just like you said. It makes sense. If humans could stumble upon this hiding place, then why couldn't horses? We're not all that different, in the end. Would you get a load of little baby Beacon?"

"Beacon?" I was laughing again, quietly, so as not to disturb the four-leggeds that had joined the periphery of our hiding spot. Joy broke open inside my chest. Tigress had just needed to get away from it all. She was okay.

So was her baby.

If only Ivy had taken a page from Tigress's book. When the mama horse had tired of her herd mates' antics, she sought solace.

That solace had brought forth the opposite of destruction. It had brought forth Beacon. What if Ivy'd had the presence of mind to do something similar? Put some physical distance between her and Seth, until her emotions blew over? The result wouldn't have been his death. The result would have been the kindness she believed in choosing. Cadence's big feelings? She'd come by them honestly. Inherited them from her mother—whose purest intentions had gone horribly awry.

"It took me all afternoon to track them," Geri-Lynn said. "Tigress is one smart, determined mom."

Across the clearing, the mustangs nickered. Beacon swished her short tail, and Tigress rubbed her nose against her baby's.

And then, I became aware of yet another problem. Needles.

They were striking the backs of my hands. Silver pinpricks streaked down my wrists, leaving trails in the dirt stains. The needles tapped my cheeks. My chest. The top of my head.

My eyelids sagged. I couldn't keep them open.

This was it. I was sliding away. Forever this time. Under a downpour of needles.

The last thing I remembered is sticking out my tongue.

Splat, splat, splat.

And realizing—just before my world whirred into silence—they weren't needles.

They were sweet little drops of rain.

74

I came to as Geri-Lynn was pulling me to my feet. "You need to get *your* legs underneath you," she said. We began a long stumble out of the woods. The rain became a full-on downpour, driving as if shot out of nail guns, pelting us. I drifted in and out of deliriousness. My head felt heavier than a medicine ball, my ears were screeching, and my legs were rubber. But I was upright, putting one foot in front of the other. Geri-Lynn hauled me along, talking all the while about how much she appreciated me taking care of her when she was in a bad way, and Mother Tigress and Baby Beacon seeming entirely healthy, and Dr. Heather would soon examine them both, her first official duty as herd vet. Geri-Lynn said the footpath wasn't far, and from there, it was only a couple hundred yards to civilization, and she knew I would make it. She knew I was strong enough. "Take heart," she said at one point. "Isn't that what Rosie told her horse, Roger? *Take heart?*"

"We can't leave them," I said. "Tigress and Beacon—"

"We have to. They'll be fine. They're wild, and they're survivors. And so are we."

At some point, through the trees, sirens wailed and red and blue lights strobed. Cruisers and fire trucks sped past. By the time Geri-Lynn and I tumbled into the parking lot, we were drenched. A squad car had just arrived. Chief Jurecki barreled over and gathered us under the biggest umbrella I'd ever seen. He guided us into the back seat.

"Cooper Payne," I said, my head plunking against Geri-Lynn's shoulder as the squad car ripped out of the lot. "Cooper Payne and Ivy O'Neill. They—"

"We nabbed them both," Jurecki said from behind the wheel. "Mr. Payne called 911 from Mustang Beach. That sick creep was bawling so hard, dispatch could hardly make out a word he said. But you must have talked some sense into him, Callie, because he turned himself in. Told us where we could find Addison Battle, safe and sound. Mr. Payne gave up Ms. O'Neill too, but he needn't have, because Fusco was already on the case. She had been following up on a lead—*your* lead—and stopped by the O'Neills' rental cottage, to find your car, but not you, and Mr. O'Neill and his daughter wondering just where in tarnation their wife and mother had run off to. Fusco put out an APB for the family Nissan, and we found out, right about the same time Mr. Payne's call came in, that Ms. O'Neill had been seen speeding here, to Mustang Beach. Unbelievable, Callie. Unbelievable."

75

I spent that night in the hospital. Next morning, as Hudson and Antoinette rushed into my room, I felt so happy I could have cried. Actually, I might have cried—just a little—as they proudly explained the repairs they'd made to the Cattale Queen, and its replenished supply of lovingly used books. They reported that Addison was going to be fine, and back to cutting hair in no time.

A few hours later, Toby pulled a chair close to the bed and held my hand—the one that didn't have an IV in it. He fed me ceviche tacos, which Turo had whipped up especially for me. Made with pink Cattail shrimp, they were limey, salty, and delectable, and proved to be the most revivifying tacos of my life up to that point.

Late afternoon brought Geri-Lynn, eggplant-hued bruise rimming her eye. My handiwork, from the previous night's flying elbow. "Oh my—I am so, so sorry, Geri-Lynn," I said.

"All in a day's work." She assured me it looked worse than it felt, and no damage had been done. "What's a black eye between Cattailers?"

"How are the trees?" I asked.

"Only one casualty. The rest were saved by rain and firefighters. And I've got something else that's going to make you smile."

I scooted over, and she plopped next to me on the bed. The video she pulled up on her phone was shot at Mustang Beach; I recognized the isolated shoreline, the fence that sank beneath the waves. Two men patrolled the sand, wielding grabbers and trash bags. A third guy—wiry blond hair, chunky black glasses—watched on, hands on hips. I pointed to the guy who appeared to be in charge. "Is that . . . Ezra Metcalfe?"

"Sure is. You should recognize one of the trash pickers too."

I brought the screen closer to my face. The wind obscured the audio, but I heard Ezra say something like, *Hey, you two, got any words for the camera?* One of the trash pickers glowered. He had a rat-tail ponytail and a cowrie-shell necklace.

"Are they the two guys who sped off in the boat?" I asked. "You caught them?"

"Not me. Fusco." Geri-Lynn giggled. "I agreed not to press charges—if *they* agreed to put in some volunteer time for the Mustang Beach Sanctuary. Ezra is supervising so I could come visit you."

"But who are they? What were they doing on the beach that day?"

She told me the tale. The boat owner lived locally and, during an impromptu booze cruise, had explained to his visiting friend—who wore the Zimmerman T-shirt—about the forbidden Mustang Beach land. When the visitor scoffed at the notion of horses having their own private multimillion-dollar beachfront parcel to roam, the Cattailer challenged him to swim ashore, run across the sand, and tag a horse without getting caught, nipped, or kicked in the head.

I couldn't help thinking their punishment wasn't much of a punishment, seeing as they got to walk a stretch of gorgeous, protected beach. But Geri-Lynn was tickled by the arrangement, so I didn't pooh-pooh it.

"Mustang Beach is cleaner than most, of course," she said. "But I still get the occasional washup. You know—wasted buoys, blown flip-flops. Ezra's making sure they don't discover anything cool, like a message in a bottle or a fossilized shark tooth. Any of that treasure will get a prime spot inside Sanctuary Bungalow, on display for all to enjoy."

Resting her head against mine, she showed me her most recent Instagram post of mustang mother and baby, nose to nose, the Atlantic glistening in the background. Little Beacon was Tigress's mini-me, a leggy rendition of her mother, minus the facial scar. The sweet image had garnered thousands of hearts.

Much more important, though, were the donations and new membership pledges pouring in.

That night, feeling groggy, I lay alone in the dark. From the hospital hallway, intermittent voices drifted. Somehow, every voice belonged to Cadence O'Neill. I'd be thinking about that girl for the rest of my life. During odd moments, quiet moments, three a.m. moments. What would she learn about her mother's failings? Her mother's fierce love? When Cadence finally came to comprehend it all, what inside her would die? And what would be born in its place?

Her life wasn't bound to be easy, but at least she'd have her faithful dog, and her father, who spoke up for her and protected her, while at the same time gave her freedom and seemed to have a handle on which battles were worth fighting.

She'd also have books.

A tall shadow appeared in the doorway. Startled, I wriggled onto my elbows. The shadow approached the bed. Clicky footsteps.

"Dang, A.C." Fusco took me in. My bandaged head. My scratches and bruises. "If I looked up *death warmed over* in the dictionary . . ."

"Thanks." I steeled myself, waiting for a scolding about how irresponsible I'd been. How I'd risked not only my life but the lives of others who'd come to bail me out. You know, the typical Fusco guilt lecture.

It didn't come.

Instead, she drawled, "The horse doc coughed up the dough." Apparently, Dr. Heather Westerly, when pressed about the money she owed the artist Denise Sawicki, apologized profusely.

"Heather didn't get off on the right foot with Cattail police, did she?" I asked. "What with the lie she told, about not knowing who D.S. was."

"In the great state of North Carolina, willfully misleading law enforcement is a Class 2 misdemeanor."

"So she'll be punished in some way?"

"That'll be up to the courts." The detective came closer and smoothed out my blanket. "Anything I can do for you?"

My forehead crinkled; Fusco actually seemed serious. I didn't have to think very long to come up with a favor she might perform on my behalf. I reminded her of the kids' book she'd asked about, that night she came into the MotherVine.

She nodded. "*The Legend of Somebody or Other.*"

"Rosie Beacon. That's the one." Warmth filled my chest as I thought ahead. I'd inscribe a copy of *Rosie Beacon* with two special, simple words: *Take heart.* Tin Man could inscribe it too, leaving his inky pawprint. I'd wrap the book in brown paper and decorate it with fluffy raffia bows. I'd even adorn it with a freshly snipped bunch of Tinnakeet grapes. "Can you get it to Cadence O'Neill before she and her father leave the island? I know that's not a detectivey task, but—"

"Text me when it's ready, and I'll stop by the MotherVine."

"Really? Okay. Tomorrow, sometime. They're letting me out of here in the morning."

Her carrot-stick eyebrows tilted. Like she wanted to say something, but didn't know exactly what.

"Listen, Fusco." Sighing, I collapsed back onto the pillow. "I broke the rules. I put myself in an extremely dangerous situation. I shouldn't have stuck my nose in police business. But—" Something strange was going on with her face. She was . . . *smiling*?

Turns out her smile was pretty and wily and made me think of a fox.

"Callie," she said.

I blinked a few times. I didn't think she'd ever called me by my name. To her, I'd always been A.C. I angled my head, pressing it into the pillow. "Yeah?"

"Call me Iona."

76

Two days later, at five a.m., I keyed into the MotherVine Bookshop. Tin Man ushered me inside with a flurry of meows. Purring louder than an Evinrude motor, he pranced over to the new hobbyhorse—cocoa-colored stain gleaming, bronze-black tail and mane sparkling—and brushed against it. The best bookshop cat in the world then watched approvingly as I placed my tiny origami foal front and center in the display window. I imagined real-life Beacon gazing upon the starlit Atlantic. Kicking her hooves through moon-cooled sand. Greeting, one by one, the forty-five other creatures just like her, the creatures that would become her companions in this life.

A text came in, breaking my Mustang Beach reverie. Toby.

Is that you inside the bookshop right now?

I called him. "You're up early," I said.

"Couldn't sleep. I came to the dojo for a workout. I saw the light on inside the MotherVine. Figured you couldn't sleep, either. Want some company?"

I grimaced. Bacitracin coated half my face, a butterfly bandage spanned a cut on my forehead, and a fat wad of gauze adorned my leg. Nonetheless, there wasn't much to be done about the fact that Toby Dodge's company was exactly what I wanted. "I'll be upstairs, getting the summer decorations together."

"Summer's just around the corner, isn't it?"

"Antoinette takes her cues from Meeks Hardware, and they're already pushing the pool toys. I'll leave the door unlocked for you."

On the second floor, predawn light spilled in through the uncovered panes. I opened a window. A breeze caressed its way in, raising goose bumps on my skin and fragrancing the air with grapes and brine. Outside, the vine shined like clusters of emeralds, freshened by last night's rain.

I was unfurling a sunflower-themed flag when Toby arrived. I could tell by the rhythm of his footfalls that he bounded up the stairs two at a time. When he appeared in the doorway, an immediate calm settled over me. "Morning," I said, drinking him in. He wore workout clothes and running shoes. His hair was pulled back, accentuating the handsome planes of his face.

"How do you feel?" he asked.

"Like I got choked out, then swallowed a gram of antihistamine at gunpoint, then puked it up, then staggered through the woods in the dark during a hard, driving rain, then spent two nights in the hospital." I managed a weak smile. "Oh, and I forgot the part about getting shot."

"You were . . . what you did . . ."

"I was just trying to do the right thing."

"That's what I like about you, Padget. Because of you, my dojo is going to make it. But even more important—honestly, I can't imagine what this past year would have been like without you in it."

A tear spilled down each of my cheeks. Ridiculous. I hadn't cried for decades, and the past couple of days had turned me into a waterfall. Sniffling, I hung my head. I wanted to say so many things—about how much I liked him, how at home in my own skin he made me feel—but the words just wouldn't form.

"Hold that thought," he said. He ducked into the stairwell. When he reappeared, an old-fashioned picnic basket, the kind with a dual-hinged lid, hung from his forearm.

In spite of my tears, I laughed. "What's this?"

"Our first date."

"Right now?"

"I don't know about you, but I can't wait any longer." From the basket, he produced a checkered cloth, which he spread at my feet. Out came two champagne flutes. Pouring from a thermos, he filled them with fizzy juice.

"Mimosas?" I watched as he unpacked cinnamon muffins, a wheel of Brie, a carton of raspberries . . . "Where'd you get all this?"

"I told you, Padget: I've got a lot of surprises in store for you. This is the first of many. Come on. Let's eat." He stepped forward to take the flag from my hands. But before I knew what was happening, he was cradling my face. Gently, he thumbed away my tears. His forehead brushed mine, and our breath mingled. The smell of his clove cologne enveloped me. A delicious tingle shivered up my spine.

"Favorite season?" he asked quietly. "I love them all, but for me, summer's got the edge. I'm guessing you feel the same?"

"Toby, with everything that's happened this week . . . what I mean is, I know you've been through a lot. I know it's been intense. If the time just isn't right, between you and me—"

"If there's anything this week has taught me, it's that the time is now. It's always now." He dipped his face, and his lips found mine. The kiss—our first—was all silk and velvet. It deepened, and I dropped the flag and threw my arms around his neck and pressed into him. His arms wrapped me tight, and his hands rolled down my hair, and the red bird that was my heart soared against an endlessly blue Cattail sky.

There was summer according to the calendar, and then there was summer according to Cattail Island.

The latter was officially underway.

ACKNOWLEDGMENTS

While Mustang Beach Sanctuary is fictional, wild Banker horses exist in real life—and need human help. For more information on actual mustang populations on the Outer Banks and on the heroism of their caretakers, check out the Corolla Wild Horse Fund; Outer Banks Forever, the official nonprofit partner protecting the Ocracoke herd; and the Foundation for Shackleford Horses.

Many intelligent, dedicated professionals made *Murder on Mustang Beach* possible. They include my total pro agent, Adam Chromy, and my dream team at Berkley, especially Michelle Vega, Mary Geren, Tina Joell, and Daniela Riedlova. Designer Sarah Oberrender and artist Michelle Pereira created the beautiful cover. Meanwhile, Xuni.com created my beautiful website. It's a joy working with you all. I'm grateful for your expertise.

To booksellers, librarians, reviewers, bloggers, bookstagrammers, podcasters, and other champions of literacy and words, including Susan Hinkle, Zandria Senft, Carissa Schanely, Susan Scott, Jo and Huck Truesdell, Julie Beddingfield, Gee Gee Rosell, John Charles, and especially Jamie Anderson: thank you for getting behind *Smile Beach Murder*, and thank you for all you do to get books into the hands of readers.

When it comes to the factual research that made its way into *Murder on Mustang Beach*, any errors are mine. Thank you to Detective Katie Mitchell of Loudens County Sherriff's Office,

Robbery/Homicide division (Virigina), and to Officer Lora Gil-reath of Kill Devil Hills Police Department (North Carolina), for generously answering my questions about police procedure.

To my friend Kat Morgan: thank you for the laughter and encouragement. I cherish you.

Gratitude to Celie Florence, Matt Huband, Emily Midgette Pharr, Dr. Kristine Rook and Julius, and Jennifer and Dr. Corey Shagensky, who, in their own unique and meaningful ways, provided invaluable support as I produced these pages.

The first time I ever saw Banker mustangs in person was when my buddy Adam Morgan aired-down his Jeep tires for an epic four-wheeling Carova adventure. Much obliged, Adam's Horse Tours.

It takes a strong man to cultivate strength in a woman. My husband is such a man. Matthew, these five words aren't nearly enough, but I'll write them anyway: Thank you. I love you.

During the writing of this book, our salty gentleman Scottie dog became terminally ill and passed away. Sir Desmond Snuggle-bottom, PhD (aka Starview Rococo by Design) was a ten-inch-tall furball, a show ring dropout who excelled at dozing. When I took a bath, Desi dozed on the bath mat. When I played piano, he dozed beneath it. When Matthew and I were writing in our respective offices, he chose the most equidistant spot—the foot of the stairs—and dozed with paws in the air.

In the strange way of terriers, Desi made our home not only cozier but feistier too. At the sound of the doorbell, he barked viciously, only to wag himself into a blur no matter who was standing on the front steps. He once picked a fight with a 160-pound deerhound and came out the victor; later that same day, upon discovering a fly had invaded the house, he hid under our bed. He won many admirers up and down the beach, earning nicknames such as The General, Classic, and Sweet Man. I've never met any dog so content to simply sit and gaze out a window, and I doubt I ever will.

Fictional pets can live forever. While I sometimes wish that were true of real pets, on my better days, I know that nothing properly cracks open the heart like a good dog's brief companionship, and were it to last indefinitely, we might not learn vital life lessons—namely, that a curious scent is worth investigating; that a stroll around the neighborhood should not be undervalued; and that sand in your beard means you're doing something right.

When Desi's cancer diagnosis came, I expected having some months' preparation would ease the sorrow of his departure. I was wrong. This book is for you, Dez, my irreplaceable old earthdog friend. I miss you, and I thank you. We'll meet again someday to share popcorn and watch for dolphins, warm breezes tussling our hair. Until then, as you cavort with die-hard brethren in the great Scottish Highlands in the sky, may the road rise to meet you, and may the wind be always at your tail.